I0673712

LYRICAL LIGHTS

Maria La Serra

This is a work of fiction. Names, characters, places, brands, media, and incidents are either the product of the author's imagination or are used fictitiously. The author acknowledges the trademarked status and trademark owners of various products referenced in this work of fiction, which have been used without permission. The publication/use of these trademarks is not authorized, associated with, or sponsored by the trademark owners.

Copyright © 2018 by Maria La Serra

All rights reserved. Without limiting the rights under copyright reserved above, no part of this publication may be reproduced, stored in or introduced into a retrieval system, or transmitted, in any form, or by any means (electronic, mechanical, photocopying, recording, or otherwise) without the prior written permission of the above copyright owner of this book.

Library of Congress Cataloging-in-Publication Data

La Serra, Maria
Lyrical Lights — 1st edition
ISBN-13: 978-0995097926

Want to be notified when Maria La Serra's next book releases?
Visit http://eepurl.com/bVUV19 or maria-laserra.com

For Agostino,
you make me feel like the world is my oyster

For Andrea Castro,
true friendship goes beyond borders

.

Not my circus, not my monkey
– Polish proverb

To all the girls that think you're fat because
you're not a size zero, you're the beautiful one,
it's society who's ugly
– Marilyn Monroe

You Meet Someone ... Something Starts to Happen

Mable

They say there are two dimensions to the first impression, and it happens the moment your eyes land on your subject. Then, the only question you should ask yourself is: is this person out to help me or harm me?

When I first met Simon, somehow I knew it would be both. Our lives collided on an ordinary night ... but then again, was anything ordinary when it came to Simon Rowe? Could you say that about someone who would change your life forever? I don't know; it's hard to tell.

The Little Orange House was the latest trendy bar in the Meatpacking District, a hot spot for the arts and fashion crowd. With an unfinished degree in computer science, I was still trying to figure out where I fit into the fold.

The bar itself was chic, a mix of Spanish and industrial

revival. To my left, there was a concrete wall lit up by candles, each in their individual compartments. All the way in the back, past the iron gates, was where I sat alone on a rust-colored leather couch, away from the crowd and the rhythmic music that played on the speakers. Rather, I assumed it was music, because everything sounded like ruckus. I rarely liked to come out to these places; the commotion and the background noise would annoy the average person, but it could be very stressful for someone hard of hearing, like me.

I had been waiting here for an hour, and it was clear that Jason wasn't coming. But hey, I wanted to make it official. Besides, the martinis weren't half-bad.

Jason?

How can I explain my relationship with Jason? I guess you could say it was in eternal purgatory—it fell anywhere between hooking up and something of a real relationship. A girl can get lonely in a big city with no other prospects in sight. You take what you can get. Besides, I didn't have time for a real relationship.

That's a lie; time was what I had in spades. I was a broke model, working part-time at an Italian deli on the Upper East Side. Technically, I wasn't allowed to work anywhere while under contract with the NY Model Agency. They literally had me on standby, waiting for the next job, but I hadn't heard a peep from my agent in over three weeks, and my debts were on the rise. With what I got from my dad and what Johnny paid me under the table, I managed to survive. Working at the deli was not my dream job, but the owners treated me well, especially the little one they called Nonna. She heckled me every time I got in her line of sight. *"Eata, eata ... you too skinny.* Don'ta worry, you make the model anyway."

I was damn fond of them, but holy cow, what was with these people and their obsession with food?

I only wished my agent Dania had the same philosophy.

The last time we had spoken, she'd said, "Darling, you need to lose three more inches, okay? Around your waist and thighs." The sound of paper crackling came through the phone—what I assumed was my contract compressing into a nice little ball— and I swallowed. "That's if you want to work. If you don't, it's not going to happen, not here in New York City or anywhere else."

She was oblivious to the fact that I was two layers deep in my lasagna.

"I'm sorry, Mable, but it's not working out … I have to let you out of your contract." She'd sighed. "I wish you luck."

It was business; if she didn't make money, then I couldn't pay my bills, and, unfortunately, I was the product she was selling. We weren't having any success with each other.

But the worst of it hadn't come from Dania—it had come from the designers themselves, who had related their concern that I wouldn't be the best match to represent their label, since I was hard of hearing. It caused me to talk funny.

I asked myself, constantly, why the hell I put myself through this. It was straightforward: the dream was bigger than me. It was like an entity of its own, making me believe that, if I held on a little longer, if I could prove to them that my disability was an asset, I could represent girls who were different. I thought things would happen, just maybe.

So tonight, I had hoped Jason would be able to console me, like I had many times for him. I should have known better. When a guy said, "I'm not looking for a serious relationship," it most likely translated to, "I have no intentions of having one with you—like, ever." But my mind was a tricky little gal, the kind to concoct a better truth, one that suited me better. I had failed miserably at conforming him to boyfriend material, but I couldn't blame the guy. He had laid it out for me, but did I deserve better? Sure, I did. But I had allowed this shit-show to run its course for several months because I believed it was better than being alone. With every passing minute living in this metropolis, my views on dating had reformed into something more cynical. After a while, you realize that everyone around you complains about dating in New York.

As soon as I finished my glass, I ordered another one. I thought, *I surely deserve it.* I had a plan. Tomorrow I would call my dad and tell him he was right, that this whole modeling thing was a waste of time. In a few weeks, I would return home to Montreal and continue my studies, like we'd agreed. But on the bright side, at least, after a year of putting my body through hell, I had been fortunate not to develop an eating disorder like some of my colleagues.

Within minutes, the waitress brought me an apple martini, and I reached over for my purse beside me. I swept my hand on the soft leather ... nothing. A surge of anger came over me.

"My purse was here just a minute ago, and now it's gone," I said, looking up at the twenty-something waitress, who looked like she couldn't be bothered. She repeated something, but I had no clue what Miss Muffet was saying. The music was blaring in the background, drowning the sound of her voice. All I could see was her bright pink lips flapping in the dark, but they were moving way too fast for me to catch anything. It's a misconception that a deaf or hard-of-hearing person can read lips—that we have developed a sixth sense to compensate for our disability. If that were true—I was still waiting for mine to kick in.

"Can you ask the bartender if anyone found a purple boho bag ... with a gold clip?" I was yelling at this point—I couldn't hear my own voice. She stood there, showing me my bill, and those damn lips still flapped.

"Yes, I would like to pay for my drinks, but someone took my purse ..." *This is crazy.* "I can't understand—I'm hard of hearing ... can you please write it on your phone?" I saw her smartphone peeking from the pocket of her black apron. Talk,

4

talk, talk … Her mouth kept going, and I was getting annoyed with her expressions. I was raised in the hearing world and had never deprived myself of anything any other twenty-one-year-old like me was doing. Never allowed my disability to impede anything.

Good grief, talk about an off night.

"Okay, just give me a second." Obviously I wasn't getting anywhere, and instead I focused on finding my bag. It was possible it could have fallen on the ground or gotten kicked under the couch. I got on all fours to look around, and that's when I stumbled across a pair of navy oxford shoes. I forced my eyes up the length of the muscular legs attached to them. Then a set of hands appeared, guiding me up, and I straightened my body.

When I did, my eyes met the most expressive, soft, ultramarine eyes I had ever seen. And I found myself speechless. I would have expected no one to come to my rescue, but there he was, with a laid-back vibe in his style. He'd come with a gorgeous smile and light tousled shoulder-length hair. Without a doubt, I knew I was in for some trouble.

"Are you all right?"

"Someone took my purse," I replied. I looked past him and realized Miss Muffet had disappeared.

"No worries. I took care of it." As he spoke, I looked at his face.

"Do you want to talk outside?" I pointed to my ear underneath my hair. He nodded, but I was aware he didn't grasp my situation. It was pointless to explain, but he would soon find out.

Meet the Dreamers

The tall stranger directed me through the crowd and toward the opening, leading me onto the sidewalk, the boisterous music now muffled behind the glass door.

"I can't thank you enough for picking up my tab. For a moment I thought I would have to make a run for it," I laughed over my shoulder. When I turned, I caught him with a confused expression on his face. I knew that look. He was probably thinking to himself, *Why is she talking like that?* It was a general question I got asked all the time. No big deal.

"Well, I couldn't have that on my conscience, but I'm not going to lie—seeing you in handcuffs would have been a real turn-on," he said, his eyes jovial.

Usually, I would have played along, replied with something witty or sultry, but I had only known this man less than ten minutes.

"Sorry. I was trying to be funny." He laughed nervously; he thought he might have offended me. But I was a cool girl.

"Somehow I imagined you would be the sort of fella who enjoyed a woman in handcuffs," I replied.

His expression turned serious. "Nah, restraining a woman is

not my thing." I watched him pull out a cigarette from his pack and offer me one.

"Thanks, but I don't smoke." I frowned, feeling a little uneasy. My mother had been a smoker; maybe she still was. Who knew? I hadn't seen her in sixteen years.

"Sorry, does this bother you?" He didn't wait for my reply and moved slightly to the right, and the cloud of smoke didn't reach me.

"I would like to pay you back. Maybe if you give me your number, I could—" I began.

His mouth widened again. "Do I look like I would make a girl pay me back for two martinis? I was happy to help. Look, if I didn't have this thing to go to tonight, I would have liked to grab a coffee somewhere and get to know you better."

He was trying to let me down easy. Inside the bar, he'd thought I was attractive enough, but now, listening to me speak, he wasn't interested anymore. No surprise.

"I'll tell you what. Why don't you give me your number; we could meet sometime." He rolled up his sleeve. Good grief, he had nice arms.

Look away, Mable, look away.

"You want my number?" I looked at him with curiosity.

"Or I could give you mine, if that would make you feel more comfortable." When he realized my hesitation, he continued. "Look, you seem like someone I'd like to get to know, and if you walk away now, I will never see you again." He was right. I had decided—I was leaving the city.

I felt the heat radiate from my skin. I liked the attention, but it would only lead me to another disappointment. I was willing to bet he got plenty of attention from girls, so why would he be interested in someone like me? A girl who talked funny? Not that I had any self-esteem issues, but I had learned too many times that guys who were all brawn and good genes had no substance.

Case in point—Jason.

"Maybe dinner? I'm free tomorrow night." He grinned, picking up on my bewilderment.

"I can't," I said, avoiding those longing eyes.

"You can't, or you won't?"

Normally I liked to play hard to get, but this time it was not the case. I needed to get home, but somehow I couldn't make myself go.

"Something tells me I should say no to you." Our eyes locked.

"Why would you want to say no?" he said with a playful grin.

"I have a boyfriend," I blurted out. The truth was, I wanted to give him my number, but then I would make the same mistakes, another smile, another gaze, and I would be back in the game with my heart left trampled and exhausted.

But a soft voice somewhere inside told me, *this right here is not like that other mess.*

Within minutes of meeting this stranger, I felt transfixed by him. He seemed older and more experienced in ways of life that I couldn't describe. He wasn't a boy, like Jason; he was a man. Anyhow, what would be the point? I would move away in less than two weeks. Good grief, where had he been a year ago? When I had thought there were no single men left in New York. I'd been in a big funk and just needed some love. Maybe that's why I'd settled for Jason. If we'd met then, I would have been all in, wearing bells and whistles, even blowing an alpenhorn.

The truth is, I wanted to stop it right in its tracks, whatever this was. I wanted to build a wall right between us, because in the back of my mind I knew—if I should see this man again, I would do something stupid. Who was I kidding? I wanted to do something stupid with him right then, all the way into the next week.

Maybe if he thought I had someone else in my life, he'd

give up and walk away.

"The guy who stood you up?" He turned back at the glass door, and then his eyes found mine. He must have been watching me this whole time, consoling my weak heart with martinis, refraining from sending Jason a gazillion texts.

"He's not your boyfriend." He had a slight accent. *Australian? British?* I always got them mixed up.

"Of course he's my boyfriend!" I nodded for emphasis, trying to hide my smile. *I don't know why my lips curl up when I lie.* Which was why I tried not to be deceitful—my stupid facial expression always revealed my secrets. So what, he was right. What I had with Jason was nothing serious, but he didn't need to know that.

"So tell me about this bonehead of yours," he said as I shoved my hands into the pockets of my gray linen romper, taking a minute to respond.

"He's a model." It came out sounding more important than it was. Jason wasn't even famous; he had done a couple of spreads for magazines here and there. I quickly forgave myself for being so prudish; it wasn't like I'd see this guy again, right?

"So is half of New York, love." He smirked. "Full name?"

"Jason Webb." I tried to brush the strands of hair away from my face, but gave up fighting the summer breeze.

"Wait, Jason Webb is the guy who stood you up tonight?" He clucked before turning serious.

"You know him?" I saw it in his eyes. Of course; all narcissistic jerks knew each other.

"I didn't get stood up," I retorted.

"Maybe you're right," he said as if he knew something I didn't.

"What?"

He swallowed before speaking. "I don't want to be the one to break this to you, but he's moved on to greener pastures." His eyebrows knit together. My mouth slightly opened, because now this man was annoying me.

"What? It's not possible, I don't think we're talking about the same person." I laughed, forcing myself to glance around to break his gaze. He made me feel bare, a little uncomfortable under those vibrant eyes. I knew what he was thinking: I was some pathetic blonde who made poor choices in men.

"Jason is from Toronto. He's been modeling about three years, and he's roughly six one, brown eyes."

"All right." I wrapped my arms around myself.

"He has a little scar on the right hand." He showed the top of his knuckles.

"Okay, okay, you've proven your point."

"I'll even give you his shoe size."

"No, that won't be necessary." I gave him a sarcastic smile.

"So how do you know?"

"Oh … that he found greener pastures?" he responded, and I looked at him flatly. He cleared his throat before saying, "I saw him walk out with a saucy brunette." He squinted his eyes and rubbed the back of his neck. He was afraid of my reaction. Maybe he thought I would break down and cry, but that was the last response Jason deserved.

"Wait, you mean he was here—inside the bar?"

"For a good half hour, aye."

Bastard!

I had always suspected Jason was brushing me off for someone else. He wasn't discreet about the way he looked at other women when I was around. Or how, when we arrived at the same event, he would ignore me, hiding the fact we were a couple, to appear to be single. I knew all this, but it still hurt, even though I'd allowed it to happen.

"Oh, I would have loved to catch that …"

"Dipshit." He finished my sentence. "Trust me, if I had known it was Jason you were waiting for, I would have approached you sooner." I was taken aback. I imagined that he was the type who wouldn't have a hard time approaching any girl, so why was he so hesitant with me?

"So, have you been watching me this whole time?"

"No," he said matter-of-factly, disposing his cigarette in the nearby trash. "Not the whole time. If I had been watching you relentlessly, then you would have had bigger issues than a stolen purse."

"Wait a minute, did you take it?" I had been so furious with Jason I hadn't seen who was sitting next to me—maybe it was him.

"Your purse?" He gave a low laugh. "You're a funny bird." He studied me for a second. "Sorry, love, I'm not that kind of man. I never take what doesn't belong to me. But you can be damn sure I'm the type that would kick the arse of whoever stole your purse."

Well, there I go putting my foot in my mouth.

I wasn't pro-violence, but it was sure sexy for a man to come to a woman's defense—even if it was just in words.

"So, why didn't you come over and talk?" I looked at him with curiosity. "Instead of swooping in at the right time."

He chuckled.

"Yeah … nah … you're right. I should have." He smiled and shoved his hands into his front pockets.

"So," he said after a short moment. "What are we doing? I need to be somewhere in the next twenty minutes, and there's no way I'm leaving you out here alone."

I didn't know what I should do, but I wanted to forget my problems. I loved the city, but it had a way of cracking you open, seducing you with its lights, making you fall in love with its possibilities, before it disillusioned you. This town could exasperate even the most wholehearted dreamer.

Arrivederci … sayonara … so long, New York!

I just had to make sure the door didn't hit me on the way out. If I stayed any longer, it would. I thought about my purse—

no point in making a police report. I figured I'd cancel my credit cards first thing in the morning. All I wanted to do was get back to my cluttered apartment and *forget* tonight had ever happened.

"What are you doing?" He watched me wave my hand in the air. Down the street, I spotted a yellow car headed in our direction.

"What does it look like? I'm going home."

"But you need money to pay for that cab." He pulled out his wallet.

"Thanks, but you helped me enough and I don't want to trouble you any further." I turned and caught sight of the cab slowly easing up to the curb. "I'll … pay him when—*ugh*, shit!" I put my hands over my eyes.

"What?" he asked.

"My keys … were in the purse, and my roommate is out of town. I won't be able to get into my apartment until she comes back on Sunday," I said, looking at him through the cracks of my fingers.

He gently sucked the air between his teeth. "You've got your night cut out for you, love. Is there anyone you can call that can help you out?"

"I do, but …"

"Ah, right, your phone was also in there—gotcha." He handed me his cell. Then he wandered past me and told the cab driver I'd changed my mind.

I didn't really know anyone in New York. Besides Jason, Gloria was my only hope. I dialed her number, and when she answered I heard the music and laughter in the background.

Gloria was always doing something cool. Her job as a freelance stylist had scored her name on the list of many high-profile parties in New York, and her lavish lifestyle had fueled my dreams even more. But I knew no one got there easy; it took hard work and persistence to achieve your goals. I've been wondering if I had given up on mine too soon. When I hung up with Gloria, the stranger wandered back.

"So where can I take you?" he asked as I gave his phone back.

How did my problem become his?

"I'll crash at my friend's apartment, but I need to get the keys from her." At first, I wasn't sure why I didn't just say it was my cousin. Maybe I didn't want him to know I had a hard time making friends in this city.

"Okay, so let's go."

"Don't you have somewhere to be? I don't want to ruin the rest of your night," I said.

"You have ruined nothing. If anything, you've made it … interesting." He had a nice smile. The kind that could melt away walls—perhaps even mine.

"It's all right. I can find my way to the Bryant Hotel. It's not far." *Geez, I hoped.*

He thought about it for a minute. "By chance are you headed to the *Nylon* magazine party?"

"Yeah, how did you know? It's a party held for a cocky photographer who won an award or something."

"Cocky? Really?" He smirked.

"They say he's the next big thing, like a young version of Mario Testino." I hitched my thumb at my shoulder, trying to scoop the strap of my purse until I remembered there was nothing there. He was making me nervous, the way he was staring at me.

"Huh, really?" His mouth went up on the sides. *What was I missing?*

"Well, I don't know. I never met the guy." I shrugged.

"Who's your friend?" He lit another cigarette. I guessed he was in no rush to go anywhere.

"Oh, you wouldn't know her." I shake my head.

"Try me,"

"Gloria … Gloria Ericson."

13

"Huh, you're right. I don't." His expression was flat, but his eyes said something else, which had me confused. "Let me give you a ride. I'm headed that way," he said.

"No, it's all right. I will walk." I said self-consciously, moving away. "Thank you for your help," I said, over my shoulder.

"Hold on. It's forty-five minutes … but this way." He pointed his thumb in the opposite direction.

"Oh." I was a complete idiot. I wouldn't know my way around this city even if I'd lived there a lifetime.

"Are you always this stubborn? Now listen, love. I'd be crazy to allow you to wander off somewhere, the back of Bourke with no phone or money." He motioned with his hand down the street.

"Bourke? Do you mean Brooklyn? Aren't we in Manhattan?" I was kidding; of course I knew where I was, but he slightly shook his head in disbelief.

"I meant some remote place."

"Oh, sure." My voice went up.

"Yeah, I think I would feel better if I personally got you home, safely. Anyhow, let's face it, you wouldn't get far in those shoes, legs." I looked down at my four-inch red patent stilettos. He had a point.

"How do I know I won't be in more danger going anywhere with you?"

"True, but I'll get my ass kicked if Gloria finds out I left you alone and stranded."

"So you *do* know Gloria?"

"I know everyone," he winked.

But you don't know me, I thought.

"I'm not ashamed to say it but Gloria Ericson scares the shit out of me." He chuckled.

He definitely knew my cousin; she could have that effect on people. You didn't want to mess with Gloria, and I'd gotten the scars to prove it. When we were kids, I'd once decapitated her Malibu Barbie. Let's just say I never touched her toys again.

"You're two for two … All right, I'll allow you to drive me, but only because your life depends on it."

"How thoughtful of you." He brought his hand to his chest and gave me a slight bow. I followed him up the street, and of course his choice of transportation was a two-wheeler.

"I'm Simon, by the way," he said when we stopped in front of his motorcycle. He held out his hand for me to take.

"Mable," I replied, shaking his hand.

"Mable." I liked how he said it, especially with his deep, gruff voice. "I don't think I've met anyone with that name."

"Well, more of a reason not to forget me after tonight." I said, laughing. His eyes glanced at me, like a man who looks at a woman with desire.

"*Oh*, you're anything but forgettable, love." He paused. "But I don't remember Gloria ever mentioning you before."

"Well, Gloria is a private person."

"Yeah, don't I know it."

Before I could ask any more questions, he handed me the extra helmet—it made me believe there might be a significant other in his life, even though he was alone tonight.

"All right, Mable, have you ever been on a bike?"

I looked down at the black matte motorcycle, which had as much sex appeal as its owner. If I was honest, I wasn't sure which one made me more nervous. "No, it's my first time."

"Ah, a virgin," he said playfully. I hadn't been a virgin for the past three years, but somehow he still made me blush.

"Well, I have two rules. One, you have to be in sync with my movements. You lean in when I do." He smirked, watching me struggle with my helmet, and took matters into his own hands by strapping the helmet down for me. "Two, watch out for the exhaust pipes; they get hot fast, and I wouldn't want you to burn those beautiful legs of yours." He winked.

I felt the blood rush from my neck to my face. "Don't worry. I insured my best feature." I smirked.

He glanced at me. "Oh, you've got a great pair of legs, but they're not your best feature."

"They're not?" My eyebrows gathered together.

"No. Your eyes ... and smile." There he went again—got me blushing like a schoolgirl.

"So, do I look like a bobblehead?" My head was feeling like it was twice its size.

"Well, I don't know much about that," he said, strapping on his helmet.

"Come on, say it, you know I'm rocking it." I gave him my cutest pose while batting my eyelashes.

"Yeah, sure—you're rocking it." He let out a short laugh. Only when I took my place behind him did he lean back into me and say, "I'm surprised; I would have never guessed Jason was your type."

"Oh yeah? And what would be my type?" I said over the loud noise of the revved-up engine.

"Me," he said, grinning wide and sexy. Maybe he was trying to get me to smile, but sweet Jesus, I was very tempted to take a bite out of that apple. I needed to be on my way before this night got any crazier.

"Are you really with that idiot?" he asked. When I didn't answer, he continued. "Yeah, I thought so. He doesn't deserve you—a smart bird like you can do so much better."

What could I have replied? My mind was in this zone of complete, utter fever. The sweet smell of his cologne rising from his cotton shirt was making my body feel things I hadn't felt in a long time.

"You could wrap your arms around me. I promise I don't bite," he said.

Nope, couldn't argue with that. One look at his smile, his sultry gaze, and I was back in the game. I willingly pressed my body up against his back, under the bright lights, in this city I had called home for a short time. Then we drove off, disappearing into the darkness— from the view of anyone who might have been watching us.

The Cat Lady in the Cellar Bar

"Thanks for getting me here in one piece." I handed back his helmet, knowing this was goodbye.

"No worries."

I stood there, close enough to see the downcast look in his eyes, and I knew something was brewing. For some unknown reason, I was the one to break away from the gaze. I had never felt this nervous.

"Well, I better go," I said. To my surprise, he got off his bike, hooking the head protectors to the back of the seat. He took a slow, deep breath as his eyes ran up the length of the black brick building, then descended back to mine. Something seemed to have changed since we'd left The Little Orange, like he had forced himself to come all this way. One thing was for sure; the man was a mystery. *Too bad he's not mine to solve.*

"Let me walk you in?" His eyes held mine for a beating moment.

"Okay." My voice squeaked. I should have said goodbye and been on my way. Why couldn't I let this go? Sure, there was some unexplained gravitation pulling me to him, making me wonder if there was something else. I hated myself for wanting to read more into this than there was … that's what always got me into trouble. I knew at this point it was not love—just raw attraction. But there was a question that kept crossing my mind every time I met someone new—*the what if.* What if he were my red thread? The myth that attaches two people: no matter the circumstances—the thread will knot, twist and bend, but never break. No matter what, we were meant to be lovers. I knew this was a long shot, but it was always nice to hope.

Inside, just off the lobby, was the entrance to the Cellar Bar. But when I got to the top of the staircase, I paused. If I had had any inclination that tonight would involve descending so many steps, I would have chosen a pair of flats instead of my stilettos. Simon shot me a glance like he must have read my mind.

"Are you okay getting down on your own?"

Before I could answer, he slipped his hand into mine, offering support as we descended. I didn't even flinch. I welcomed it like it was the most natural thing. The velvety multicolor leather bands he wore around his wrist lightly brushed against my skin—such an insignificant thing, but it caused such friction inside me, and suddenly I wanted more. Even though Simon was a stranger, I knew just one smile from him would disarm me, relinquish any small doubt still pegged at the back of my mind. As we took each step down, I could feel his warm eyes burning on me. I knew if I looked at him there was something I would see on his face. Maybe we both wanted something to happen—or continue—*I don't know.* The only sure thing I knew was that I shouldn't be ready for it, because the logical side of me told me I was in the midst of a kerfuffle. I was planning to leave the city. So why bother to start something you couldn't finish?

But the other half of me waited desperately for this moment to pass, to pick up the pace. I didn't want to behave the way I should. Every molecule in my body wanted him to pin me up against the wall. I wanted him to kiss me. I wanted to see him again.

At the last step, I knew this wouldn't play out.

Inside, the décor had the allure of a grand reception hall within the walls of a Gothic castle, but it was nifty enough for me not to dislike it. My eyes scattered over the heads of people who were dancing to the tune coming from the DJ in the corner.

"Did you spot your friend?" he asked, letting go of my hand, only leaving me further disappointed. I looked up; he was now standing much closer than I had expected. At least this way I could try to read his lips. With the loud music and the excitement that the night had brought, my brain was in state of exhaustion, making it difficult to stay focused.

"I know. I'm late," he said, but not to me. I followed his eyes to find Gloria walking closer to where we stood. Her expression was flat, almost matching her hairstyle, slicked back and tied into a ponytail. She wore a button-down navy silk shirt and white tailored pants, a charcoal knitted top knotted around her waist. Only Gloria could pull that off, making something simple look so chic and indispensable. I guess that's why everyone in New York wanted to work with her.

"Hey, what happened? Are you all right?" Gloria looked puzzled, her eyes darting from me to Simon and back again.

"Yeah, I got my purse stolen, along with everything I owned."

"Shit, that sucks," Gloria said, her eyes never leaving Simon.

"Simon was nice enough to help me." I felt I needed to clarify, but I wasn't sure what to make of Gloria's straight face.

"So you guys know each other?" I asked, but what I wanted to know was how they were connected.

"We work together." He was quick to say. That's when it hit me.

"*Oh* ... Simon Rowe?" I let out, and he nodded. "So you're the up-and-coming photographer." I glanced at him. "But you're not what I imagined."

"Up-and-coming?" He frowned.

"Well, you know what I mean."

"Cocky?" Simon playfully narrowed his eyes at Gloria. "What have you been telling her about me?"

"Only good things." Gloria waved him off.

"Ah, well, I've added that part in," I said, intertwining my fingers together. "I mean, I've only known you, what? About an hour?" I glanced at my watch. "Who am I to judge?"

"You're drowning." He let out a laugh.

"Anyhow, being cocky is not a bad thing, you know? Some girls even find that attractive," I said, and this piqued his curiosity.

"And what about you?" He radiated interest, but *in me*?

"Um, well, not really." I gave him a sideways smile.

"I'll tell you what. Why don't you find out for yourself— hang out with me a little longer? A drink at the bar?" Simon was staring at me.

How could I say no to that smile? I forced myself to look at Gloria and wished I hadn't. "I would love to, but I can't …" I said. "Anyway, it's true what people say about themselves. So if you say you're not cocky, then I'll just take your word for it."

"Well, I can't be cockier than Jason," Simon said, tilting his head in amusement.

My eyes widened. "Oh, you just had to go there?"

"Come, we'll talk about your poor taste in men over a martini."

"*Hey*— I'm beginning not to like you." My eyes zero in.

"So, what did you mean by that—that I'm not what you imagined?" Simon crossed his arms.

"Well, can I be honest with you?"

"Sure," he said, but his little laugh made me think otherwise.

But before I could respond, Gloria stepped between us.

"I hate to break up—whatever this is," Gloria gestured with her hand in the air as if she were polishing us off. "Simon, you need to get your ass out there and have a serious tête-à-tête with the editor and chief of *Nylon* magazine. He's the one hosting this party for you, remember?"

But before Simon could reply, people swarmed around him, prying us apart, and the space between us only grew. I looked back to find Simon talking to someone, but his eyes never left mine. I only turned around when Gloria tugged on my arm. She wanted me to follow.

"Mable, of all the men in the world, why Simon?" she asked.

"What's your problem? Look, Simon was kind enough to pay my tab, and then he gave me a ride over ... that's all that happened," I squared my shoulders.

"I thought you were meeting up with Jason?"

"He never showed up." I feigned a smile.

"No surprise." She half-rolled her eyes. "I hope you've learned your lesson, and that you forget about that idiot now."

"Yes, I'm done. I never want to see his face again." Even if I said it out loud, it didn't make it true. I knew I would have time before my departure, and if Jason should call somewhere in between me packing my things till the day I left town, I might be tempted to make one more mistake. Unless I had another suitable distraction.

"Simon has to be off-limits, please." She caught me throwing a glance his way. *Well, there goes that idea.*

"Why?"

"Because I said so." Her eyes softened. "Look, Simon is a great guy, but—"

"So if he's that great, what's the problem?"

Gloria's eyes focus on her wine glass. "He's going through something ... I'm not able to talk about it right now."

"Oh, I get it. You think I wouldn't be a good match?" I

asked.

"Mable, you're missing the point."

"This is so funny. You're protecting him from me?"

"We work together," Gloria said, like I should get it.

"I thought you said he's not your boss?"

She put her hand out to stop me from talking. "Right, but we have a great relationship. Enough that when he's working on a new project, I'm the first person he calls." She looked at me straight on. "What happens if you start fooling around?"

"Nothing is going to happen, okay?" I said, but she kept on going.

"He hasn't been in a serious relationship in—like ever. He doesn't even date."

"Who said I wanted a healthy, steady relationship?" I teased, taking her glass and proceeding to drink out of it.

"I know you better than you think, Mable Harper. Everything starts off loose, and you act like you're okay with it until you realize you want more."

"That's not true. I never wanted more with Jason." Shit. Was I smiling? I hated when she was right. It would never be enough for me—a half relationship—because it never was. The need for more, to have someone you can depend on, a reassurance of love. Isn't the whole point in life to find someone to connect with? The only thing is, my connections had been tangled and mangled up like a set of Christmas lights, long forgotten in the attic for years. But just because the lights were in boxes didn't mean they weren't good anymore. *Or were they?*

"What are you afraid will happen?" I asked.

"I'm worried if things go south, who's left picking up the pieces? How do you think my relationship with Simon will continue?" she asked.

I wasn't buying it. I knew for a fact she got plenty of jobs without Simon's help. There was something she wasn't mentioning. Or maybe Gloria was trying to protect me. Simon was an attractive man who took pictures of beautiful people all day. Who was to say he wasn't some womanizer?

"You're selfish. Don't you ever think of my happiness?" I was coy with her, but it only intensified her agitation.

"I *am* thinking about your happiness," Gloria sighed out of frustration.

Then I realized that maybe she had feelings for him. "*Oh* ... are you guys …"

"What? Are you crazy? No! *Never!*" She adjusted her black-framed glasses. "I'm in a committed relationship with Tracy, remember?"

"I know, but you also left Jerry for Tracy." My eyebrows went up slightly. How weird would it be to be interested in someone your cousin also wanted? It wouldn't be cool.

"Jerry was a mistake, and you know it. Look, just because I don't have romantic feelings for Simon, it doesn't mean I'm giving you the green light." Gloria looked past my shoulders, then diverted her eyes back to mine. "Simon is like the annoying brother I'm glad I never had. He comes with lots and lots of baggage." Her eyes softened. "What I'm trying to tell you is—if he breaks my cousin's heart, I won't be able to work with him, because it will get nasty between us. Just trust me, okay?"

"I get it. Don't worry, all right? Soon I'm going to schlep my irresponsible ass back to Montreal, and I'll be out of your hair."

"I didn't say you were irresponsible. Shit, Mable, you always hear what you want." She snapped her head back. "Wait, you're going back home?"

"Uh-huh. I've decided I'm not looking for another agent, so there is no point of me staying here."

"*Oh,* I don't want you to go," Her voice cracked.

I shrugged. "It's for the best. So you have nothing to worry about. Nothing will happen between Simon and I." I paused, taking in her expression.

"Why are you looking at me like that?"

"Because you're smiling."

"I'm not." I looked around the room, and my eyes found Simon. He was in the corner now, talking to an older couple. His eyes focused in my direction, amused by the fact that I was being scolded.

Do you want me to rescue you? I thought he mouthed. I smiled, shaking my head discretely, so that Gloria wouldn't pick up on it.

"I swear … I'm not interested in Simon." *I can't keep a damn straight face.*

She looked me over, relinquishing the air from her chest. "You're impossible," she said in a monotone voice.

I placed my hand on my heart. "Okay. I, Mable Harper, swear on my cat's head that I will never sleep with, or have anything to do with, Simon Rowe."

"You don't even have a cat," Gloria pointed out.

"Well, not now, but you realize you might have cost me my last chance of happiness. Now I have to resort to a lifetime of being a spinster living with cats."

"So we're good?"

"Perfect," I chirped.

"Great. I'm glad we cleared that up. Now give me back my wine, crazy cat lady!"

Somewhere in the Middle

"Hey, I thought you'd be gone by now."

I looked up at Simon, who was pulling up a chair beside me.

"I'm staying at Gloria's place tonight, so I thought I'd wait," I said, my face resting in my hand.

He studied me for a moment. "You don't look like you're having fun."

"What gave you that idea?" I smiled wearily, gazing into the eyes of the man I was forbidden to even look at. But I couldn't help but like the way he stared, making me feel like I was the most interesting person in the room.

Ugh, too bad I don't break promises. Those damn cats!

"Yeah, I'm not crazy about these parties either," Simon said. I cast a watchful eye as he took a sip from his glass, then leaned forward, resting his elbows on his knees.

"Can I get you something to drink?" Simon glanced at my empty hands, but I shook my head.

"That's ironic," I quipped. I straightened myself, thinking about what he'd said.

"What's that?"

"You don't want to be here? But this is your party." I hiked my eyebrows.

"It's all right, I guess, but I didn't ask for any of this. I love what I do … to some degree," His eyes didn't meet mine, instead focusing on the black slate floor. "It's the circus lights that I hate."

"Circus lights?" My smile grew with amusement.

"You're familiar?"

"Um, I'm not sure. Unless you're literally talking about circus lights, then I have no freaking idea."

"No, I'm talking about the bullshit that comes along with success. It's a false illusion, you know? Making you believe you're more important than you really are. At some point, if you live long enough under the lights, you become blinded to what reality is."

I can't relate; I have none of those issues. I had been modeling since the age of sixteen, and I was nowhere close to finding any success. Simon had established himself as a young fashion photographer, and though we had never met before, I had seen his work on the spreads of high-profile magazines. His photographs were works of art, and his night should have been celebrated, a huge achievement for any artist in his place. So I was baffled, staring into a pair lapis lazuli eyes, to discover that there was desolation living inside those walls.

"Tell me something. Do you wish to be unimportant, Simon?" His eyes didn't meet mine, instead diverting back to the cluster of people in motion. I had sensed it from the moment I'd met Simon. I knew there was more to him, but it was his prerogative if he wanted to talk about it. Why would he? I was a stranger.

"To be honest, I don't deserve this kind of attention. I thought things would get easier, you know? Maybe after having a few of these." He smirked, looking into his glass.

I knew for a fact that, since we'd arrived at the Cellar Bar,

Simon's hands hadn't been empty. It had seemed like he was just celebrating, but I couldn't ignore the feeling that there was something off.

"Is that why you were hiding at the Little Orange?"

He gave me a knowing grin. "I intended on coming … eventually. But I got distracted by a beautiful blonde." A big smile spread across his face.

"Oh, you're blaming me? You could have left anytime, you know?" Feeling flushed, I pushed my hair away, exposing the side of my face. His eyes trailed to my ear. My hearing aids were small and inconspicuous, but sitting this close I knew he saw them. If he asked, then I would have told him I had lost most of my hearing at the age of four, but he didn't.

"I couldn't leave you," he said, but something about his words moved me inside.

"So when I mentioned the party, why didn't you tell me who you were?"

"And what? Save you from putting your foot in your mouth?" He gave a slight grin.

"So funny," I shot him a glance. "Anyhow, even if you'd told me, I'm not easily impressed."

"I know, that's why I like you."

Oh.

"What's not to like about an Aries?" I said, trying to play it cool.

This made him pause. "So am I."

"Come on, you're not."

"You calling me a liar?" He chuckled.

"No, but Aries are supposed to be optimistic." I raised my eyebrows in amusement.

"I am. Just maybe not Monday to Friday."

"Huh, now I know why you're single." I was assuming.

"*Oh,* you're funny too!" He bobbed his head, as if he was reconsidering my statement. "Yeah, maybe you're right." He took out his driver's license and handed it over. I looked at his date of birth, a few weeks before mine and five years before me, which made him … twenty-six. A lot younger than I'd expected. I didn't know what it was about him that made him seem more mature.

"Well, it's a good thing we're not in a relationship—two Aries. There's a good chance this would be a very intense love-hate relationship."

"I enjoy a little chaos now and then. It keeps life interesting, you know?" He flashed a mischievous grin. *I don't doubt it.*

"Have you done any modeling? Is that how you took up photography?" It came to mind and I asked.

"No, I never modeled. I started off as a photojournalist, but my wife thought it was a job hazard, and so fashion was a safer bet."

"Oh … you're married?" My heart tightened.

"No, no … we're no longer together." There it was again, in his eyes … sadness. *He's too young to have been married and divorced; maybe this is the baggage Gloria spoke about.* I diverted my eyes back to the plastic card. There was something else written on his driver's license that piqued my interest.

"Your middle name is *Walter*?" I glanced up, and he made a funny face. "What? You don't like it?" I asked, handing back the laminated card.

"Not really."

"I think it sounds sophisticated, like Sir Simon Walter Rowe of … wherever you're from," I said, feeling playful.

"Perth," he added. "No, I have no royal blood running through my veins. My granddad was Walter."

"You must have been close."

"Ah, yeah … nah—well, sort of, I guess. The man was all right; not very affectionate."

"You can't choose your family," I said. *It's a statement that resonates with me. I should know.*

"No, you can't," Simon reaffirmed.

"Are you close to your family?"

"Sure. I would like to believe I am. My mum can be overbearing, and my dad is a bit of a workaholic, but they're both amazing. I haven't seen them in a while, though. I hope this summer to make it back home," Simon said.

Now he had me thinking of my dad, whom I hadn't seen since Christmas.

"So why are you sitting in this corner?" He lifted his glass to the crowd in front of us. "You should be showing me your moves."

"If you haven't noticed, Walter, I'm hiding," I mused.

"From what?"

"The clowns and the jokers." I flashed him a smile.

"And me?" His brow furrowed. I straightened myself to get a good look at him.

"No, with you I'm stuck right and center."

"Hey, isn't that a song?" He sang a few lyrics to the tune he was thinking about, off-key.

"Wow, you have an amazing … singing voice," I said, trying to keep a straight face.

"Liar!"

"I'm serious—oh wait, I think I hear the dogs howling outside," I said, and he burst into laughter. When I met his eyes, they softened. It was as if I could read his mind. I wished everyone around us would disappear.

"I don't mind being stuck anywhere with you," he offered, and I was the first to break away from the gaze that was making me feel so vulnerable.

"So, it's quite an accomplishment to be recognized tonight. You must be ecstatic at least for that?"

"Ah … well, a way to earn a crust, I guess. It has its perks. I get free breadsticks and I don't have to pay any taxes." He grinned.

"Wow, lucky you. So that's what happens when you win fashion photographer of the year?" I smiled at him.

"Pretty much." Simon leaned back in his chair. "Don't get me wrong, I work long hours and I'm very passionate about my job, but I didn't discover a cure for cancer or anything."

What was it about Simon that made me think I'd never met someone like him? Why did he feel less deserving of something he had a right to? I looked across at the crowd, and after a quiet moment, he said, "You know, we could turn this night around."

Something mischievous flashed across his eyes.

"We can? What do you suggest?" I shifted in my chair to get a better look, meeting Simon halfway.

"Well, I have something in mind, but first I want to know … are you in?"

His breath gave off the scent of whiskey, and the blood rushed through my veins.

Usually, this kind of proposition wouldn't catch me off guard, but coming from Simon, it felt almost surprising.

"Wow, you're straightforward, Simon." My cheeks burned. From the moment I'd met him, something had told me he wasn't the kind of guy who was up for an instant gratification. Now I wondered if I had been wrong. Yet here we were, in this environment, in the basement of a hotel where influences came into play. He was a man, I was a woman, and this undeniable raw attraction had spiraled between us, threading us together. There was nothing wrong with the laws of nature, but I knew how it worked. They say the faster you go, the more destructive the crash. *The only issue: someone will be left broken, and it will most likely be me.*

It's always me.

"Look, I don't want to act like some porcupine whose quills are up, but I like to get to know someone first before anything goes further." It was not always my rule of thumb, but that night I decided it should be.

"Oh, no," he chuckled. "That's not what I was implying," He jolted back up in his chair. "You've got a dirty mind, Mable Harper ... I was thinking about ditching this place and going to another bar." He gave me a charismatic smile, but I knew better. No man would refuse a girl if she were willing.

Men.

"Gloria warned me to keep my distance from you."

We both knew where tonight would go if I left with him. I would misbehave in the arms of this stranger, but what good would it do? I'd been down this path before. A man just had to smile, and I would swear that he was different and I was down for the game until they got bored of me. Maybe I was only destined to meet people who made me feel unfulfilled, repeatedly. But I was also the only one that could change that. Gloria was right. Even though I pretended to be this carefree girl, there was one thing I always wanted, even if it was impossible to gain.

Love.

This quest for love—it was like searching for the Holy Grail, and after a while, I'd come to believe it was only a myth. Love is the daughter of a trickster; no magic happens. It was nothing more than an idealism that made a relationship between two people appear more romantic or meaningful, I thought. The problem was, if you didn't know love, how the hell did you stop yourself from looking for it? Especially peering into a pair of eyes that were trying to convince your mind of anything otherwise. Good grief, all of a sudden I had this crazy craving for a spoonful—no, make it a crater-full—of Nutella.

"She's right, you probably should stay away." Simon glanced down at his glass, giving it a swirl. "If I go anywhere near you, she'll have my head on a silver platter and my arse in the binner." He emphasized the word *binner*, referring to Gloria's favorite word.

"I hate when she says that," I laughed.

"You reckon? I hear it thousands of times on the set."

He smiled, and our eyes met.

"Mable, I hope you haven't made up your mind about me. You have the most important aspects I look for, what I'm attracted to."

He sensed it, I knew it, and we'd already begun this tango, this two-step dance with each other.

"And what is that?" I drew myself in.

"A great personality, beautiful eyes … full, full lips … the kind I would like to kiss, if given a chance."

I knew there was a reason I liked this man. *What can I say to discourage him and myself?*

"Ah," I said, laughing, trying to shake off whatever had gotten me bothered. "Great personality? Ha, you haven't seen my full potential yet. I'd like to hear what you have to say when you do … I'm pretty feisty and stubborn. A woman who always speaks her mind," I said, and he studied me for a second.

"You seem harmless enough. I'm not afraid of your full potential … I like feisty, but stubborn … hmm." He gave me a wide smile. "I'm glad you speak your mind. It will save me the trouble of trying to guess what the hell you're thinking."

"You're intolerable." I shook my head.

"I'll take that as a compliment." He sucked in air, making me wonder how long it would be before I wore him down, or before he lost interest. "Look," he continued, "I understand you don't want to give me your number, and I don't want you to do something you're not comfortable with, but can I at least give you mine? I would like to see you again. I'll leave it up to you … tell me when and where, and I'll be there."

"I don't think it's a good idea. You'll get me into so much trouble." I averted my eyes around the room. *If I take his number, I won't be helping myself. I'll break my promise to Gloria and my future cats.*

"Why?"

"I promised Gloria that I wouldn't go anywhere with you or near you." I studied the space between us.

"She wouldn't have to know … I can keep a secret if you can."

I playfully narrowed my eyes. "You're relentless, Walter."

"So I have been told. I hope you can understand." He searched my face. "I can't go without trying."

"Do you always get what you want?" I said, forcing myself to pull back, because I realized how hard it was not to be drawn in by this man.

"No, I don't," he said honestly.

"Hmm, why do I find that hard to believe?" I glanced around the room—there were attractive women everywhere—and it was making me wish I was wearing more than just lip gloss. He could have gone after any of them.

"You're surrounded by hot girls all the time. You don't fool me, Walter."

"You're right, I am, and I take my job seriously. I don't mix work with my personal life. Even though I don't have much of a life these days." He scratched his jawline. "But to be honest, what attracts me goes beyond someone's attributes. I guess you could say I'm searching for truth in a world where everything is staged. I'm looking for authenticity in a person, and in this business, you don't come across much, or any at all. When you find it, you could never doubt it, and that's why it would be so hard to let it go."

"Do you see the truth in me?" I stared at him, because somehow his answer mattered.

"Yes, I do, Mable." His eyes delved into mine, like he was satisfied with what he saw. "You're more real than anyone in this room." There was something honest about his admission and it made me wonder exactly what he saw.

Good grief, here I'd thought I was doing a good job of holding off, but if he'd kissed me then, I wouldn't have been able to hold my ground. "There's nothing you can do or say to change my mind. I'm a brick wall." *Way to go, Mable; why not give him a challenge?*

"Do you know what happens when an unstoppable force meets an immovable object?" He leaned in closer, and chills run through me, making me wish he'd kiss me.

I guess I'll never find out; Gloria was approaching. "I got to go," I said. I stood up, disappointed, but it was one last desperate attempt to pull myself away from him.

"Will you be okay?" I nodded to the almost-finished drink in his hand.

"I had my limit … I'll get someone to take me home."

"Promise?"

"I swear, you have nothing to worry about," he said, and I believed him. His eyes shifted from Gloria to mine. "Well, it's a shame you have to go. You seem like a cool girl."

Cool girl …

I felt a twinge in my stomach. There they were, those two little words to set the tone, to disqualify me from anything more. No, I wasn't a cool girl—*not tonight … Tonight I'll be alone, feeling good about refusing to go down that rabbit hole.*

"You're a cool guy yourself, Simon Rowe." I answered him the only way I could, with the truth.

"Hey, Mable," he called back as I made my way to Gloria. I slightly turned in my step.

"Yes?" The way Simon made me feel under his gaze, I didn't think I'd ever get him out of my mind.

"You still think I'm cocky?"

"Hmm … I'm still on the fence," I winked, and this made him laugh.

I nodded, following Gloria toward the exit, hesitating a split second to turn back to find him still watching. The unstoppable force. *With all his efforts, he will never know how close he came …*

I braced myself on the edge of the border. But something told me it wouldn't be the last time I would see Simon. When you're attached by an invisible thread, you're never too far apart from each other.

Trouble on the Set

I should have taken the subway instead of Uber to the SoHo studio apartment. Maybe once I moved back home, I'd put money aside.

I doubt it.

It was still dark outside when I got into the car. I'd slept terribly the night before and felt like crap, so it took everything for me to leave the house at five in the morning without first having my coffee. But I didn't want to be late and deal with Gloria's annoying looks—it was too early for that. Gloria was the one who'd thought about me when her assistant called in sick the night before, and of course I was interested. The pay wasn't anything to crow over, but still, money was money. I was excited, and I thought that, if I tagged along, maybe it would inspire me in another direction. At this point I had no idea what I was about to do with the rest of my life. I'd postponed college to pursue a career in modeling, and there was only so long I could depend on my father financially. I had to figure out my next move, and fast.

Inside the loft, there were roughly thirty people on the set: a styling team, which Gloria managed, a tailor, hairstylist, and makeup artist, and the rest of the crew: handymen who'd built up the set for the backdrop. It was a two-day shoot; you needed a big group to make a quick project happen. After Gloria introduced me to the team, she led me down a hall that opened to several rooms. We continued to the end, coming into a large room that was to be used for prepping models. Inside, there were already two girls getting their hair and makeup done. On the opposite corner, racks and racks of earth-toned clothing were all gathered up against the wall.

"Hmm, this dress." Gloria held out a floral, embroidered tea-length gown.

"*Oh*, how pretty … I want it."

"Sure, it can be yours for only twenty thousand dollars."

"That's all? What a steal," I said. Before I could look through the rack, Gloria reached over and held my arm.

"Wait! Are your hands clean?" Gloria asked, and my mouth hung slightly open. I could deal with Gloria's antics, but this was too early in the morning, and I still hadn't had my coffee. I was beginning to think she was the real problem on the set—not Simon.

"Yes, they are, mother." I laughed because she was giving me a dead-on stare.

"Don't think I didn't see you wolf down a doughnut earlier. I just want to make sure you don't get any chocolate on a five-thousand-dollar skirt," Gloria said, checking off a list in her hands.

I'd enjoyed that doughnut, too! Getting dropped by Dania was the best thing that could have happened. Now I could eat whatever the hell I wanted without feeling guilty about it.

"What? This little thing cost five thousand dollars? Seriously?" My mind couldn't get around the fact that this tiny piece of fabric was worth more than I had in my bank account.

"Yes, and the designer will have my head on a silver platter and my ass in a binner if her samples come back damaged."

"Binner? That's not even a word," I mused.

"Yes, it is … the bin," Gloria said. "Trash can?"

"You're so weird." My eyes focused back on the collection. "Shit, if I had these clothes in my closet, I would never complain that I had nothing to wear." I sighed, my fingers touching the delicate fabric of the ruffled garments. I wished I could play dress-up, because these clothes were a work of art. Bruno Ortiz's designs embraced many types of women and sizes. His passion was reflected in the clothing he creates; that's what the Colombian designer did best. *Good grief, if only I weren't so broke.*

"Who are you kidding? You'll still complain." Gloria looked down at my feet. "Good choice of footwear, by the way. It's a good thing you're wearing *my* loafers, because the first day of the shoot is always the longest."

She took a sip from her coffee cup. Gloria was four years older and shorter than me. She wore a bare minimum of makeup, her dark hair worn long and straight like it always had been.

"Tell me something. We don't live together, so how the hell do you get your hands on my stuff?" Gloria's job was to select styles and accessories to create a whole storyline behind a fashion photo, almost like they'd became characters on their own. Her experience was vast; she'd done everything from print to television advertising campaigns. In my opinion, she had the best job. It gave her access to designer duds, sometimes all at a fraction of the price or even better—free. So, naturally, why wouldn't I go dabbling in her closet from time to time?

"I have a key to your apartment." I beamed. "Kidding. Tracy lets me in when you're out of town."

"Hmm, I'll start charging you a membership fee." She readjusted her black-framed glasses and put her cup down on a nearby table.

"Don't worry. You'll get them back before I skip town," I said.

"Keep them. I never wear them anyhow. So are you ready to start?" She smiled wickedly; *God knows what she has in store for me.* I had been on sets before, but never anything of this magnitude, and I was grateful that Gloria was allowing me to be a part of it. Even if it meant fetching coffee and unpacking boxes.

"Okay, so let's do this," I said, like I was ready to take over the world.

She laughed. "*Oh*, don't get too excited … you will hate me after today." Gloria walked a few steps and stopped in front of six boxes all stacked up.

"First, I need you to go through the packages and place the accessories on this table." She pointed to a long white fold-out board next to the boxes.

"After that, then what?" *I have a feeling I'm going to be stuck doing a lot of boring stuff.*

"That's when the real magic begins." She smiled at me.

"Hey, Gloria," said Steve, the makeup artist.

"Should I leave the lip bare until you decide what Jenny will wear?" Steve hovered over a model in his chair, getting her glammed up for the day.

"That sounds good." Gloria looked around the room. "Ah, where's Vanessa?"

"She's not coming," said the other model who was getting her hair blown out.

"What do you mean she's not coming?"

"When I left the apartment this morning, Vanessa was coming in from a night of partying."

"Well, he called it." Gloria bit her lip and looked down at her phone. "This is not good … have you ever seen a six-foot man have a tantrum? Well, Mable, it's your lucky day." I couldn't believe someone like Simon, so calm and in control, could have a temper, but then again, Gloria knew him better.

"If you have questions, Mable, I'll be in the other room,

trying to track this girl down. Shit, wish me luck," Gloria said over her shoulder, walking into the hallway.

I was halfway through emptying a box when I heard footsteps coming from behind me.

"Nice view," a deep voice said, and I stood up quickly, realizing someone had full sight of my back.

"Excuse me? That's inappropriate." I turned to find Simon standing there. Something on his face made me realize he wasn't talking about me.

"Yes, it would be if I were addressing your assets, love." He frowned. "But I was talking about the view from the window. I was thinking of having a few shots taken along this wall." There was a low laugh coming from a girl steaming out the clothing in the corner.

"Oh." I should have felt like an idiot, but I didn't.

I knew that the fashion industry was surrounded by predators, and harassment was not uncommon. You needed to protect yourself, because if you didn't, nobody would. I, unfortunately, had had to find that out for myself.

Once, my agent Dania had sent me on an audition test shoot, and I was excited because the photographer had worked with several luxury brands. But things quickly became weird when the photographer talked about how he always had sex with models. He asked me to remove everything but my underwear. I knew I had to get out of there quickly. I went back to my agent and told her what happened, and I was surprised by the lack of support. She laughed it off like it was nothing. "You need to grow a thick skin. It's part of the business, darling. Men will be men, and they creep around when it comes to young pretty girls. Yes, he's a flirt, but he's harmless. The next time just tell him you have a boyfriend and that should set him straight." This was my job; I didn't sign up for any harassment or abuse. I wasn't delusional. I knew this wasn't normal behavior, and it shouldn't have been acceptable. I would always stand my ground, no matter who it was. But, then again, there were good guys in this business; you just had to figure out which wolves wore sheepskin. I hoped Simon wasn't a creep.

"What are you doing here, anyway?" His tone was assertive, a way to intimidate me.

"Well, I thought you were okay with it. Besides, I'm here helping you out." I caught him suppressing a smile, and I knew he was messing with me.

"I didn't know you were Gloria's cousin," he said finally, fiddling with his camera.

"Yeah, her mom is my dad's sister," I said, opening another box filled with custom jewelry, all individually wrapped.

"So ... a spitfire ... Does it run in the family?"

"I heard that!" Gloria's voice came from another room.

"Shit, I forgot she has bionic ears." His eyes shut for a moment, then opened again, focusing back to mine. "Sorry, I didn't mean it that way ... I'm such an arse," he said.

The first thing I notice when people first learn of my disability is how uncomfortable it makes them, like everything they say might offend me, even if the comments are not directed to my hearing loss. But I don't get offended, and I'm not ashamed of my condition. This is a part of who I am. This is my normal.

"It's all right. I'm not super sensitive," I said, and he went quiet for a minute. "You said nothing wrong."

"So, Gloria tells me you're giving up on modeling and leaving New York."

"Well, it's for the best," I said with a wry grin.

"Funny, I didn't take you for a quitter."

"What?"

"Well, you said you were stubborn ... a brick wall."

I glanced up. *He's trying to figure me out, and I don't know how I feel about that. I like to read people, not the other way around.* "I am, but I'm not a quitter, Okay. I got dropped by my agent."

"So what? Doesn't mean you should throw in the towel."

"Apparently, I have nothing to offer," I said, my tone carrying an easy nonchalance.

"Who said that?"

"Like, all the agencies in the vicinity of New York." I lifting my hand to the window.

He walked toward me, kneeling down to my level. At first, I was mystified at what he was doing.

"The main thing I've learned in this business is that the ones who think they know it all are those who know jack shit. Don't allow people to make you feel you have nothing to offer when you do." He dragged his eyes across my face. "They're nothing but puppets, looking for the next person to exploit and cash in. Nah, you don't want to work with these people, anyway."

His eyes softened, and I wanted to believe him. There was nothing I desired more than to travel the world and have a job I'd always dreamed of doing, but how could I break through and make it happen?

"I've made up my mind."

"Well, maybe you're right. You're just not cut out for it … You don't have the hunger or the drive, so what's the point, right? No one will hire you … no other agency will want you."

"I—Well, it's more than that." I faltered. "I made a deal with my dad. If my career went nowhere within a year, then I would come home and continue my studies."

"Tell me something," he said, eyeing me. "What made you want to do this in the first place?"

As I stared at him for a moment, I was trying to figure out how much I wanted to reveal.

"Growing up, I was made fun of because of the way I

talked." I swallowed, turning away to empty out another box. "I don't know. I thought if I were pretty enough, maybe all my troubles would go away. So it became a long-held dream of mine." My mom had been a model in the eighties, mainly for catalogs, but she gave it up once I was born. I guess I wanted to be just like her, but I left that part out.

"You don't need to be a mannequin to validate your self-worth, Mable. You're beautiful, and I think there's nothing wrong in the way you talk. But if this is your dream—"

"It is." My stomach flipped. The thing that stuck in my mind was that he wasn't bothered by the sound of my voice— he thought I was beautiful, was nice too.

"So, what's stopping you?" He frowned.

"I told you."

"No, that's not a reason, it's an excuse," Simon said. "The only person who's stopping you is—you. This agent ... whoever the fuck she is, I bet she's never modeled a day in her life. You should respect only the opinion of someone who's been through it." He gently brushed my hair away from my face. "You need to find someone who will push and support you. Bottom line, you need the right person to represent you."

He was genuine, wanting to encourage me, even though he barely knew anything about me.

"You need to fight for the things you want in life, Mable, or else what's the point of breathing?" His eyes expressed tenderness, and it touched me more than words could say.

"Try not to destroy the dress, Emily. I have to get it back in one piece." We both looked up to find Gloria talking to the girl steaming the dress in the corner.

"Uh—Simon? We've got a problem." Gloria watched Simon as he straightened up.

"Don't say it."

"Vanessa—"

"Nope, I'm not listening."

"She didn't show up." Gloria quickly added.

He sucked in a breath. "And that's what I was afraid of." He walked a few feet and set up his equipment.

"So what's the plan?" Gloria said, following him in his steps.

"Not my circus, mate," he answered without glancing up.

"*Oh* no, no—this is your spectacle, and you're the ringleader," Gloria said, glancing my way. "Simon, seriously, we have so many samples to go through and I don't want to be here all night. What's the solution?" She leaned over, smacking his arm.

"Mable, you're my witness, see the abuse I get?" He gave me a teasing smile, sighed when he glanced back at Gloria. "You want me to repeat it? Vanessa is unreliable, a poor choice for the shoot. This is Elaine's fault. Either she comes up with a quick fix, or we'll handle it."

"Ugh. You know it will blow our budget. Maybe we should call Elaine and let her decide what to do."

"What? Is she not here? Hmm … I was wondering why the temperature hadn't dropped." Simon smirked.

"Get serious, will you?" Gloria looked at him flatly.

"Who's Elaine?" I asked.

"The most wretched woman you'll ever meet," Simon said, allowing his camera to hang by his side. "That woman is off her rocker."

"The editor of *Elite* magazine," Gloria clarified.

"Hey, Simon, the first drama of the day and you're mellowed out?" Noah said from across the room.

"I'm calm, mate, but internally it's a whole different story." Simon tapped his chest and shot a look my way. "I have to keep a cool head; we have family here today. I don't want to scare her off … not just yet."

He winked at me, bringing his attention back to my cousin.

"Please, Gloria, see if you can get ahold of Vanessa."

"Not my circus." She sang his words back to him. "I'm the stylist, not your assistant."

"Come on, mate. I'm asking you for a favor—as a friend. You know it's bad enough I have to work with Vanessa. I can't call her, and you know that." The way he said it led me to believe that there was something that had happened between them.

"All right, but you owe me, Simon."

"Whatever you want, consider it yours."

"I'm not joking; one day I will collect," Gloria said, storming out of the room.

"Mable?" Noah, the hairdresser, was cleaning his brushes and setting them aside.

"Yes." I looked up from the table. Gloria would be proud that I had everything unpacked and color-coordinated.

"I couldn't help listening to your conversation with Simon. I know someone who works at Next agency. I could call them, if you like?" Noah's dark hair flopped when he spoke.

"I appreciate it, I really do, but I don't think it's for me, quite frankly." I smiled.

"Well, don't feel bad, honey. It's not for everyone. The competition is fierce, and this business has its setbacks. I'm sure you'll find something better for yourself."

Before I could say another word, an unrecognizable girl came rolling in. She walked in with such force, as if expecting people to stop what they were doing just to look at her.

She tossed her glasses on the table, revealing the dark circles under her eyes. Her auburn hair had a straw-like texture that was hidden under a black beanie. She looked so defeated, I almost didn't believe it was the same person I'd seen on the cover of all those fashion magazines. And, for a moment, I caught her attention.

"What are you looking at?" she yelled, and I diverted my eyes away. I didn't bother getting into the drama. Instead, I piled up the cardboard boxes and placed them off to the side.

"You're late, and you look like shit. A night of partying when you know we have the biggest issue to shoot the next morning? Not smart," Gloria said, walking into the room.

"Why don't you mind your own business? I don't have to answer to you," Vanessa snapped.

"Hey, don't speak to Gloria like that. Her job depends on your showing up—have a little more respect." Simon glared, walking in right behind Gloria.

"What are you, my father? I could talk to her any way I want," Vanessa hollered back.

Simon's expression went flat.

"Noah, Steve, let's get her prepped and see what we can work with before Elaine shows up," Gloria said, trying to defuse the situation.

"Gloria, forget it. There's no amount of cake that will cover a night of partying. Send her home." Simon turned to walk away. "I can't work with unprofessional people."

"Oh, screw you, Simon," Vanessa shrieked.

Simon paused in his steps before turning around.

"You're embarrassing yourself, Vanessa, and you're embarrassing me. It's obvious you're not here to work, so just go home, please," Simon said calmly. Realizing everyone in the room was watching, he walked out.

Vanessa grabbed her purse with such force, darting straight after Simon and slamming the door to his office on the way in.

"Drama, drama, drama," Noah murmured.

"Crap, if we don't shoot soon, we will lose the light and this day will be a complete loss," Gloria said, picking out a few accessories and placing them aside.

"What's her problem?" I asked.

"She—" Gloria stopped, interrupted by the loud voices coming down the hall.

"Yeah, well, I'm fucking done," Vanessa yelled. "Who do you think you are? This is bullshit … I will sue your ass off, Simon," the model said as she stormed down the hallway, her exit followed by a big thud.

"Vanessa! Vanessa," Gloria called out.

"Let her go." Simon appeared, leaning against the doorframe.

"Way to go, Simon." Gloria looked utterly defeated.

His lips were tight. "You know I refuse to work like that, and I've given her plenty of chances before."

"So now what? We're definitely in a pickle," Gloria murmured.

Simon's eyes pegged me from across the room. "No, we're not."

"Plan B? Oh hell, Simon. Elaine won't agree to it."

"She will. I'm Simon Rowe," he said, his eyes radiating with confidence.

"You can't just do whatever you want."

"Watch me." Simon pushed himself off the doorframe and walked farther into the room. "Let's get Mable ready." He turned to Gloria, talking as if I weren't even in the room.

"Ready for what?" My heart raced.

"What's the worst that can happen?" Simon shrugged.

"We won't get paid," Noah snorted.

"Hello? Guys?" I was trying to get a word in, but no one was listening.

"If Elaine is not happy with the results, I'll pay for everything," Simon said.

"You're insane," Gloria pressed.

"Sure I am." Simon gave her one of those confident, sexy smiles that I loved. "Trust me, she'll be right."

"Guys! Can someone please tell me what's going on?" I asked. They were both staring at my face as if they'd seen me for the first time.

"We have a problem, and you're the solution." Simon stepped closer.

"Me? But you haven't seen my portfolio—I'm not."

"I don't need proof. I know how the camera will react to you. But I have to warn you, I'm very demanding on the set. I don't want you to hold back, not from me—ever. I want it all … all of you."

I gazed at him for a moment. I was balancing on the fence. On one side, I wasn't willing to move away from the pain of disappointment, and on the other, I wanted to give him my wholehearted all. This was my opportunity to see my face inside *Elite* magazine.

"I don't know—" I twisted my fingers in my other hand.

"Mable, don't throw in the towel. You walk away now, think about the future you might be sacrificing. If you don't buy the damn ticket, how do you expect to win the lotto?"

"It's kind of impossible to win." I gave him a sideways smile.

"Not with me." A big smile plastered across his face; his eyes had magic in them, like he could make anything happen. Simon thought this could be monumental for my career. He believed in me, and when someone has that kind of faith in you, you can move mountains.

"So are you in?"

And an unstoppable force squeezed a *yes* out of me.

One Way or Another

The following morning, Simon found me sitting in a chair while Noah separated, pulled, and straightened my hair, getting me ready for the last day on the set. I was taking mental notes from Noah, who was offering me pointers on how I should take better care of my hair. *Good grief, Noah has way too much energy this early in the morning.* I sat there like a noodle, the rhythmic sound of the blow-dryer putting me into a trance. My eyes were half-closed, exhausted from yesterday's shoot— not that I was complaining. *Actually, am I even getting paid for this*? It would have been smart to ask before we'd started, but I was so blinded by excitement to be part of the shoot that I'd jumped at the chance without thinking about anything else. Then again, some opportunities can't be summed up with money.

"Howzit goin'?" Simon sat in the empty chair beside me, giving me a side-glance. "I hope I didn't tire you out from yesterday?" he said, as I straightened myself higher.

"Are you kidding me? Please, yesterday was a piece of cake." What he didn't know was that, when I'd gotten home, I'd passed out in my bunk bed. Slept like a total baby. "There's nothing you can put me through that will slow me down. I got stamina." I smiled. Yeah, maybe after a morning coffee—or two.

"Stamina?" Simon repeated it. "You think you could keep up with me?" He slightly shook his head.

"Haven't I already?" I raised my brows.

"True, but I can't wait to hear what you'll say after today."

I caught myself staring at Simon. His hair was worn back, but not snug enough. Some sandy-brown locks had come undone, trailing in front of his face when he looked down at the papers resting in his hands. I wouldn't say Simon was eccentric, but he had hints of it in his style. On his wrists he wore an arrangement of colorful leather bracelets with silver links. I didn't know any other man who wore that much jewelry, but on Simon, everything suited him.

"So, what did you want to talk about?" I said, now able to reposition my head, catching his eyes through a large, cheap, black-framed mirror that leaned against the wall in front of us.

"I wanted to bounce ideas with you before we shoot." He playfully rolled the papers in his hands.

"Sure," I said.

"I think we'll do the first half on the roof, and, if the lighting is perfect, we could get some shots in the studio, too." His voice was deep but cheerful. "So, Gloria went through the collection, and she has this idea of a theme … a mixture of seventies rock and downtown art scene vibes." His eyes scanned the walls. "Think … Debbie Harry." He motioned with his hand. Another thing I'd noticed about Simon was the use of his hands as a way to express himself. He accentuated it more when he talked about something he felt passionate about.

"Debbie who?"

"Are you kidding me?" Simon's eyes grew wider.

"No. I kid you not. Does she, um … have a reality show or something?"

Simon made a clicking noise with his mouth, like I'd said something offensive. "How could you not know? She's a legend." His voice went up at the end.

"Surprising, right? Not all intellectuals know about *everything*. So spare me." I shrugged. "I'll just Google her later." My phone was out of my reach.

"You know who I'm talking about, mate?" Simon looked up at Noah, who was now teasing my hair, which stumped me, because he had spent twenty minutes smoothing it out. But he was the stylist, who was I to question him? *I'm going to have so much fun getting those knots out later.*

"She's the lead singer of the band Blondie ... 'Call Me'?" Noah said to me.

"But you're right here." I winked.

"It's a song, love," Simon added.

"Yeah ... I got that."

It went over Simon's head, and he sang a few verses.

"God, here we go again." I murmured. "Oh-oh, the dog's howling again."

I glanced at Noah, and he chuckled.

"For heaven's sake, Simon, cut me some slack. I wasn't even born yet." I groaned, but it was useless. Another thing I'd learned about Simon: he didn't know when to let go.

"Know this one?" I watched Simon scroll down his phone. When Noah caught me in the mirror, I half-rolled my eyes.

"Aye?" He held up his phone for us to hear. Noah sang along and swung his shoulders, getting into it as I laughed. My gaze found Simon's bright eyes reflecting back.

"Sorry, Simon, I'm not from your generation ... old geezer," I said, finally seizing a moment to drink my now-cold coffee.

He stifled a laugh. "Who are you calling old?"

"Well, close to thirty is pretty ancient," I teased, giving Simon a wide grin.

"Oh, I see how it is." Simon playfully narrowed his eyes at me.

"What?"

"Don't tell me you're one of those girls?"

"What girls?"

"Crazed fangirl who likes bands that don't know how to play an instrument, and it takes six guys to sing one song," he laughed.

My mouth dropped. "First, there's five of them. And don't judge me or make fun of them." *As we speak, there's still a poster of Harry hanging up on the wall of my old bedroom, but I'm not about to tell him that.*

"They're top blokes, but the most untalented bunch of guys I ever met," Simon said through the mirror.

"Wait? You met them?" My voice got louder at the end.

"Yeah. I shot them for the cover of *Rock* magazine last year."

"Seriously?"

"Seriously?" He mimicked me, his voice hitting an upward inflection. "Oh, that got your attention. Which one are you crushing on … Liam?"

"No way … I'm more of a Harry kind of gal."

"Huh."

"What?"

"I would never think the dude with the messy hair would be your type." He stood and tapped my knee with the rolled paper and walked away. I couldn't help but think he was on to something. *Maybe I have a weakness for guys with messy hair. Like Simon.*

"Hey, Simon," I called out.

"What?" His voice echoed from the other room.

"Can you get me Harry's number?" I howled out. *Joking, but not joking.*

"No." His voice bellowed. And suddenly the music changed on the speaker … Simon blasted the music, playing some seventies song that I had never heard of. Noah and I laughed.

Later, Simon had me sitting on a stool in front of a deep green curtain with props behind me. He took a couple of shots, then stopped and walked over to his laptop, where he analyzed the pictures. He leaned over to Gloria, said something unclear, but my eyes watched the shape of his mouth, which spoke some sort of praise just before he returned. I repositioned myself, and we started the process over again. *A hundred shots will be taken before one is considered good.*

Chick che ... flash.

Chick che ... flash.

Nobody ever tells you how exhausting this process can be, the continuous lights flashing in your eyes. The repetitive movements: bring my collar up, put my collar down, extend my leg, retract my leg. Sometimes I ended up in the most awkward positions, but it had to look natural. *I'll do anything to give him that perfect shot.*

At this moment I was fighting for Simon's approval, offering my all to get something back from him. Praise, admiration, maybe even love. In this case, I wasn't talking about romantic love, but the kind that every model wants from a photographer. If you make him fall in love with you, make him believe the most amazing shots are created only when you're around, then he will ask you to work with him again ... and again. This was supposed to be a one-time deal, but I still couldn't help wanting to be Simon's muse.

"Beautiful, perfect, great ... keep doing that," Simon said.

Chick che ... flash.

Everything was going well until *she* showed up.

I would be lying if I said I was surprised to see her again. After witnessing what had happened yesterday, I would have been crazy to think she would go quietly.

"What are you doing here, Vanessa?" Gloria met her at the doorway, trying to block her from coming in farther. "I thought Simon made it clear to you we won't be using you for this shoot. You need to go home."

Everyone in the room stopped what they were doing, including Simon, who now placed his camera down on the floor.

"I need to talk to Simon." Vanessa plowed through Gloria, making her way toward Simon.

"Vanessa, I'm working … please go home." Simon attempt to take her by the arm, but she jerked away.

"I'm not going anywhere until you tell me why you're not returning my calls." Vanessa's eyes only focused on Simon, disregarding everyone else in the room. Her uncombed long brown hair clung to her bare face, and her sweatshirt and jeans looked stale. I wondered if Simon was the reason for her condition.

"I'm not doing this in front of everyone. Let's take this outside," Simon said, his head slightly tilted down. When Vanessa looked away, her eyes settled on me, and her face went to a paler white.

"Who the fuck is she? Is she taking my place? I can't believe this … are you fucking her now?" Her eyes felt like daggers, her long finger pointing right at me. "A fucken retard?"

"Oi, that's enough." Simon's agitation reached its boiling point. "Leave Mable out of this. It's me you have a problem with."

This was not the first time I had had someone direct their hate without a substantial reason for it. Though I wasn't new to the drama, I'd once lived with two other models, and there was never a shortage of melodrama in the apartment. Still, this was something else altogether. I'd been called a *retard* before, and I'd thought, as an adult, I would stop attracting bully behavior. It's funny how people seem to focus only on what makes you different instead of seeing the person you are. But I wouldn't let her get under my skin or engage, because I wasn't the one with the problem.

"I will not allow you to come in here and abuse the people I care about. You lost this gig on your own merit, so own up to it … go home." This time he caught her by the arm, and she didn't resist. She stopped halfway and turned back.

"Hey, bitch, watch out for this guy. He will screw you over like he did with me," she yelled out, flipping me the bird, sending everyone in the room into a shuffle.

"She's delusional," Noah said, when they were out of sight. We stood there, all fifteen of us pretending not to eavesdrop on the shouting match outside the door. I couldn't help wondering, what made Vanessa so out of control? And had Simon played a part in it?

"Are you okay, hon?"

I looked up and met Noah's velvety brown eyes.

"Oh, I'm fine." I wasn't, and I couldn't bring myself to smile.

"Don't take it personally. That girl … she's got a lot of issues." His mouth slightly hung in midair. "Look, what she said back there, making Simon out to be a jerk. It's not what you think."

I nodded. I didn't know why Noah felt compelled to clarify. Nothing was going on between Simon and me. Whether what Vanessa had said was true made no difference. But I felt something. Vanessa's attack had triggered heavy emotions. Even if I knew her anger wasn't intentionally directed at me, it didn't make my feelings less real.

My eyes caught the camera resting on the floor, and something came to mind. I'd once read somewhere that there is a spiritual belief that taking a photograph steals a person's soul. After witnessing Vanessa's behavior, I had to question it. Vanessa was a model at the top of her game, and I guessed something must have happened that got her caught in a downward spiral. Who knew— maybe the business had stolen Vanessa's soul. I felt it in her eyes. Past the anger and the jealousy, there was an unmistakable essence of loss.

The lights are so bright, and just like a moth to a flame, the outcome seems inevitable.

"Oh shit. I'm so sorry … I didn't mean to walk in on you." Simon diverted his eyes away from me. "I thought you were dressed." He had come into the back room, catching me in the middle of getting ready to go home, and I made no effort to cover up. I was only glad my undergarments matched, and that they were half-decent.

"It's alright."

I felt good in my skin, and you had to, to be in this line of work. But I found it endearing the way Simon was showing signs of embarrassment.

"Is there something you wanted to do over?" I asked, pulling on my light wash jeans, thinking the shoot hadn't gone so well in the second half. After Simon got Vanessa to leave, he'd come back in the room like nothing happened, but his demeanor had changed. He went from being playful to tight-lipped on the set. Simon couldn't even meet my eyes, which was hard, since we were still shooting. I understood. He was exposed, his dirty laundry out for everyone to see. That was probably why the crew didn't make a big deal about it, which made me believe either this had happened before, or they didn't want to agonize him any further.

"Ah, no … No, everything's great. I was heading out with the gang to the bar across the street. You're more than welcome to come along."

He still couldn't bring himself to look my way, and my smile widened. Where had the overconfident man I met at the Little Orange gone? I couldn't say he appeared different from the man I'd first met—just a little less self-assured. Maybe the dynamics of our relationship had changed. Whatever it was, it only made me like Simon more, in a platonic kind of way. *Or at least that's what I keep reminding myself.*

"Are you always this well behaved?" I asked, sliding on my black bomber jacket.

"What?"

"You have a half-naked girl in front of you, and you haven't attempted to sneak a glance."

He took a second to reply. "I'm always a gentleman ... when I need to be."

I couldn't see his face, but I could hear the smile in his voice. I rather enjoyed these innuendos between us. I grabbed my purse and secured the long strap across my chest. *I'm taking no chances this time.* If anyone wanted to take my satchel, they would have to take me along with it.

"You could turn around now. I promise not to scandalize you any further," I said, walking closer to him. "So now that we officially work together, we have to keep this strictly professional," I teased. Was it wrong that I wanted to provoke him to cross the line?

"It would be best. Well, you had your chance." His lips curved slightly, the look in his eyes making me think he wanted to say something more, but it remained unsaid. Though, if I wanted to, I knew I could change his mind.

But I had rules of my own. Never chase after a guy—ever. I was interested in them until they weren't. So I dismissed, deleted, and moved on to another horizon. I swept my hair to the side, placing the right hearing aid in as Simon stood there watching.

"How long have you had them?"

"Since I was a kid," I replied.

"Can you hear without them?" I like the softness in his eyes and the fact that he was curious about it, about me. This was more than just a disability; it was a part of me.

"Yes, I can, only the sound comes to me muffled. It's like being under the water, and the aids help filter the sounds." A smile grew on my face. "Do you know what the best part about having these things is?"

"Tell me."

"I just have to take them out, and I don't have to hear your jabbering, Walter," I said.

He laughed, and he pointed at me, his hands fluttering across his face.

"What did you say?" I giggled, amazed he knew ASL.

"You don't know sign language?"

"No, I was raised in the hearing world. So there was never a need to learn."

"To be honest, I'm not fluent, but I know some signs. My cousin Jack is deaf," Simon said. He was always surprising me. The more things I discovered about him, the more I wanted to know. *I wish I had more time.*

"Shall we go?" I asked, knowing everyone was waiting for us. I didn't want to give any more reason for them to gossip today.

"Hold up, what's that you're wearing?" Simon asked as I walked past him. I shook my head, not connecting.

"I thought you didn't listen to seventies music," he said, taking a second glance.

"I don't."

"So why on earth are you wearing a Black Sabbath T-shirt?" He chuckled.

"Because I liked the print." I tugged at the cotton fabric that I had found it at a thrift shop. Simon gave me a cocky smile just before he distanced himself from me.

"Hey, are you going to tell me what you signed?" I asked.

"I signed … you're a cute and funny bird. But if you call me Walter one more time, I will kiss the hell out of you," he said, over his shoulder, just before disappearing around the corner.

Play to Win, Even if It Means You Lose

S imon and I were the last to arrive at the Liquored bar, and I could feel all eyes on us. Just like I had imagined, we had gotten the rumor mill started. But I didn't want to live up to the cliché of the model who slept with the photographer to get the job. I was not that kind of girl. I knew I shouldn't care what other people think, but I did.

"What are you having?" Simon turned to me.

"I'll have a vodka cranberry—but wait … Hey, hold on, I'll give you the money." I was reaching into my purse, but Simon put his hand over mine, and something inside me fluttered.

"No, it's on me. After what you did for us, let me at least buy you a drink."

I sat next to Noah, watching Simon walk over to the bar.

"Hey … can I ask you something?" I continued when Noah nodded. "How long have you known Simon?"

"We've been friends for a while, give or take five years. Why?"

Those past two days I'd gotten to know Noah, trusting him enough to divulge my personal struggles. We later discovered we both had our share of mommy issues. My mother had been absent from my life since the age of six, and Noah's mom couldn't come to terms with him being gay. They hadn't spoken to each other in the past two years.

I felt we shared enough that we could speak freely, so I asked the question that had been scratching me all day.

"What's the deal with Simon and Vanessa?" I said. In one movement, I gathered my hair into a bun.

"Oh, honey, don't go there." Noah swirled the mint leaves in his glass with a clear stir stick.

"Were they an item?" I frowned. After what I'd witnessed, I felt compelled to know. Maybe Vanessa was one of Simon's scorned lovers. Simon had once told me he never got involved with people he worked with. I wondered if she was the reason for his rule.

"Truthfully, it's a hell of a story … Too long and complicated to get into it. Get my drift?" He knitted his brows together.

No one was willing to talk about it, and I had to respect that, but it only made me want to know more.

"Now it's my turn to ask a question." Noah smiled like he knew he would put me on the spot.

"Sure."

"Are you involved, or … contemplating getting involved?"

"With Simon? No."

"Right," he said. *I wouldn't believe me either if I were him.*

"Why would you say something like that?"

"Oh, I don't know. The way you look at each other, I guess."

I laughed. "Well, we have to. I mean, how else are we supposed to work together?"

"I'm not talking about what happened in the studio. I'm talking about that night at the Cellar Bar." He grinned. "You two were mighty cute and cozy." Noah's eyes twinkled, which made me wonder who else was watching us that night.

"Ah, yeah okay, I won't deny there's a certain chemistry between us—but it's strictly professional." *For now.* "To be honest, I don't know Simon that well. But hypothetically … would it be a bad thing?" I tilted my head in Simon's direction. He stood at the bar, talking to the other model. I observed his body language; he wasn't into her the way I imagined any man in his right mind would be. *Her, on the other hand …*

"It's not for me to say." Noah looked into his glass, then his eyes met mine, as if he wanted me to understand something without revealing too much.

"Simon is very selective in the people he surrounds himself with. He's the type of guy who'll give you the shirt off his back, but also the kind of person who can retreat within himself with no warning. He's got issues he needs to work out, and I don't think he's found a way just yet. I want to be honest—because I like you."

Noah pushed his glass aside and looked at me.

"You're leaving, and Simon travels a lot. I'm not sure how this will work out for you two."

I didn't know why Noah's words were so disheartening.

"Honestly, I'm not in the slightest interested in Simon. I mean, he's an awesome guy, but we wouldn't have anything in common," I said, watching Simon from across the room. I felt relieved when I found him alone again.

All this talk about Simon, but I hadn't given any thought to my baggage—a messy, worn-out duffel bag with stale clothes. At this point in my life, I could say I was a professional when it came to being rejected.

We could start at the root of it: my mother was at the top of that list. The runner-up was Marc, my first real boyfriend in college. Things were great until I ruined it by telling him I loved him. Well, I'd never imagined he would break up with me over it. I was a mess for weeks. I had allowed someone to wreck me because I sincerely cared for them. It sounds kind of cruel, doesn't it? After Marc, I'd never allowed those words to come out again, not to anyone. Yup, that's baggage for you. I hoped that, miraculously, my dirty laundry would get washed on its own or disappear at customs, but I guessed things couldn't get resolved on their own. You have to come up with your own resolutions. I just wasn't sure if I was ready for it yet.

"Hey, the next time you're in town, we'll get together with a couple of mojitos. Maybe I'll tell you all about it then."

"Sounds like a plan." I smiled. Simon came around the table, placing my drink in front of me, but before I could thank him, he raised his glass.

"Okay, guys, let's cheers to a fantastic shoot that almost went to shit. I couldn't have done it without you fuckin' amazing people, and Mable, thank you for saying yes. It seems you're always there at the right time." He glanced down and smiled. It sent chills of excitement throughout my body.

"Cheers," everyone yelled, bottles and glasses clicking together.

Gloria slid into the other chair next to Noah.

"Hey, you know what I wanted to ask you? How did you keep Elaine away?" Noah said to my cousin.

"Oh, she was supposed to come, but had a flight out to L.A. at the last minute. She thought there was no need to come since we had everything under control. Little did she know. Anyway, it all worked out fine," she said, taking a sip from her wineglass.

"That's not like her. She puts her nose into everything— like, everything!" Noah said.

As I sat there listening to their conversation, I remembered that, at one point, during my emptying of the boxes, that there had been a very sophisticated-looking woman who had walked into the room. She had taken one look at me—or, I thought she had— it was hard to tell; she was wearing big sunglasses.

"She was there," I interrupted.

"What?" Gloria peeked her head around Noah to get a better

look at me.

"Yeah, the first day of the shoot. She came in, but left before I could ask her anything."

"What did she look like?" Gloria asked.

"Late fifties, Chanel suit, big glasses, and blond pageboy haircut."

"Yeah, that sounds like Elaine Furstenberg," Noah said, taking the last sip of his drink.

"Weird. Why would she leave like that?" Gloria said, looking at both of us.

"You think she was spying on us?" Noah asked.

My attention shifted to Simon, who was sitting in front of me, talking to one of the crew. *I'm not sure what to make of Simon.* At times he seemed hard to read, but I was never afraid of the unknown. While everyone at the table slowly scattered around the room, I found myself alone with Simon. He sat across from me, and we smiled at each other like two kids playing some sort of game.

"So what's next for you?" I yelled over the loud music.

He picked up his bottle and chose the seat next to me. "Sorry, what was that?" His leg gently brushed against mine. I wished he would do it again.

"What's next on the agenda?"

"I'll take some time off. I say that, but I never do." He smiled. "I wish you could stay."

"What?" My heart stirred up, shaking the dust off. Only now, with the sound of Simon's voice, did it respond.

"Stay in New York, and we could work together again."

I yearned to say yes. What if he meant something more than just for work? This was flat out clairvoyance. I knew how this would play out, and if I stayed Simon would become the biggest rejection of all.

"You've got something special ... going at it like an apparatus, full of energy and postures. For a moment I thought I wouldn't be able to keep up." He smiled gently before he continued. "It was a real pleasure to shoot you."

"That's very kind, but I'm no different from any other model—"

"No, you're definitely something else. Not everyone gets it the way you do. Everyone thinks modeling is about showing up and putting on a beautiful face, but it's more. You understand that every garment has its own personality, a fluid quality to it. You have to love what you do; that's the only way it's captured on film."

"Where were you when my agent gave me the boot?" I smirked, peeling back the label on his beer bottle.

"I'm surprised you're not doing this full time. Obviously you had a bad agent. Let's prove her wrong ... And stay."

How can anyone say no to this man? "Oh, I—"

"I could use someone like you, because you're not a model."

"No? So what am I?" I smiled.

"You're a muse ... my muse, a feast for my creativity," Simon blurted out. "Something about you stirs emotions inside me. You make things happen. To be honest, it's something I've never felt. This kind of connection—you can't make this up."

Settle down, heart.

"I guess it feels natural. When the makeup and the clothes come on, it reinvents me." I directed my eyes back to him. "It's nice to escape from being me."

"Why would you want to escape from who you are?" His eyebrows crashed together.

"Doesn't everybody?"

"I think it's funny you say that, because under all the characters you felt you were playing today—the ones you thought you were hiding behind—I saw a girl who wants to be let out. The truth is you were playing yourself all along," he said, looking at me with those loving eyes. "The thing is, you don't believe what you're capable of. Don't allow your ambitions to come undone because of self-doubt. Only you have control over that. You're ready to take the world by storm. No more fears, Mable. Set out and do what you're meant to do."

"I don't know what to say." I looked up at him. "Thank you?"

He let the words sit there between us before he continued. "I should be the one to thank you for helping me out of a jam. You might have saved my career."

"So was I your plan B?" I now suspected Simon was the reason Gloria brought me along.

"No, you were my plan A," he said, his eyes going clear. "Look, I didn't know how the day would work out. I simply aligned my ducks, and everything happened as it should have."

I leaned my head back into the blue-tufted chair and tilted it lightly, looking up at him. He smiled in a way that made me believe Simon Rowe never left anything up to chance. He was a man who made things happen, and I couldn't help but wonder if he had every intention of making things happen inside of me.

"The first moment I saw you at the Little Orange, sitting on that run-down couch … You just lit up, hooking me in. I only regretted not having my camera with me that night."

God, am I blushing? Pretty sure I am.

"There was a lot of tension on the set today." I had to bring it up, because I was trying to convince my heart how wrong it was about Simon. *Pay attention, heart. I'm doing this for your own good. There could be someone else in his life.*

"Yeah. I'm sorry for the way Vanessa acted. It was uncalled for."

"It's not your fault." I said. His lips parted, but he diverted his eyes away, focusing on the corner of the room.

"Hey, you think you could kick my arse in a game of pool?" I liked how he changed the subject, but I took note.

"I can," I said matter-of-factly.

He was taken aback. "Wow, very confident bird. I like that."

"I enjoy playing games, and it so happens that I'm fantastic at winning—like a lot." I smiled brightly. "You should prepare yourself, because you will do a lot of losing."

"Oh, uh … that good, hey?" His expression cleared. "No worries, mate, I'm sure I could take you down. Win with my eyes shut."

"Listen, Crocodile Dundee, this is not my first rodeo," I replied. He laughed louder, watching me get up from my chair, removing my jacket.

"Well, Mable, you better put your money where your mouth is." He got up, making his way to the table, and I followed.

"Oh, I'm planning to. Eight ball?"

"Sure," he said.

"What should we play for?" He leaned closer as I racked in the stripes and solids. *Good grief, what cologne was he wearing?* The scent interfered with my every thought. I need to move away from him if I wanted to win.

"What else—money."

"Okay, twenty?" He tied back his hair with a black elastic from around his wrist. I thought to myself, *not much help that will do.*

"Come on, you've got to do better than that, you cheap bastard." I gave him a cheesy grin.

"Wow. I don't know how I feel about this side of you." He quirked a brow.

"Am I scaring you?"

"Um, no. Oddly, it's turning me on." I half-rolled my eyes. "Okay, fine." He inhaled deeply. "I just didn't want you to lose your shirt over this." His eyes flashed wickedly.

"Thank you for being such a perfect gentleman," I said. "But I told you I will not be the underdog."

"You really think so? That's cute." He dragged out a bill

from his trifold wallet, placing it on the edge of the pool table. "Hundred bucks, how does that sound?"

He smiled; he was enjoying this way too much. But I knew something he didn't: I'd been taught by a three-time national champion pool player. *I think I will only disclose that trivia after I wipe that overzealous smile off his face.* I flashed him a knowing look as I hauled out five twenty-dollar bills from my purse, placing them on top of his. I planned to win, because I needed that money to survive the next couple of days I had left in the city. He handed me a cue stick. Unsatisfied with its condition, I passed it back to him and took another from the wall.

"Solids or stripes?"

"Solids." I chalked the top of my cue stick.

"Okay, Mable, let's have a fair go." Simon leisurely leaned against the table behind him. "I'll appreciate the view from here." *I know what he's trying to do—rattle me up to distract me—but it's not going to work. I can't wait to show him who's boss.*

"Look all you want, Simon. Soon you'll kiss it," I said, knowing he would have full regard of my backside. I placed the chalk down and made my way back to him.

"That wouldn't be a bad thing," He looked slyly at me. "Don't give me that look, you stepped right into that."

He had me there.

"So you're super competitive?" he asked.

"Oh, you have no idea." I swept my hair to the side and caught his eyes while doing it.

"I'll tell you what. I'll take my shot standing on one limb and with one hand behind my back," Simon approached, a little too close.

I stood there, anxiously idle. "Oh, how generous, but that won't be necessary. Now get out of my way and let me show you how it's done." I nudged him with my hip to scoot him over—he was a beast—and it made no impact. He laughed and moved over, anyway.

"This will be fun, seeing you lose." His eyebrows playfully went up. I got down to my stance. I was sure he had a full view of me, but I focused on keeping low on the cue ball and struck hard as I could. The balls scattered all around the table.

"Not bad." He walked around, then leaned in to line up his shot. Simon sent four balls into the sockets. He slowly glanced up.

Shit.

"Not bad," I said coolly. *I hate losing, even more to a man who's getting under my skin.* I had to up my game. I took my shot, and more balls went in.

"How did you learn to play?" He took his turn, and I was not happy with the outcome.

"My dad." I smiled, trying to line up my shot, but I could see Simon goofing around in front of me, moving his stick side to side and making me lose my focus.

"I know what you're doing," I said, placing my hand on my hip.

"What?" Looking innocent.

"Please don't stand in my shot."

"Oh, was I distracting you?"

I saw how this was going; I had to come up with something better. He made his way around the table, found his opportunity, and leaned over.

"Simon?"

"Yeah."

"I'm considering getting a tattoo."

"Hmm."

"Do you think it would look stupid if I get one right here?" I brought down the waistband of my pants, but not low enough to reveal anything more than I wanted. It seemed to have worked, because he missed his shot, narrowing his eyes at me.

"You have no intentions of getting a tattoo."

"Maybe." I smiled wickedly. "I think I'll get one of an eight ball to commemorate this win." I winked. As I leaned in to take my shot, Simon took his white T-shirt and pulled it over his head.

"What are you doing?" I swallowed.

"Now see, Miss Harper, two can play that game," he said, and I had a full view of an exceptional fit torso. I laughed nervously, not because I felt uneasily hot, but because now we were drawing attention from everyone else, and soon enough we had an audience. *It's a good thing it's slow for a Tuesday night.*

"Are you guys playing strip pool? You know that's indecent exposure, right?" Noah's voice came from behind us.

I turned to Noah, mouthing the word *damn.* I tried not to focus on Simon's body and instead on my shot.

"Gah," It didn't go as planned.

"Is this distracting you?" He flexed, and I stuck my tongue out at him.

"Okay, wise guy, put your guns away before you hurt somebody. Take your shot, will you?"

"*Ouch*, somebody's not happy. Pay attention, maybe you can learn a thing or two." He winked before sliding his shirt back on. Then he leaned down, aligning his stick.

"You're sure you want to do that?" I asked.

"Go on, do your worst."

He positioned himself. Just before he took his shot, I leaned close to his ear and whispered, "I can't handle myself when I'm around you. I want you in the worst possible way." Yup, that did it. The cue ball went off the table, and the crowd laughed and howled.

"Oh, that sucks," I said. I looked down at my nails, freshly painted pink, somehow already chipped.

"*Shiiitt.*" He sighed in disbelief, and his eyes slowly trailed up the length of me. "What the hell was that?" He straightened up, his eyes filled with heat. "Explain, woman."

"You told me to do my worst." I flashed him an innocent smile.

"And that's what you thought of? You shouldn't say shit like that unless you mean it."

"Like what?" I fluttered my eyelashes.

"You like playing with fire?" he murmured.

"If it means winning, yes. I have a talent for getting what I want." *It's a total lie, but I say it anyway.*

"Well, don't entice me into wanting to explore that talent of yours," he said, close enough to my ear.

A heat rose through me, and I realized that what had started as a friendly game had become something else.

Simon's phone buzzed from his back pocket, and it put an end to the match we were playing. A crease appeared on Simon's forehead as he looked down at his phone.

"Sorry, I need to take this."

I watched him walk outside and appear on the other side of the window. It was clear from his facial expression that he wasn't happy talking to whoever it was.

───────────

Later, when Simon came back in, he made the rounds, saying his goodbyes to the gang before making his way back to where I was standing.

"Hey … I'm so sorry. I have to go. A friend is in some sort of trouble, and I need to check up on them. Will you still be around in … about an hour?" Simon slid his hands into his front pockets.

"I wish I could, but it's been a long day," I said. God, I was so bummed out. I knew I was being selfish, but I wanted him to stay with me. But I wouldn't hold it against him.

"So this is it?" Simon asked. There was a hint of sadness in his eyes. "I'll never see you again?"

It felt like a defining moment for us—all that could happen, all that, now, would never happen. *I could stay and wait for Simon to return*, I thought; but on the other hand, there was a good chance he wouldn't come back. Whoever was on the other line must have been important enough for him to leave. If he wanted to stay, then he would.

"Not unless you come to Montreal," I replied, hiding my disappointment behind a smile.

"Maybe one day," he said, but I knew it would never transpire. "Well, I appreciate your helping me out." He nodded.

"Yeah, no problem." My voice must have sounded flat, because he looked like he wanted to say something more, but we remained in limbo, not sure what to do next. *Do we hug? Kiss?*

"Take care of yourself." Simon was the first to step forward, and it was like time slowed down. I felt every detail of that moment. The way his hand came around me, touching the small of my back, the way he pulled me in for a kiss on the cheek. What a letdown, but it was better than a handshake.

My heart sank into my stomach as I watched him go out the door, and that's when I realized his hundred-dollar bill still lay on the pool table. I grabbed it and rushed out after him.

"Simon! You forgot … your money." I waved it in the air, and he walked back.

"Keep it."

"But we didn't finish the game—"

"You would have won, right?" He flashed me a grin and I stood there, watching him go.

"Hey." He spun around in his steps, looking back at me. "It will give me an excuse to see you again—winning it back from you." He winked. "I want to finish what we started, okay?"

What that could have meant, I would never know, because with one last smile he was gone.

I went back inside and found Noah and Gloria together.

"There he goes again. That bitch has him wrapped around her finger," Noah said to Gloria.

I couldn't help but instinctively know who that person was. It would be the first insight into the oblique illusion, the three-way circus I was to be a part of. She would always be placed before me.

Life, and Whatever Forms It Takes

I learned that it's difficult to return to your old life, especially when what you had imagined for yourself was far better. I had this condition called dreamer syndrome. There's no known cure. Only Nutella can help—just maybe.

I refused to look back at my time in New York as a flash in the pan—you can't sum up life experiences like that. The fact was, I tried, and that was some form of success, right? Failure meant defeat, and I wasn't defeated just yet, not when I had more days ahead of me.

Maybe that was the reason I hadn't unpacked my bags when I'd arrived back in Montreal. Instead, I went through the old clothes I had left behind. Or, subconsciously, I wanted everything to be back to the way it was before I left, but I knew it wouldn't be possible. By leaving home, I had somehow altered the makeup of the thread that was woven into my old life. I was foolish to believe my world here in Montreal would be put on hold, ready for me anytime I wanted to come back. You can't stop time. Things evolve, and people move on, with or without you.

I decided to enroll at Concordia University, mainly picking

up my studies where I left off, only this time I knew no one in any of my classes. Everyone I had started off the program with was a year ahead of me now. The only thing that didn't change in my world was my dad; even though his chestnut hair might have gone a little gray since the last time we were together, he was still the same supportive father I appreciated so much. At some point I would have to live my life, making my home, but first I had to pay off the debts I'd accumulated with the advancements from the agency. I was still trying to grasp things. I made twenty thousand before taxes, and it was all gone with the wind. Agencies will charge you up the wazoo just about anything, and they know they can get away with it—exploit models— because there are no regulations. So here I was, back in my childhood home. Honestly, I didn't mind my old pink-and-purple bedroom with posters of Harry on my wall. Hell, it beat living in a model's apartment with underwear and bras hanging everywhere. I didn't have to put up with endless dirty dishes in the sink, and seriously, I could do without the drama.

Though my dad would never admit it, he was never keen on my moving out and pursuing the whole modeling thing. He never expressed it verbally, but I knew if I had given him the opportunity, he would have told me to stay in school. Yes, that would have been a smarter idea—sure, even a safer choice—but I was a dreamer who forged her own path, going out into the world to spread her wings. It was essential for me. Charlie Harper understood that, or else he would have said otherwise. Maybe he didn't want me to be marked like him. Ever since my mother left us, Charlie had never dated anyone, dedicating his time to raising me. I wondered if he was waiting for her to come back. But I had given up on that dream long ago.

"Hey, kiddo, you're not going out?" My dad found me sitting at the kitchen island with my textbook open in front of me.

"Patricia invited me out with her boyfriend to the movies,

but I didn't feel up to being a third wheel, so I think I might stay home tonight. Is there anything good playing on Netflix?"

"So you want to spend time with your old man?" my father asked, opening the fridge door. Truthfully, I liked being home, easing my way back to life as a girl who enjoyed being solo and meeting my friends once a week. Living in New York City, I got to understand firsthand why they call it the city that never sleeps. I went out with my roommate almost every single night. And I realized that, when you live in a big metropolis, you have to meet new people all the time. You never wish to find yourself alone. So I welcomed the change of pace.

"Dad, you're not old."

"Really?" His head popped up from behind the fridge door. "Because I sure feel like I am."

"Anyway, I'm not the one you should hang out with on a Friday night." I said.

"Why not?"

"Because you're a silver fox … you should hit the town with Lauren." I gave him a broad smile, leaning back in my chair.

He groaned. "I should never have told you what Lauren said yesterday."

"Oh, it's not something I don't already know. Your hairdresser has the hots for you, Dad."

"She doesn't. I'm an old geezer."

It drove me crazy how my dad underrated himself. Even though he was fifty-five and wore beige all the time, he was still considered handsome. I grew up aware of the fact that women at the supermarket or in schoolyards had their eyes on Charlie Harper, ogling every time he would walk on by. My dad was— still is—an excellent catch, and it was my mother who should have taken the blame for my father's insecurities.

"Dad, please stop with the self-pity. Don't you think you deserve a bit of happiness?"

"Do you see a frown on my face? Who said I wasn't happy?" he closed the fridge door. "I have you, and one day you'll get married and have children, and I'll be the happiest grandfather on earth."

I shivered just at the thought of it. "If you're waiting for me to give you grandchildren as your last wish, then I really feel sorry for your hopes and dreams," I said. I had never envisioned myself as a mother. "I think you'll make a cute couple," I teased. I couldn't read his mind, but I had gotten quite good at interpreting his body language. *He knows I'm right.* "You don't find her attractive?"

"No, no. Lauren is beautiful; she has a great sense of humor, and she's smart." He got a glazed look in his eyes.

"Ask her out," I continued. I wanted to encourage him. Even though Lauren might not be the one, it was a venture out of his solitary life he'd built for himself. I wanted him to have someone else, because I knew it was only a matter of time before I left again.

"Oh, I don't know …" The look in his eyes made me believe he had already considered it at some point. "I'm out of practice."

"It's simple. Call her and ask her out to dinner. It's obvious she's interested, or why would she give you her number?" I watched him lean against the kitchen counter. "What are you afraid of?"

"That if it doesn't work out, I would have to look for another hairdresser," he said matter-of-factly.

"*Pssh*, if she turns you down, I'll cut your hair."

He laughed, running a hand through his hair. "Yeah, like we never did that before, remember, kiddo? You gave me a mullet once."

"You should thank me—that's how you found Lauren." I winked.

He sighed. "I'm going to check out what's playing on

Netflix."

"Dad, I'm not finished talking."

"Oh, but I was." He grinned. "You'll make the popcorn?"

I know what he's doing, changing the subject. My mother had made us feel we are less deserving of anything else, making ourselves hostage of the past, but the past can't rent any space in the present. It was time to open the doors, giving our hearts a chance of feeling again. I wished my father would understand that.

"Sure, Dad."

He planted a kiss on the top of my head and disappeared into the next room. I closed my books, stacked them up, and pushed them aside.

My phone rang. I didn't recognize the number, so I let the voice mail pick it up. As I walked into the pantry, reaching for an unopened box of popcorn kernels, my phone rang again. I opened the package and placed it in the microwave, setting it for two-and-a-half minutes. As I reached for a bowl, my cell phone rang again, only this time I answered.

"Hello?"

"Quick question: what's the point of having a phone if you're never going to answer it?"

"Who is this?" I asked, but my heart already recognized the tonality. *Only that sound can get my heart to race.*

"Wow, forgot me already? Well, love, now I'm jealous. How many people do you know with a 'Stralian accent?"

"Only a few, but they're not as interesting—Walter." I smiled.

"You're just asking for it, aren't you?" he said.

I didn't know why I got a real pleasure in teasing him. I caught myself wondering what it would be like to be kissed by Simon Rowe. *Am I asking for it? Sure, maybe just a little.*

"Uh, not that I mind, but how did you get my number?" Why was he calling me? I thought … a date? *There I go again, dreaming like Walter Mitty.*

"Who else—Gloria."

"Oh, okay … so you're calling me because you miss me?" I baited, waiting for a reply, but all I could hear was his breathing, and it gave me no satisfaction.

When he didn't reply, I continued. "Simon? This call will cost a fortune." I opened the package and filled the bowl with buttered popcorn.

"Oh I don't know, it shouldn't be too bad," he said. "If you open the door, love. And please hurry, I'm freezing my arse off." Wasn't it summer for Simon? I guess he never got around visiting his parents in Australia.

"Where are you?" I asked, throwing the popcorn packaging into the trash.

"What the hell is this? Don't you put stuff away in the winter?" A deep laughter came through the phone. After some rustling, he said, "What's up with the gnome wearing a mankini?"

"What?" The plastic bowl slipped through my fingers and fell onto the floor. "You're here? Outside my front door?" My eyes glanced at the digital clock above the stove. It was seven thirty P.M.

"Yes, I am! Now be a doll, love, and open your front door. I'm losing the circulation in my feet."

I was walking in circles, not sure what to do with myself. I was wearing my flannel pajamas and it was too late to get changed. I removed the elastic out of my hair, and I flipped my hair.

"Mable? Are you still there?"

"Yeah … yeah, hold on, I'm coming." I rushed to the front door, swinging it wide open, and there stood Simon, sharing the most captivating smile that could have melted any amount of snow.

"I miss you," he said in one breath. His eyes sparkled,

knocking the air out of me. My face burned, turning every possible shade of crimson.

"I miss you pestering me about my singing—"

"Or your bad taste in music." I quickly added.

He leveled his eyes at me. "That's debatable."

I laughed, stepping aside to allow him in, but he didn't venture farther than the foyer. I studied him for a minute—no wonder he was freezing. He wore a black leather jacket, no hat or scarf for this minus twenty-five-degree weather.

"So what are you doing … here?" I quickly shut the door behind us, not allowing the cold air to follow him in.

"I thought I'd surprise you with a rematch." His voice was low and husky, and his eyes glanced around before meeting mine. I couldn't tell if he was being straight with me; Simon always looked serious, even when he was joking.

"Not to brag, but it's pretty sad for you to come all the way to Montreal only to get your ass kicked by a girl." I smirked.

"You wish." He chuckled. "The only reason you were winning was because you weren't playing fair."

"Neither were you," I reminded him, leaning against the wall.

He didn't deny it and took a step forward. "Actually, it's not the reason I'm here." He placed a hand above my head. I hoped he realized I didn't live alone. My father was in the other room, unaware we had a guest.

"I wouldn't believe it would be." I swallowed hard.

His eyes trailed down the length of me, and something amusing caught his eyes. "Nice pajamas, Batgirl."

"Thank you." I smiled as he straightened his body back up, his eyes never leaving mine.

"I have some exciting news for you."

"You could have told me over the phone." I knit my brows.

"Yes, I know, but since I was in town, I didn't want to pass up the opportunity to see your face when I told you."

"Tell me what?" I searched his face for some plausible answer as to why he was here. The truth was, I didn't know Simon well enough to understand what was in that head of his. I watched him pull at something from underneath his black leather jacket and hold it out.

"What's this?"

My eyes flickered to the image, but my mind couldn't comprehend what I was looking at.

"Oh my God, is that me?" My hand touched my mouth. "This is a joke, right? If you're messing with me, I'll never forgive you."

"No, I promise I'm not. Congratulations, love, you're on the cover of *Elite*'s April issue. One of the biggest magazine publications in the world." He beamed brightly. I was afraid to take the glossy magazine into my hands. *If I touch it, I'll wake up from this dream.*

"I don't understand … how is this even possible?" I shook my head.

"The editors are fond of your look, so they made one of the editorial pictures we shot the cover." The way he looked at me was overwhelming. He seemed proud, and he should have been—we had done this together.

"That's not all. They want me to work on another editorial next month, and they want to use you as their model."

"Really?" As he was telling me this, my mind couldn't understand how this could be possible.

"Gloria knew?" I asked, and he nodded.

"Why didn't she say something?" I was thinking there was still a chance of some mix-up.

"I wanted to be the one to tell you."

"Wow … *Wow*, I can't believe it …" I shook my head, taking it all in.

"Well, believe it … only I'm embarrassed to say the pay isn't much." He pulled something from his back pocket. "I tried,

Mable, but this is all I could pull out of them." His lips were tight, like he was disappointed for me.

"I had never expected to get paid, so I'm grateful for what I got." My eyes lagged over the piece of paper, and the first thing I noticed was that it was a check, Simon's personal check. Before I could question it further, he placed his hands on my shoulders.

"You realize this is a big deal, right?" His words hit me like a ton of bricks, and I folded myself in half. I had never wanted something so badly, but yet deep down I knew it would never happen. I was sure that, no matter how hard I tried, the universe would never fulfill that dream. And just when I had finally given up, the fates had decided to answer.

"Hey … hey." He gently touched my arm, and I felt my body slowly rise, but when his eyes met mine, Simon found them filled with tears.

"What's the matter?"

"Sorry … I don't know," I said, looking into a pool of bright blue. The heat rose to my face, and I wished he couldn't see me like this.

"Look, Mable, I know this is overwhelming. And this crazy industry is filled with more than a few arseholes, but not all of us are like that. If you let me help, I will find you the right person to represent you. Right now, I need you to focus here." Simon took the magazine out of my hands, resting it back on his chest for me to study the cover. "See this girl? She's the real deal. These crazy gorgeous eyes I'm looking into right now. That's the truth. This is your chance, Mable. I want this for you, and I want you to want it, too." He said it with a deep contentment.

All my life I had been teased for the way I was. But then this happened, and it put everything into perspective, reinstated that I should have had faith in myself, to keep doing what I love.

"You're stunning, you know that? So dry your tears, love, because all you need is one person to think you can do this, and it's you. Come home with me to New York," he said.

But the only word that stuck was *home*. *I'm not sure where that is anymore.* I had spent the past few months trying to fit into a life I had thought I was okay to go back to, but then I realized why I was struggling so much with my choice. Ambition likes to test us—push to see how much we're willing to bleed just before we luck out. I wanted this bigger-than-life kind of dream, and somehow I was going to find a way to make it work. *Whatever it takes.*

I threw my arms around Simon, which took him by surprise along with myself, but I couldn't help getting caught up in the moment. He was clearly receptive by the way his arms tightened around me, his hands bringing me closer.

"Thank you. If you didn't give me a chance, this would never have happened." There were no words that could explain what I was feeling, and when I looked back up to those amazing eyes—*I'm feeling everything.*

"No worries." He pulled away enough to see my face, and that's when his stare paralyzed me, making me want to divulge something more. They say if you look at someone in the eyes long enough, you'll fall in love. More than anything, I wanted to drop.

"Mable? Who's this?"

We both turned to see my father standing in the hallway, and Simon quickly lets go of me.

"Is everything okay?" he asked.

I wiped the remaining tears that had found their way to my chin with my sleeve. "Yes, more than okay, Dad." I cleared my throat. "This is Simon, the photographer from New York that I spoke to you about," I said.

My father observed Simon through half-shut eyes. His initial reaction was understandable. If I saw a stranger in my house and my daughter in tears, there would be a need for concern.

"I'm sorry for intruding so late, Mr. Harper." Simon quickly gave me a glance. He had to know I was living with my father. *The effects of being poor.*

"I had something for Mable I wanted to drop off."

My father's features softened. "No, please call me Charlie." He smiled. "Well, pleased to meet you, Simon. It's just Mable didn't tell me anyone was coming over tonight." He held his palm out, and they shook hands.

"Look, Dad." I held up the magazine.

"Hmm, look at that." Charlie adjusted his thin-framed glasses and plucked the glossy booklet out of my hands. I turned back to catch sight of Simon in the foyer, smiling.

"Can you believe it? They put me on the cover!" My voice rang through the corridor.

"Why don't we talk more about it in the kitchen?" my father said, glancing over my shoulder at Simon.

"Why don't you come in, Simon? Can I offer you something to drink?"

"Thank you, but it's late. I should be going."

"Please, Simon, stay for a bit?" I didn't want him to leave so soon.

"All right. I can't stay long, though. I've got an early-morning shoot."

———

I would be lying if I said the air didn't feel awkward at first, but once Simon and my dad got on the topic of sports and cars, everything seemed to roll after that. So much so that I suspected they had forgotten I was in the room. I didn't mind. I liked to watch them connect, and for a moment I could feel what it would be like if Simon were mine.

"Yes, sir," Simon said when my dad asked if he was Australian.

"My mum is 'Stralian, and my father is French, but New York is where I call home for the moment."

"It must be tough to be far from your family."

"It is, but I see them when I can." Simon swallowed before continuing. "My sister and her American husband live about two blocks away from me."

"That's nice, at least to have your sister nearby." My father smiled, but I could see he was trying to assess the situation. *If I know my dad—which I do—he's trying to determine how relevant Simon is to me.*

"It certainly is. I feel a little less homesick." Simon's eyes caught mine from across the kitchen table, then he rose. "It's getting late, and I've imposed on you long enough." Simon grabbed his jacket from the back of the chair and, with one swift move, slid it back on.

"Well, it was nice meeting you, Simon, and the next time you're in town, you should come by for dinner."

"I will do, thank you, sir. And sorry again for disturbing your evening."

"There's no need to apologize. It's understandable now, knowing the reason."

Simon's eyes diverted to mine. "Mable, do you mind seeing me out?" I walked Simon to the front door, and I watched him slide on his shoes. *I don't know why, but with Simon, parting never seems final.*

"Meet me tomorrow?" His voice was more than a whisper, and my heart tightened. "I have a friend and I think she could help you out."

"Okay," I said. Wanting to say *yes* to every moment possible with Simon.

I'm feeling everything.

Altering Your Perspective Changes Your Life

"**H**ey, you're still up?" my father cast his eyes around me. I had my legs stretched out on the living room floor, surrounded by old photographs and unfinished albums. There were several pictures of my mother mixed in the batch. I wasn't sure if it hurt my dad to see the photos, but I didn't try to shield him from them, either.

"I couldn't sleep." I looked up at my father, with his hair going in every which direction, a gray terrycloth robe wrapped safely around him.

"It's been a while since you've had them out, but never at two in the morning." He frowned, sliding down next to me. "The last time was the night before you left for New York," he said, like he'd already figured me out.

I took the photos out when I was missing my mom, or when there was a significant milestone in my life, critical moments she was never there to share with me. These old photographs were the only tangible things left. In them, Joyce, my mother, frozen in time. I liked to think that, if she should come walking back, she would still look like the last time I saw her through the kitchen window.

I remembered the day Joyce left, the way her long blond hair flowed frantically around as she dragged and loaded her green sedan with her luggage. The baggage I had watched her pack earlier that day. Those hollow eyes focused only on my father's car as he pulled into our driveway, arriving from work.

"Where are you going?" he asked.

"I'm leaving."

"What are you talking about?"

"I don't belong here ... I'm leaving you, Charlie."

"Joyce, let's go inside and talk about this."

"Stay away from me!" Joyce barked when my dad got closer. *The neighbors were walking out of their homes.*

"What is the matter with you? I just want to talk."

"Don't. Touch. Me." She reached the handle of her passenger door.

"What about your daughter?" He pointed to the window without realizing I was standing there. *"You're just going to walk away from her?"* he said, but she continued to look at him with a far-off distance in her eyes.

She was already gone.

My final glimpse was of her in her blue couture tracksuit, sliding into the driver's seat, heading off toward her new life. We were left to return to ours, a single father raising his daughter. That damn tracksuit ... I get hives every time I see something made of velour. It's crazy how you remember the most insignificant details, but I guess that's better than remembering something far worse, your heart being smashed, trampled, and kicked to the curb.

I always wondered what had motivated my mother. The reason was never sufficient to overshadow that I still wanted her in my life. How can you omit someone who's given birth to you? Initially, when Joyce was around, there were moments when I felt her love, and that was why her departure had been so surprising.

"What was she like as a kid?" I leaned my head on my dad's shoulder, holding out an old photograph of my father and Joyce, well into their teens. They were sitting on the steps of what must have been my grandparents' home. My dad once told me they had known each other since kindergarten. He had stolen her red Crayola from her desk, and she called him out on it. They had remained friends through the years—until they weren't. It amazed me that, after all this time, he had never once spoken a bad word about her, at least never in front of me. I guessed it would be difficult to do about someone you'd known and loved all your life.

"Your mom was wild; she wanted to do all sorts of crazy things." He took the picture in his hand. "Well, your grandparents never liked me very much." My mother's family came from money and my dad's didn't. Possibly that might have played a part in it.

I felt his breath on my head.

"Does it hurt you to talk about her?" I asked, sitting up and placing the picture on the pile nearby.

"Well, it's always difficult to speak about your mother, but then I figured it would be harder for you not to." Charlie ran a gentle hand through my hair.

"Why do you think she left?" I asked the question I had always been afraid to ask. All my life I had wanted to know the truth—what had happened the day she disappeared—but knowing wasn't as important as hurting him with the pain of reliving it.

He inhaled a long breath before turning to me. "I can't tell you how many nights I spent thinking about that question, but your mother is the only one who could answer that." He rubbed his eye under his glasses. "When we were young, your mom and me, we would spend hours talking under the stars. I thought I knew everything there was to know about her, but what I wasn't counting on was that people never stay consistent ... we grow toward each other, and sometimes we grow apart. I guess at some point she stopped being the person I thought I knew ..." He shook his head. "Because the Joyce I knew would have never abandoned her daughter." His eyes softened.

"Where do you think she is?" It was a question I asked myself all the time, but this was the first I'd said it out loud.

He focused his eyes on the wall across from us. "To be honest, I don't allow myself to think about it. I haven't heard or seen your mother in years, but somehow I can't stop myself from believing she will come back one day."

"But she won't." I was livid that my dad refused to move on, especially from someone who didn't deserve it.

"You wasted almost two decades and—what—for her? She broke your heart." I turned to look at him.

"You will understand one day. Love is one of those things you don't forget how to do, like riding a bike. The only thing is ... God, I still want that same damn bike." He paused. "Maybe that's why I don't have the heart to find someone new. Your mother was my best friend, the love of my life, and that's something you can't forget."

"See, that's why I'm cynical about love. Even if you find it, it will ruin you."

"That's not true," he said. "No matter what happened between your mother and me, I wouldn't have changed a single thing. I hate to think you see me as someone wrecked by love. I'm not. It enriched me, because now I have you. My little light in the midst of clouds; that's all I needed to keep on going."

I sank into his side, feeling like I was six all over again. *How can I leave him?* I felt guilty that I had been flirting with the idea of moving back to New York.

"It's time to let go, Dad."

"I thought that's what I've been doing." He knitted his thick eyebrows together.

"You don't see it, do you? Living in the same house, still

holding on to the same phone number. You're like a train that should move forward, but's been stopped at a station waiting for a passenger that will never come"

"I like this area. I have sweet Mrs. Shaw next door, and what's wrong with having a landline?"

It concerned me that my father's social life comprised of a bunch of people well into their golden years. So much so that he dressed like them.

"She's not coming back," I said with the utmost sincerity.

He sighed. "So, what can I do?"

"Go to the next station, where your friend Lauren is waiting."

"Do you think she would be interested in someone like me?"

"Yes!" I shrieked. "Why else on earth would she give you her number? You've got to swing into action, Dad."

"Yeah … Yeah, I think I will," He said, more defiantly. "I will ask her out next Saturday, maybe bird watching on Mount Royal." He looked down at me. "No?"

"No!"

"Dinner and a movie?"

"Now you're talking! Geez, we have so much work to do," I said to him as he slowly got up.

"Where are you going?"

"I'm going to call Lauren." He nodded his head, and a sudden light went on in his eyes that I hadn't seen in a long time.

"Hold on, Romeo, wait until it's at least eleven A.M." I laughed.

"Right. I guess I got carried away." He grinned, coming back down, picking up the magazine off the floor.

"What does this mean now?" He sighed, making my heart dip a little. "You know, I let you go off to New York … secretly hoping it wouldn't work and you'd come back. Am I selfish, that I want to keep my little girl here with me?" He inhaled deeply.

"But you're an adult, and this is your decision alone to make."

"I hate leaving you again."

"I'll be here whenever you need me, Mable." He smiled. "When does this go on sale?" He held the magazine higher.

"It will hit newsstands in March."

"Well, I'll buy a few copies and show them off on bingo night." His eyes cast down at my face. "I'm proud of you, Mable. I really am, but please forgive me if my insecurities are stopping you from following your dreams, because you're all I have left, the only thing that matters."

"I will always need you, Dad. You'll never lose me." I sat closer, nestling in the crook of his arms.

"Just promise me one thing? Go live out your dream, but please hurry back when you can," he said, while I hugged him tighter around his waist. He reminded me of a particular guilt I had held on to. I had spent the holidays in New York not because I couldn't pay for a ticket, but because I couldn't tell my father that my aspiration had been a complete bust. Now, thinking back, I was so foolish, because none of it mattered. We are never failures in the eyes of the ones that love us.

"Let's get to bed," He said, and I pushed myself off the floor, but my eyes trailed down to the glossy paper, looking at the girl who was staring back at me; her eyes had never looked so bright.

This is a big deal. Simon's words echoed through me, ringing like a brass bell. This was a dream on the verge of blossoming. I knew what this meant, but I didn't think about the fame.

No.

I didn't think of money.

Nope.

I thought about her.

If Joyce saw this, would she come out of the woodwork? Maybe seek me out, because now I might be something worth having in her life?

A Call of The Wild

I wasn't sure what Simon had planned or who he wanted me to meet, but I spotted him outside the restaurant, looking down at his phone, balancing a half-finished cigarette between his fingers. The substantial amount of snowflakes that rested on his thick, wavy hair only made me feel dissatisfied with myself. As the pedestrian signal counted down, I made my way toward Simon. It was impressive how unbothered he was with the cold, exposed, only wearing a leather jacket worn open, revealing a black cotton tee underneath. It made me wonder if it was some small penance he liked to subject himself to. When I got a few feet from him, Simon's eyes snapped up, revealing discontent. Well, he wasn't the first person to discover I was a complete letdown, but for some inexplicable reason, it bothered me.

"Hey, I was worried about you." His voice was tight.

"I tried to get here as fast as I could." My voice came out breathless. Guilt had kicked in the last few blocks, so I had run the rest of the way to get here.

"What happened? Don't you read your texts? I thought I told you this was important." His tone didn't sound furious, but

94

his eyes expressed disappointment.

"I'm sorry. I got stuck between stations, so I couldn't call you, but believe me, I tried to get here as fast as I could." I had the urge to smile.

"Mable, from here on out, I can't put enough emphasis on the fact that being on time is of the essence in this business," he said. "I'm putting my name on the line for you. You think it's no big deal, but it is for me."

He saw right through me. Being stuck between stations was partly true, but it only counted for five minutes of the forty of tardiness. The remaining I had spent chatting with a classmate and a quick detour to Starbucks for a cappuccino. It made no sense. I mean, deep down, I had wanted to be there on time, but somehow I had gotten sidetracked. Maybe I was trying to derail this, because if I showed him how untrustworthy I was, he could finally stop believing in me. Why should he, if I didn't believe in myself?

"Do you want this?" His voice was quiet but firm.

"I'm not sure what *this* even is." Now it was my turn to be annoyed, on top of the fact that he was so secretive.

"You will know soon enough." His eyes softened. "Look, there are many doors that could open to you, Mable. I want you to take this seriously. You only get one chance at this, so don't earn a reputation for being unreliable."

"Do I at least get an A for effort?" I half smiled, holding the faux fur-trimmed hood of my coat from flying backward.

"You're forty-five minutes late. Where's the effort?" He exhaled a long breath. "You're lucky I like you," he said, without smiling.

"You like me?" I teased, but he didn't answer, not with words, anyway.

"Let's go inside. We've kept her waiting long enough."

I walked past Simon as he held the door open for me. Then we walked together all the way to the back of the trendy restaurant, where I saw a very recognizable South Sudanese woman, sitting alone at a round table.

I suddenly stopped, pulling on Simon's arm, causing him to retract back into me.

"What's the matter?"

"Oh my God, Simon." My voice came across as a mixed whisper and scream. "Is that who I think it is? Why didn't you tell me it was Amanie?" I leaned my forehead into his back. I was a little starstruck. Maybe nobody in the room knew who she was, but if you followed the fashion world like I did, then you would know that Amanie was an international supermodel in the nineties, now well into her forties. She had retired from the business about two years ago.

"Would you have been on time if I had?" He cast me a side-glance.

"Possibly."

"Possibly?" He shook his head in disbelief. "What am I going to do with you, Mable Harper?" he said, looking me over in a sincere way that made my heart leap. *He's doing this for me, and I'm acting like a complete jerk because I'm suspicious that everyone wants something out of me.* They always did, but I wanted to believe Simon was different.

"Do you need a moment?" he said, turning around to face me.

"No … I think I'm good." I breathed in a sufficient amount of air. Simon smiled, like he wasn't sure what to make of me, and continued to walk ahead, but this time he held on to my hand.

"Sorry, Amanie, we've kept you waiting." Simon moved to the left, allowing me through. "This is my friend Mable."

"It's nice to meet you, Mable." Amanie stood up, holding out her hand. "Simon talks so much about you. He believes you're capable of building a long, productive career."

I accepted her hand and looked up at Simon, who was

standing right beside me, smiling like there was a bright sun in the room, unaware that the dark clouds were rolling in behind him. *I'm the cloudburst; he doesn't know it yet.* My heart tugged farther down, and I was not feeling good about myself.

"I apologize for my hands being so clammy. It's just— I can't believe it's you. I don't want to sound like a crazy fan, but it's a dream come true to meet you," I rambled.

"That's so sweet, and now you're on your way to inspire other young girls. It's a big responsibility to be in the spotlight, but you'll learn that soon enough." She was tall and slender, and when she smiled, it seemed to light up her round face. Her eyes went from me to Simon and back again. "Congratulations on the *Elite* cover. I don't have to tell you this will open doors."

"So where do you see yourself, two years from now?" Amanie asked after we sat down and placed our orders with the waiter.

My throat tightened. "Um, I don't know … I mean, this is so unexpected. I've been home for a while, throwing myself back in my studies. I thought my career in modeling was over," I said, glancing at Simon sitting across from me, trying to figure out what he had up his sleeve, because this was feeling like an interview.

"You're thinking of retiring when you just got started?" Amanie hiked up her brows. "Life can be funny. Sometimes doors spontaneously open, and you have to make a quick decision to bounce through them or not."

Do I bounce? I believed the only thing that could prevent me from crossing that threshold was another possibility of disappointment. But aren't we all destined for a shortfall at some point? Maybe the difference is having a healthy outlook on failure. Now how did that translate to the industry I was trying to break into? It was a good question.

"How did you get discovered?" I asked, digging into my salad as the waiter placed it in front of me.

"I was approached in a grocery store, back when I used to live in London." She looked up for a minute. "Hmm. About twenty years ago. You two were babies back then." Amanie winked at us.

"Simon was probably watching *Power Rangers*." I gave him a side-glance, imagining for a minute what Simon must have been like as a child. Unruly, for sure.

"Never heard of it. I don't think we had that back home," After a short moment, he said, "I used to watch *Ocean Girl* on the telly."

"*Ocean Girl*? That doesn't sound like something a five-year-old boy would watch." I was aware we had contrasting upbringings. Besides having an age difference, my world comprised of living under six months of snow, and his consisted of none at all. And yet we somehow managed to get along. Too well, I reminded myself.

"Yeah—don't judge if you haven't seen it. It's about a girl with superhuman strength who lives on a deserted island. She was a little hottie too." He grinned.

I shook my head. "Ah, your first girl crush? Is that what kick-started your fascination for photographing beautiful women?"

"No, in fact, I always wanted to go into journalism. Fashion is something I fell into," he said, leaning back in his chair. I wasn't sure what I caught in his eyes. A hint of disappointment?

"So, Mable, have you given any thought about coming back to New York?"

I diverted my eyes to Amanie.

"I'll be honest, I'm a little apprehensive. I've spent a little over a year living in New York, and it left me deflated. The thing with the magazine cover is amazing, but it doesn't guarantee something will come out of it." I was now aware that Simon had brought me here because he thought Amanie could guide me in the right direction, but I was more stubborn than I'd originally told him. "I don't think I can muster the energy to go through with it again … spending countless hours in casting and playing yo-yo with my weight. Um, really, I don't think I fit into the mold."

"And yet you've been chosen to be on the cover of the biggest magazine publication in the fashion world." Amanie leaned in closer, like she was about to share a secret. "Let me tell you something: molds are made to be broken, or at least break what people believe the mold is. In life, you will inspire people without knowing it, just in being yourself. So never apologize for who you are." She smiled. "You're different, but it doesn't mean you have nothing to offer. Your distinctiveness makes you stand out from the rest. I should know." She sat further back in her chair. "When I first started in this business, I was a bit controversial, especially for those days. I think for high fashion, they didn't know where I would fit. I wasn't beautiful, not according to the norms of what designers thought a model should be. I'm dark as night with small eyes, and I didn't have long, silky hair like the mannequins," Amanie said. "In my first shoot, the photographer was appalled because the stylist had me in this long blond synthetic wig." Amanie showed from the top of her head, painting with her fingers how long the hairpiece must have been.

"The late Michael Thompson was the photographer, and I'll never forget what he said. *"Amanie, that's absurd get rid of that cheap-looking thing. It's not authentic— it doesn't look like you."* So I thought, you have to know yourself before someone takes notice of you. That's where it begins. I draw all my energy from within, being self-assured in who I am so I can be confident in what I do. Pictures don't lie. You could be beautiful in every definition, but if you don't feel comfortable in your skin, then you have nothing to bring to the table as a model."

The waiter came by, refilling our glasses with water. I caught Simon staring from across the table, and it felt so surreal.

How am I even here, talking to Amanie Melak? Growing up, I'd seen her on TV, on countless magazine spreads. She was the model who had redefined beauty in fashion.

"Have you guys worked together on a shoot? Is that how you know each other?" I asked.

"Funny thing is, fashion had nothing to do with us meeting," Amanie said, glancing at Simon.

"We met several years back, working for a charitable cause," Simon said.

"It's because of Simon that I met my husband," she added.

He was full of surprises. A matchmaker, humanitarian, and a photographer, and yet there was something offbeat about Simon. Any woman would be drawn to that magnetism; no one in their right mind would pass him up. *I'm questioning my sanity, and if I should die before Gloria, I will make sure she inherits every single one of my sixty cats.*

"All I did was introduce you two." But then he added, "Mac is a good friend of mine."

This reinforced my belief that he genuinely wanted to help people with no sinister motive behind it. And all that rugged, tough exterior was only a front. Simon hid his gentler side behind a wall, and of course I would know, because it was my favorite hiding place, too. I had my reasons. What was Simon's?

"So what kind of humanitarian work do you do?" I asked Amanie.

"I'm an ambassador for Humanity Matters. I'm so grateful that this job has given me a platform to do more than just modeling. See, with fame comes opportunity, and it's my responsibility to shed light on a third-world reality. I was fortunate to have escaped a civil war in my country, and not everyone is as lucky as I am. When you're blessed with this sort of influence in the spotlight, you can't go without wanting to do more for undeveloped countries."

After the dishes were cleared off the table, and after we'd talked for a while about designers and Simon's upcoming projects, Amanie turned to me and said, "You're wondering why we're all here today."

"I'm beginning to piece things together," I said.

"It's been a couple of years now since I retired from modeling, but there's one thing I always wanted to do: to have my own agency. So, last spring, that's what I did. I opened one. I want to run a firm that breaks the barriers. To change the way the fashion industry is behaving. Designers will have to evolve their own images of women in fashion, but it starts at my level. Fashion is not created for one body type or culture. We come in a wonderful variety of forms and colors, and that should be praised, not shamed or abused. I know it will take time, but the progress has already begun." Amanie looked me straight in the eye. "My question to you is, do you want to help me break the mold? Because I'd like to represent you."

"Wow, you really throw yourself into everything," I said, looking at Simon from the passenger seat of his blue rental car. After we had parted ways with Amanie, Simon offered me a ride home, and I, not wanting to let go just yet, said yes. When it became clear that he knew the area well, I asked him about it. Simon explained that he had worked for a short time as a still photographer, taking pictures on movie sets, and that had brought him to Montreal often for work.

"Photography is my great passion, but I have this innate restlessness inside me, which inspires change every so often," he said.

I got what he was saying, but I wondered what this might mean for me. I was thinking that maybe Simon was a nonconformist, never constrained by anything or, possibly, by anyone. Perhaps being tied down domestically might have led to the dissolution of his marriage. Let's face it: you can never tame a free spirit, and more than you can control the ocean.

"So you're trying out everything for size?"

"Nah … yeah, I guess you can say that. I want to try everything at least once." He shot me a smile. "I can't imagine doing one thing for the rest of my life."

"What happens when you run out of things to do?" I played with the zipper pull of my black parka coat.

"You could never run out of things, as long as this heart beats … the wind blows, and I go."

I imagined my mother for a moment. Was it her restlessness that had caused her to go? I believed this feeling existed for some people, like Simon. When they are anchored in one spot for too long or suppressed, they have no choice but to break free for their superficial survival, like answering some private call of the wild. They need to change the scene no matter who they hurt or what the consequences are. I wondered if I had it in me, like my mother. Since I'd been back, I couldn't seem to shake the feeling of being contained. It was like hearing the whispers of an inner intuition, calling me back to the concrete jungle. How can anyone defy nature?

"Amanie is so inspiring. I wish I could do something like that." I peered out the window.

"Like what?"

"Make a difference in the world." I turned my eyes back to him.

"Nothing stops you from doing what you want in life, Mable." He quickly glanced my way. "I knew you guys would hit it off, and to think it almost didn't happen. I had to beg her to stay. I never grovel—ever. You owe me *big* time."

"Yes, I'm grateful for everything you've done for me. I don't know how I'll ever repay you."

"Just buy me a bevy the next time we go out, and we'll call it even," he said, and I was amazed by how this pleased me, the possibility of seeing him again.

"You'll be in good hands should you sign on with Amanie's agency," Simon said. "Have you thought about the offer?"

"It's a lot to think about. My dad is ecstatic to have me back, and I'd feel terrible leaving him again. What should I do?"

"Mable, I'm the last person you should ask,"

"Why? You're the one who set this up; why wouldn't I want your opinion? You have a hand in my career, and all the good things that have been happening so far."

He slightly opened his mouth, taking a moment to choose his words. "I can't tell you what to do because my answer would be blinded by my own motives, Mable." He bit his bottom lip, stopping himself from saying what he wanted to. So there *was* a motive, and at least he was admitting it. But what could it have been? It wasn't difficult to see that Simon was a man restricted by self-imposed restraints, whatever drove him to help me, whatever it was that we meant to each other. Half of the time I wasn't entirely sure of it, but there was this force between us. This invisible wall we might never scale over, because there was something we wanted from each other but didn't really need, not just yet.

"You know, before we met, I had heard stuff about you ... through the grapevine." I raised my finger in the air.

"What kind of stuff?" He gave me a quick glance.

"I don't know, the way people spoke of you, I got the impression you were ... a little unhappy, I guess." I inspected my hands as I spoke.

"Uh-hun ... but you've told me something like this before." His eyes became small, and the lines on his forehead became more pronounced. I would have said nothing if I imagined he would take it personally. Since when did it matter what I thought of him?

"Have I? No, I don't think Gloria let me finish … What I said was you're not what I imagined," I gave him a side-glance. "But then I met you—"

"And you thought … Oh my God, he's so hot," he said in a girly voice.

I laugh. *"No way."* I playfully shoved his arm. Maybe, but he didn't need to know that.

"Go on." He signaled with his hand for me to continue, without removing his eyes from the road.

"It's so surprising you can be such a goofball."

"Why is that surprising?"

"I don't know. Maybe because you act so serious most of the time, and it made me wonder if there was anything in life that made you smile."

"You make me smile," he said, and my heart picked up the pace.

He shifted slightly in his seat, contemplative in thought.

"Well, I'm not an angry person … maybe just tired of feeling sad." He sighed. "But I don't want you to think I'm depressed, either."

I could feel it with every breath he took. *He's trying to tell me something, but he's not sure if he can trust me yet. I can't understand why this frustrates me.* The reality was that we were nobody to each other, yet I felt like I'd known him my whole life.

"Maybe I'm like you said, but then you came around, pestering me with your enthusiasm and fun-loving attitude, at least for the little time we spent on the set. You made me forget." He gave me a quick side-glance. *What did he want to forget?*

"So my point is, you're a good guy, Mr. Rowe."

He stifled a laugh. "That's absurd." He looked in his

rearview mirror and changed lanes.

"Aw, I'm making you blush."

"I'd rather you thought I was sexy and dangerous."

"Maybe I do."

"Yeah?" He flashed a knowing smile.

"I see you, Simon Rowe. You helped me so much, and I'm not sure why."

He sat there quietly for a second. "Well, you kind of remind me of myself." He shrugged. "I've been there before … big dream and a passion to match it. I know how it feels when all the doors are closed off. Look, I'm sorry I was such an arse to you back there."

"You were right. I was the one being unprofessional." I realized now that he had every reason to be upset with me. He was the one who had put his reputation on the line. But I had never expected him to.

"So the next time when I tell you it's important—be punctual?"

"Fair enough, but only if you promise no surprises, all right?"

"We make a good team, you and me," he said, matter-of-factly.

When he looked at me with those wild eyes, I had to fight the urge to kiss him. I understood the depths of my situation. Maybe I hadn't realized it before, but something had happened that day in the studio I never expected. With Simon, it was easy to communicate, without uttering a single word. We knew what we wanted from each other. Gloria later told me it was beautiful to watch it happen, almost poetic. Like witnessing two people falling in love. I never questioned what she meant, but I always wondered, the day that the axis shifted ever so slightly: did she mean love between a photographer and his muse … or did she see something that Simon and I weren't aware of?

"What should I do? Tell me, Simon. I trust you."

"You trust me?" He pulled into my father's driveway, putting the car into park.

"Of course I do," I said with all honesty. "You've proven to be a good friend, and what you think matters to me." The more I got to know him, the more I wanted to know, and the further my heart opened.

He looked deep into my eyes. "If it's up to me, I want you …" He turned and leaned in closer.

"Want me?"

"I want you to come to New York and work with me." His words were restrained, filling the air with what my heart had been whispering all along, like a call of the wild.

A Beat of a Dream, a Flutter of the Heart

W hat is it about New York City: that when you're there, you can't wait to get the hell out, and when you're gone, you keep wishing to go back? You realize you can't live without her, that grand metropolis, because it has the kind of magic that can revive your dreams, shine them up and make them brand new again. And then, with just the change of the tide, with no recognition of diplomacy, she will swallow you whole. One way or another, you can't stop loving her. No doubt, you're screwed.

Since I'd been back to New York, things had progressed. Auditions turned into callbacks. Callbacks turned into job offers. My new agent, Amanie, believed I had a unique look, the potential for a promising career well into my thirties. The feedback was positive; the designers said I had a great presence when I walked. I should have been happy, but for some unknown reason, I couldn't help but feel that something was missing.

I didn't think Nonna's lasagna could have helped me with this hitch. So I did the next best thing. I sought him out. I realized this was becoming a habit. Simon encouraged me to come and see him at his studio, because he loved a good chat, and I was looking for any excuse to devote more time being around him. But lately, I had tried to create space between us, because I realized the time we spent together only intensified my passion for him. I was playing with a loaded gun, and it was only a matter of time before I would get hurt.

I ran into Gloria on her way down the staircase. From the look on her face, she was questioning why I was there.

"Hey you, what's going on?"

"Is Simon still up there?"

"Yeah … yeah, he is." She gave me an unsure look. "Was Simon expecting you?"

"No … ah, I wanted to swing by and tell you guys the good news … I'm booked! Ten shows for fashion week." In the small details, I wasn't getting paid much. A few of these gigs paid nothing at all. Amanie said I had to look it like this: I was working for exposure, hoping I might catch an editor's eye. In the modeling world, time is your enemy. I was twenty, and if it didn't happen soon, then it was never going to happen for me.

"Oh, that's great! I'm so happy for you," she said, pulling me into a hug. "I was just on my way to the apartment. Are you coming home for dinner?" Gloria and her partner Tracy had allowed me to crash on their sofa until I had myself sorted out. I would find a place of my own once I had a steady income rolling in; it wouldn't be much longer. *Hopefully. Crossing fingers and toes.*

"Hey stranger, howya been?" A husky voice echoed in the small corridor, and we simultaneously looked up. At the top of the staircase, leaning against the doorframe, was Simon.

Simon's eyes were bright. I wasn't sure if he was happy because he had had a good day or for the fact he was seeing me. *Heck, I'll go with the latter.*

"I came by to share the good news." I slid my hands farther into my coat pockets.

"Come on up, love, and tell me all about it," he said,

disappearing around the corner.

"Okay, I've got to go … Should I expect you at home?" Geez, Gloria could be so maternal.

"Yeah, sure, later, but not for dinner."

She looked me over through her black-framed glasses. "Don't forget about the cats," she shrilled over her shoulder as she walked past me.

"If you don't stop taunting me about them, I will not feed them."

"You're cruel," Gloria continued. "I'll see you later. Hopefully not too late. Don't do something I wouldn't do," She said, disappearing through the door.

Gloria knew it, and I knew it. It's always possible to go past the line, to smudge it when you're attracted to someone, but I had packaged it with a little bow and sold it to Gloria that Simon and I were nothing but platonic. We had sailed far into the friend zone, and I was comfortable with the idea. *I think.*

The way I saw it, this was safe. I didn't need to give a part of myself, but that also meant I couldn't expect anything from him either. Then again, does a platonic relationship actually prevent you from any kind of heartache?

When I reached the top step, I realized he wasn't alone. Some of the crew still lingered around.

"Mable," Simon called from his office, and I walked in.

"So where have you've been?" he asked. When I was in his view, he went back to placing his grip equipment on his pegboard.

"Oh, am I interrupting something? I could come back later," I said, noticing the cute brunette sitting in the chair in front of his desk.

"Oh no, stay. I was just on my way out," she said, getting up and sliding on her coat that rested on the back of the chair.

"Mable, this is Roxanne, my new intern. Roxanne, this is Mable," he said, placing his camera back in its case.

"Nice to meet you," she said, and I smiled. My hands remained in my pockets.

"I'll see you tomorrow, Simon?" Roxanne said, and he nodded. His eyes followed her out the door. My stomach was in knots, but it might have been because of the hamburger I had eaten at lunchtime. *It had to be the extra pickles, and nothing to do with the brunette.*

"So?" Simon studied me from across the room. "A little bird told me you went out with Noah the other night." He smiled in a satirical way.

"Are you keeping tabs on me?" I playfully narrowed my eyes.

"No, but Noah is my top bloke."

"I'm not stealing him from you, if that's what you're thinking … It's not my fault if he likes me better than you." I flashed a coy smile.

"I have no problem sharing in the sandbox. All I'm saying is it would have been nice to be invited." He held out his arms.

I wasn't sure what was bothering him, but I guessed it was the fact that he hadn't heard from me in a while.

"Geez, I'll be sure to, the next time. Only we wouldn't be able to talk about you behind your back."

"What about me?" His tone was playful.

"Ah, my lips are sealed." I casually slid into the chair, making it roll back a few inches. It was still warm from the attractive brunette. "Anyhow, I didn't want to bother you. I thought you'd be busy with your new intern."

His eyes snapped up. "Yeah, you're right, she has been keeping me busy, but not the kind of *busy* you're thinking." He frowned. "Roxanne is my intern and nothing more."

Of course, I should know. I waved my hand dismissively. The last thing I wanted him to figure out was that I cared about what he did, but it was too late for that now.

"Ask me why I'm smiling," I said, changing gears, not

wanting to talk about his intern and focusing on the reason I was there.

"Okay, why are you smiling?"

"You're looking at a new runway model!" I shrieked.

"That's awesome, love." He beamed. "We should celebrate."

"When … now?" I leisurely slouched farther into the chair, letting it roll.

"Yeah, why not. Do you have plans?"

"I do." My voice came out playfully.

"What kind of plans?" His eyebrows knit together. I thought I might have hit a nerve, or at least I hoped I had.

"I've got … plans, date plans." I smiled more than I should have. My fingers played with the zipper pull of my jacket.

"With who?" He stopped what he was doing and slowly walked over. The hard lines on his face were more pronounced, revealing that he was more sensitive to his feelings than I had thought. I liked it.

"With someone I met," I pressed on, giving him my best poker face. He grabbed the arms of my chair, pulling it toward him, pinning me to his body and the seat.

"Break your plans." His face was inches away from mine. I could feel his warm breath on my skin. I guessed the label in the back of my down-insulated coat was right. It claimed to trap heat to keep you warm even when the temperature dropped. But now I knew what happened when the temperature rose.

Good grief.

"I … I can't." I swallowed hard and looked up into his eyes, anticipating what might happen next.

"I don't care, you're coming home with me. I'm cooking you dinner tonight." The way Simon looked at me, all my senses seem to slip away. "Mable."

"Hmm." *Kiss me already.*

"Tell him something came up … Say your cat got sick and

you need to bring her to the vet." He smiled like he'd won a match. Then, with a gentle push, my chair rolled back, adding space between us.

What just happened?

"You know about the cats?" I laughed.

"What cats?"

I read his face with no signs of confusion. I continued to watch him put his equipment away on the shelves across the room when he stopped and looked up. "I highly doubt you'll remain a spinster with sixty cats. With legs like yours, love, someone is bound to sweep you off your feet."

I broke my plans with Mr. Nonexistent and took up Simon's offer to cook me dinner. *I know, I'm knee-deep in turmoil, but I got this. If Simon can be a professional, so can I.*

An hour later, we arrived at Simon's one-bedroom apartment in Central Park South. The building had all the amenities, with a concierge at the front desk. I wondered for a minute what people in this building could possibly request. I could only imagine sending him to pick me up a mushroom burger with extra fries at the Shake Shack.

"I have to warn you, though, there's a possibility my apartment is all over the place like a madwoman's breakfast," he said, putting the key in the lock.

"A … what?" I laughed, not familiar with his slang.

"A complete mess. I wasn't planning on having company tonight." He grinned.

"So why invite me?"

"Because I wanted you over," he said matter-of-factly.

"I promise I won't pass judgment either way," I said. "Unless you have a pull-up bar in the doorway; then it will be full-on scrutiny." Simon opened the door, allowing me to walk into his studio.

"Why would that be a deal breaker?" Simon said, walking into his galley-style kitchen, setting the grocery bags on the dark granite counter.

"I can't be friends with a conceited man."

He laughed. "Well, wouldn't you feel silly if I did."

I took a quick glance around; satisfied, I returned to Simon in the kitchen.

"Are we still friends?"

"Perfectly," I smiled.

Overall, his apartment was like everything else in New York: compact and crazy expensive. The way he managed his studio, it wasn't much of a surprise to find his home spotless.

"Huh, your apartment doesn't look like a madwoman's anything." I playfully frowned.

"I said that because I thought the concierge wouldn't have a housekeeper come and clean this place up while we were at the supermarket," he said.

"A maid, too?" *Can I live here?*

"Yeah. I work a lot, and the place can get pretty messy after a while." He peeled off his jacket, then took mine and placed them on a black chair in the living room. I felt something rub against my leg, and I looked down.

"There you are, old mate. Where have you been? I haven't seen you since the last time Lena cleaned up the place." He walked past me, disappearing into the kitchen.

"You have a cat?" I lowered my hand, allowing it to run through the soft gray fur. I couldn't help but laugh at the irony.

"Yes, I'm a man with a cat. Is there something wrong with that?" He laughed a little. The sound of chopping on a wooden board had begun.

"No, there's nothing wrong. It's just I never pictured you with a cat. What's his name?"

"It's a she, and her name is Captain."

"Captain? That's a very boyish name." I walked toward the opening of the kitchen, leaning on the doorframe.

"Don't be sexist, love. Captain is a perfectly good name for a feline, whatever the gender." He smirked, emptying the grocery bags.

"What made you want to get a cat?"

"She was gifted by my sister Jennifer. She thought it would be nice if I had something to come home to, especially after ..." His voice trailed. "White or red?" He bent down, removing a bottle from his wine fridge.

Did I miss something?

"Uh, red is fine," I said. "After what?"

"Yeah ... She thinks I'm lonely." He walked toward me, holding out a glass of red wine.

"Are you?"

"I'm not sure. I keep myself too busy to notice." He smiled. "Cheers, love. Here's to you, me, and the night we met." His eyes grew darker, as deep as they could.

"What can I do to help?" I said, feeling it was my obligation to change the conversation. If he kept looking at me like that, we would need to redefine our relationship, and platonic was not the word I'd use.

"Nothing. I'm better when I work alone—in the kitchen, anyway." He winked, placed his wineglass down, and continued chopping. I had never had a guy cook me dinner before. *The man wants to feed me; there's nothing sexier than that.*

"You have an impeccable home." I allowed myself the liberty to venture into his living room, just off the kitchen. A Moroccan rug lay over a natural-colored floor that creaked as I walked on it. The furniture was mostly tan or black, modern, and masculine. Pictures of his travels hung on every inch of the walls.

"I can't take credit for the décor. My sister is the interior decorator. Everything in here is her doing." He bobbed his head through a small opening in the wall that separated the kitchen from the living room. I took a sip of my wine before turning to head back to the kitchen, but I stopped to look at the family pictures that hung on the wall. My eyes came to a dead stop. Now I found myself more confused than ever.

In the middle of all the framed photographs was a picture of a happy couple. It looked like it was might have been their wedding day. I choked, nearly spilling the wine out of my mouth.

"Are you okay?" Simon asked behind the wall.

I cleared my throat. "Oh … yeah … I'm all right." My voice went high-pitched at the end.

I'm fucking fantastic.

Simon and Vanessa … married? Newly divorced? There's something very messed up about this. I mean, would anyone keep a picture of someone they had divorced hanging on the wall? From what I had witnessed, they were not on good terms. *Is she the one he's been disappearing to?* Then another unlikable thought came to mind. What if they were still married? Simon didn't wear a wedding band, but that meant nothing … And Noah had said they never dated. This had my head spinning.

I had a lot of questions, but did I have a right to the answers? Probably not, because it wasn't my business. So I chose to be silent—for now, anyway.

"If you'd like, you can keep me company while I cook," Simon called out.

"Sure," I said, already making my way back. I leaned in the doorway so I wouldn't get in Simon's way. He was already cooking up a storm.

"I feel awful standing here watching you."

"I want you to relax. Let's get to know each other more." He tossed a dishcloth over his shoulder. *Sounds like a great idea, because I want to know about Vanessa.*

"You could ask me anything you want," he said naturally.

Okay, focus on Simon ... your wife ... Vanessa? Nope, he's not a mind reader.

"So what made you want to be a photographer?" I asked. *Seriously, I'm such a coward.*

"Well, my parents wanted me to be a doctor or a dentist like them, but I never had it in me." He threw the chopped vegetables into the hot skillet that simmered over the gas stove. "When I was younger, I was more artistic than anything else. I wrote music and played in a garage band."

"Really?" I could picture Simon as a rock star. He had a look for it. "So what changed?"

"Well, one summer I came to visit my sister in New York, and that's where I met other artists. I felt more at home in Manhattan, and it sort of clicked." Simon took a sip of his wine. "I took up photography as a hobby until I wanted to take it up full time." He added herbs and spices to the pan and, with a quick wrist move, flipped the food in the skillet.

"So, against my parents' wishes, I came to live in New York. I thought it would be a good place to start. Seven years later, here I am." He took a peek in the oven, then reached for two plates from the cabinet above. I didn't know what he was making, but it smelled delicious.

"You seem to know your way around the kitchen."

"Yeah, I only enjoy cooking when I'm doing it for someone else."

Like Vanessa?

"Just curious, how many women have you cooked dinner for?" I brought the glass to my lips.

"Usually it's breakfast, never dinner." He grinned mischievously. "Nah, to be honest, you're my first in a very long time."

His eyes went soft.

"I hope you're hungry." He slid the plates in his hands.

"Famished." I smiled, but I was not entirely sure what I was starving for.

After dinner, we sat in the living area. I curled up in Simon's club chair with Captain in my lap while Simon sat across from us on his couch. The room was beautiful at night, surrounded by tall framed windows, revealing the night sky and the lights below in Central Park. We talked about my mother and his sister, his childhood in Australia, mine in Canada. Here we were, two expats, in pursuit of a dream, in a city that might deliver. But it was our dreams that had brought us here. If it wasn't for our passion, we might never have met.

"What's that?" I asked, pointing to a blue notebook with the words *Lyrical Lights* scribbled across the front cover. It rested on the clear vinyl coffee table in front of me. "Do you write your songs in there?" I asked, but Simon snatched it up before I could get my hands on it.

"Hold on—this is top secret. I let no one read my stuff." Simon smiled, but his neck turned a light shade of red.

"Oh, come on. I spent an hour pouring my heart out, talking about how I practically starved myself in the name of fashion." I never bared my soul like I did with Simon. "You owe me." I narrowed my eyes at him.

"Fair enough. Okay, but I have a condition." He set the copybook aside and passed his hand through his hair. "We have to know each other at least … two years tops before I allow you to read my poems."

"*Ohh* … poems." I smiled, raising my eyebrows at him.

"Well, I guess you could call them poems; it's just stuff I jot down." He leaned his head on the back of his sofa.

I thought about it. *Two years is a long time—what the hell was in there? Who was he, the CIA?* "Do you think this

117

friendship will last that long?" I looked down at Captain, afraid of disclosing something in my eyes.

"Well, that depends on you."

"Me? Well, Gloria doesn't believe we could be friends."

"She may be right, and I thought so too at first ... especially if you continue to whisper stuff in my ear," he said, and I smiled, not sure if I should take it as a challenge. "You're a hell of a package, Mable. Any man would be proud to have you by his side, but I make a lousy boyfriend."

I wondered if he made a horrible husband too.

"But now I feel we're in a place—I like you ... in a figurative way, and I respect you. I enjoy your company, and I think sex would just ruin things, you know?"

He looked up. I wasn't sure if he was trying to convince himself or me. In other words, he appreciated me enough not to get involved. Shit, those are the things any girl with a mad crush loves to hear. To say I was disappointed was putting it mildly, but I had to accept it.

"Sweet mercy, what a romantic. Who's talking about sleeping together? I meant Gloria was speaking about having feelings for one another."

"Well, that's generally what comes next, hopefully."

"Next? What, you're saying you could sleep with someone and not have any feelings for them?" *Where are you going with this, Mable?*

"No, no. I mean the sex is just better when you love someone or at least care about them, right?"

Where is Simon going with this? "Well, I'm not much of a romantic, but I always thought there was something magical in believing you're only meant for one person," I told him.

"Huh. I used to think that once, but not anymore." He looked away.

When Captain leaped off my lap, I got up and walked over to a black bookcase across the room. Each shelf was crammed with pictures and mementos of the trips he had taken in the past.

"Have you been to all these places?" I allowed my fingers to slide across the bindings of the travel books.

"Yeah, some for work, some for pleasure," he said. I could feel his eyes watching me, but I didn't dare to look in his direction.

"What was your favorite place you've visited?"

"My first trip alone … just before I turned twenty, I packed my bags, my camera and set off for Asia."

"Were you there long?"

"About four months, but three weeks in I was in a motorcycle accident." He shifted his glass in his hands. "I was pushed off the road by a crazy driver and ran straight into a tree."

"Yikes, were you seriously hurt?"

"I was lucky. I got off with minor cuts and bruises." He swallowed. "When I got out of the hospital, I decided I was done—time to pack my shit and head home. But on my bus ride to the hotel, I met a girl."

"A girl?" I turned. His arms sprawled against the backrest of the sofa, holding a glass of scotch.

"An American. A jewelry designer who was there on holiday. I stayed three weeks more than I'd originally planned, because of her." He nodded.

"She must have been pretty to get you to stay."

A shadow crossed his eyes, and I felt the pain. "Yes, she was." He took a moment to answer. "She changed everything."

It made me realize that Simon, too, must have lost something crucial. Perhaps he didn't have much more luck with love than I did.

"What about these?" I looked back at the unmatched frames lined up on his counsel table. "Where were they taken?"

"In Ethiopia." He pointed at the photographs.

"They're wonderful. Does everyone allow you to take pictures of them?"

"Not always. If I do, I either compensate them with money or send the portrait."

"Oh, so you must speak other languages?" I brought the frame closer.

"I try to learn a couple of words here and there. It's important for me to connect with the locals, and often people want to interact with you. I visit those places not only to snap pictures to fill my portfolio but to take the time to get to know them—to learn."

"Hmm. Sounds like you've been doing a little soul-searching." I came around and sat next to him on the plush navy sofa. He watched me in a way that caused a deep tickle in my stomach. He was *really* attractive right now.

"Maybe, but being an artist also means you have to be someone who observes the world around them. That's why most places I choose to travel are consumed with poverty. But I never put myself above those people. They are very proud of what they have, and I always say to them it's great … because it truly is. The human condition is a remarkable thing."

"Wow, quite an experience, traveling, love. So what's next?" I asked, taking another sip from my glass.

"I don't know, but all my life I've taken the offbeat path. I'm the first to admit it's a marked life, a lonely road to follow." He looked at his glass. "I'm planning to go back someday. Most likely I'll be going alone."

I thought to myself how deep and clear his eyes were, wishing I could dive right in.

An hour later, Simon helped me flag down a yellow cab.

"So when will you be back?" I asked. He had mentioned before that he'd be away working on a project in Las Vegas.

"In two weeks,"

"Well, thanks for dinner. It was fun." I wanted him to kiss me. The way he was looking at me, I thought he did, too.

"You're welcome. But remind me why I'm not driving you home?" he asked.

I believed he didn't want the night to end, but it was already two in the morning.

"I don't want Gloria to know I was here." Gloria was under the pretense I was out with friends.

"How will she know I drove you home?"

"Oh, you don't know Gloria. She's at the window waiting in the dark as we speak."

"Mother hen?" His smiled broadened.

"You have no idea. I need to get a place of my own because these days it feels like I'm living in a shoe," I said, watching him wave a taxi down.

"At least text me when you get home?" When the cab pulled up, Simon opened the door.

"Well, have a safe trip. I guess I'll see you when I see you." I lingered for a moment. I didn't know what came over me; maybe it was the wine, or the crisp, cold air that made me feel so alive. Or was it those eyes, intensely staring back at me, like something extraordinary should happen. I yanked him closer.

Contact.

I was worried when he took a step back, pulling away from me, but then he quickly recovered, pushing me backward. Soon I was leaning against the frame of the taxi door. His arm wrapped tight around me; he was kissing me feverishly. And there it was, as clear as day. Words couldn't convey what a kiss could. There was no hiding from it now.

"Hey, lady, I haven't got all night. Are you getting in or what?" the driver called out from inside. Simon pulled back and looked at me, half in shock, half not wanting to stop.

"I like you too, Simon, in a figurative way." I winked just

before sliding into the seat. As the taxi drove away, I looked back at Simon, who was standing there, thinking to himself *what the hell just happened*?

I thought we might never scale that wall—not because we were cowards, not because we were afraid, but because things between us would always be sensitive … like a fragile object, it needed to be held with both hands. This relationship meant a lot, and so delicate it would have to stay.

A Kiss and All of Its Glories

A black town car drove us to the *Elite* cover party that was being held at the Plaza Hotel. The who's who of the fashion world was to be there, including a few Hollywood stars. I felt sick to my stomach, and maybe I should have had something more than a salad for lunch, but I had to fit in a Vigi dress. I was fortunate to have been able to borrow it from the designer, a beautiful metallic purple dress with a plunging neckline. Gloria thought I needed to wear something extravagant to make an entrance, to stand out from the other models who might be there. I wasn't crazy for attention, but I cared about my career evolving to something more. So I had to do things I wasn't comfortable with.

"Stop stressing, you'll be okay," Tracy told me when I kept asking questions. "Trust me, these events are such a bore." Her wavy cinnamon hair cascaded down her black jacquard blazer, stopping an inch from a jeweled flower pin on her lapel. Tracy was a district attorney, and I think the only reason she had an interest in fashion was Gloria. They'd been dating for a while, and I was not sure what was next for them, but I had never seen Gloria so happy. Somehow her past relationships with men had always seemed forced and unnatural. Then, two years ago at a New Year's party, she pulled me aside and confessed she was in love with a woman she had met on a plane bound for London. She had wanted to tell me sooner, but was afraid that my view of her would change. That couldn't have been farther from the truth. It's easy to think we know it all when we don't. This was about love. Did it matter who reciprocated on the other end? Not for me. I was only disappointed that she had thought otherwise. I knew it took courage for someone to bare their soul; it took fearlessness to face the world and be who you were. She was finally just being Gloria.

"That's not true. They're so much fun, and it's great for networking." Gloria smiled, and Tracy half rolled her eyes, then put her hand on her mouth, pretending to yawn.

"Whatever you do, just don't get stuck with Matthew Norville. That man is such a flat tire, he'll talk your ear off the whole night."

"Don't tell her that. He's the one that signs our paychecks. *Elite* is part of Norville magazine publishing," Gloria said. Her diamond teardrop earrings dangled back and forth, a flicker of light bouncing from them. She checked her makeup one more time before snapping the compact mirror shut as the vehicle slowed down.

"I think we're here." Gloria placed everything inside her small silk purse as the car eased its way to a halt.

When I stepped out of the black town car, there was a row of photographers snapping away at anything that moved. Paparazzi—now I realized why no one smiles when they're on the red carpet. Why on earth would anyone smile at the torments of their demands and rudeness?

The arriving guests gathered quickly at the front door of the Plaza, and the surrounding security got tighter. I moved over onto the sidewalk and waited for Tracy—she was the last one to get out of the car.

"Ladies together," a man yelled out from the group of people snapping away. Gloria always said if the paparazzi wished to take your picture—let them. You never knew; it might land on a cover of some magazine, and any publicity was good publicity. The three of us gathered up and posed right there on the sidewalk, next to the crowd of people who were getting out of the black limo.

Flash, flash, flash.

Every single reflecting light made me think of him. I imagined someone like Simon would have to be here tonight. Part of me had hoped, and the remaining half felt uneasy to cross paths with him. I hadn't spoken to or seen Simon in weeks. That night of the kiss had left me wanting more, and I thought Simon had felt the same, because when I texted him I had arrived home safely, his response was, *We need to talk when I get back from Vegas, but I don't think I can wait that long. That kiss ... Can't stop thinking about it. Troublemaker, what did you start?*

But it had never transpired. When he came back to New York, I flew out to L.A ... When I got back home, he had gone to Japan. Then it had come to a sudden halt, all our daily texts. Some were flirty ... some were just shooting the shit until we went out of focus.

It was not like Simon not to reply to my text, but I wasn't going to chase him around. If he wanted me, then he would make it happen.

We walked into the beautiful hotel lobby, adorned with marble floors. Just under a big crystal chandelier, I found Amanie and her husband Mac. We spoke until a woman dressed in black with a walkie-talkie in her hand whisked me away, taking me into a large room. There I was asked to get in line behind other people waiting to walk the black carpet, getting their pictures taken behind a black screen with names of sponsors printed in white. I lowered the volume of my earpiece, which was covered underneath my hair. The extraneous sound of the background noise had caused me more anxiety, and it was only elevating. I watched a couple go before me, and I knew I had to follow their lead, since I had never done this before. You were supposed to walk the carpet, stop, pose, a hand on the hip, and continue until you made it all the way down the runner.

Here goes nothing.

"Down here to the right!" someone yelled behind the velvet rope as I began my stroll towards the end of the runner. The crowd of men were more tamed than they had been minutes before. When Crystal Z, the biggest pop star of the moment, had walked the carpet, it was total mayhem.

"Here please!" another shouted. Millions of lights going off by the second, blinding everything in front of me. I focused on not tripping on my train, because that would have been embarrassing.

"Hey, Mable, over here!" someone yelled out, and it provoked the pack of men.

"Mable, Mable, come back!" As I approached the end of the runner, a woman in black ran up and asked me to go back again.

"Guys, get back, please," the security guard yelled out to the crowd of photographers, trying his best to hold the line. I couldn't understand the excitement.

"Look over the shoulder. Yes, that's it, babe."

"This way, please ... Mable, to the left," another one yelled.

"Mable, at the top!" I moved my face, taking their directions. You couldn't understand the feeling until you were up here. There was this moment, right before the light caught you, this exhilarating feeling that anything could happen. At that moment, you were bigger than your dreams, larger than life, and with every flicking light, I knew I would be a slave to it, all in the name of fame. The final time I walked off the carpet, they still called me by name, but I had given enough of myself. Only now I had gotten a taste of what it was, and I wanted more.

"Welcome to the circus," someone behind me said.

"Careful," he said, fluidly, like we knew each other.

"Hmm ..."

"Your glass of sparkling wine ... is leaning dangerously. It would be a pity to get it all over your dress." He held my gaze. At first glance, I noticed he wasn't wearing a necktie; his silk light green pocket square was tucked inside like a flower. His velvety brown hair parted to one side. He was pleasant on the eyes.

"Oh, I ..." I shook my head. "Thank you." I had focused on the crowd, unaware of how I was holding my champagne glass.

"Don't worry about it," he said with a heavy French accent.

"About what?"

"You having troubles with the boyfriend?"

"Oh, no."

"So now I'm curious to know what's distracting you. We crossed paths back there in the entrance, but you didn't find my smile contagious." He looked me over and frowned. "I really deserve your attention, but it's difficult to prove." He slid his hands into his pockets and walked closer.

There's nothing I would have enjoyed more than to brush off this brash young man, but I had had a glimpse of Simon through the crowd, and that had left my heart deflated. I wished it were Simon instead of this stranger that was seeking my attention.

"I'm sorry ... if I'm making it difficult for you." I thinned my eyes, inhaling a breath before I continued. "But what is it exactly that you want?"

"I think you already know," he answered seductively. He looked at my eyes, then trailed to my lips. I could have walked away if I wanted, but now curiosity got the best of me.

"You want to write my autobiography?" This made him

laugh.

"Ah, not only are you beautiful, but you're very witty. Sure, if it means accepting an invitation to dinner."

"So you are a writer?" I said playfully, knowing well that wasn't the case.

"You're adorable." He smiled, looking at me in disbelief.

"Should I know who you are? Wait, let me guess … You're the French prime minister's son?" I mused.

"Not quite, but close."

"Close? So who are you, then?"

"I'm an executive …" He reached for a champagne glass off a silver tray.

"An executive?"

"Let's just say my family owns a famous French brand."

"*Oh* … which one?"

"Paris Star." He paused for a moment. "You never heard of it?" he said, not satisfied with my reaction.

"Sure, I have." Paris Star was a major player in the luxury brand arena. What I knew now was that Mr. Debonair's father was Bernard Gaspard, who had gained the company when it was on the verge of bankruptcy with no experience in the fashion business, and who had somehow managed to turn it around, making it the most successful luxury goods company in the world. The Gaspard family had a net worth of fifteen billion reported in *Forbes* magazine. I wouldn't have known this if Gloria hadn't mentioned it once. Maybe all this information should have been impressive, but money and privilege never persuaded my opinion of someone. It was all irrelevant. The authenticity of a person had me going … but what about Mr. Debonair?

"I'm Julian." He held out his hand.

"Mable."

"Enchanté, the pleasure is all mine. This is your first time, no?"

"Yes." I smiled, discreetly wiping my damp palms against the fabric of my dress. "Can't you sense my unease?" I didn't know why I was transparent with him.

"Why?"

"All these executives can make someone feel overwhelmed." I brought the glass of champagne to my lips; *it might loosen me up.*

He laughed. "I hope I'm making you feel more comfortable?"

"Yes." I smiled, trying to be polite, but I diverted my eyes around the room and back to Julian, who was still looking at me.

"Ah, that's more like it … You're stunning when you smile." He cocked his head to the side. "And the most beautiful language is the one your eyes are speaking now." To some, he would be considered irresistibly sexy, but trying too hard was a total turnoff.

"And what are my eyes saying?" I asked, amused.

"They're saying they want me to show you around Paris." His eyes grew darker. I didn't know what it was about his stare that made me feel uncomfortable. I was hoping Gloria would come to my rescue, because I didn't know how to keep up this conversation with a man of his caliber.

"I saw your book, and I'd love for you to represent our brand one day."

"*Yeah* … Okay." I deflected my eyes back to the crowd. One thing I'd learned was to beware of people who promise big things. They usually wanted something in return.

"I mean it. You have it—that magic. I knew when I saw your portfolio." He took a step forward, trying to get back in my view. "You seem like a sensible woman, and it's necessary to trust your instinct. It's a misfortune for me in this case; in your mind, you already decided about me. We are not in reality where we take a person for something they're not, and most people can invent virtues … But I promise you, I'm the one who will take you places." If I were more naïve, I would have believed him.

"Have you ever been to Paris?" He offered a subtle smile.

"No, but I will be there for fashion week," I said.

"*Ah*, fantastique! We should plan to meet up."

"Perhaps." I was vague for a reason, but I knew in this business it's who you know, and I shouldn't be closing any doors. But this was where it could get tricky. Fashion is an industry that's run by mostly men, and where there are men, somewhere there's also an abuse of power … it's almost a given. Yes, it would be a dream come true to work with Paris Star, but it didn't mean I would sleep with Julian to work for him. I redirected my eyes again, only this time I caught someone recognizable in the crowd. It was Vanessa, who seemed to be out of hand and in the arms of a man.

Simon.

"If I were him, I would have chosen you," he said after a short moment. "Well, it was nice meeting you, Mable. We'll be in touch?"

I was relieved that he'd given up, but not before he gently touched my arm and leaned close to my ear.

"I'm worthy of your time, mesmerizing Bella. I hope you'll figure that out." He stepped away, disappearing into the crowd, leaving me speechless … but not in a good way.

⸻

I picked up the bottom of my dress and zigzagged through the cluster of people, making my way to the brass doors. Outside, the crowd and the photographers had all but vanished from the spot which hours before had been total havoc. I took off my hearing aids, and life felt still for a while. My shoulders relaxed, and I stood there, feeling the cool spring breeze on my shoulders. It was my way of shutting out the world, leaving me alone with my thoughts.

I remembered when I was younger that I had never wanted to miss anything. I had wanted to hear every audible sound the world made, every beat, every murmur. Without my hearing aids, I wasn't a part of anything. Silence ... but tonight I welcomed it.

Sure, I felt hurt, not only seeing Simon with Vanessa but because of the fact that he knew I had been there the entire time and never sought me out. Weren't we friends? Maybe I was fooling myself, to think he cared for me as much as I did for him. After the kiss, he had deliberately ignored me. We were adults; couldn't we talk things out? It felt like I had just lost my best friend. Then another thought crossed my mind. Maybe Simon and Vanessa had reconciled; that's why he had never responded to my last text. *She despises me, so it would make sense.* I wouldn't lie. It wasn't easy to watch her throw herself at him—and she knew I would be watching.

I lifted my eyes only when I saw a shadow on the ground, and there he was. My heart throbbed in my chest; no need to hear something you feel. His eyes hadn't found me in the shadows because his focus was on Vanessa, who was half passed out, draped between Simon and some girl. He said something to the cab driver once Vanessa and the other girl were safely inside. Then he closed the door and watch the car drive off. I stood there, hoping I might go unnoticed, but something made him turn, and when he did, his eyes found mine.

"Mable." He made his way towards me.

"Is Vanessa okay?" I didn't care, but I asked anyway. The air seemed offbeat between us, like we didn't know how to act around each other. I placed my aids back in, and for a moment my eyes focused on the concrete floor.

"Yeah, nah ... She'll be all right, I guess." I wished I could understand exactly what was going on between them. Better yet, what was going on between us?

"Howya been?" He had no right to ask. Simon took his time to look me over, like he was searching for clues. Maybe he wanted to know things were good with us.

"I've been … great." I kept my tone fresh, like nothing had transpired between us. After all, it had only been one impulsive kiss. I had never expected it to be more than what it was, but my heart had other ideas. I came to believe my vital organ was a beggar reeling from the privation of love. It had searched for love high and low and had hoped to have found it in Simon. I had been wrong, just like those other times—love was a gutted game, and I played it so well I'd been made the captain of the team.

"Look, I meant to call you … I wanted to speak to you about that night—"

"Oh, that's great. I appreciate that, but after you avoided me for over three weeks, I can only imagine your intentions fell, hmm … a little short." My voice was steady, not even rising a notch. Few people looked at us as they walked by.

"Maybe we should go somewhere private?" he said.

"No, here's fine." I frowned. I had been waiting long enough for his bullshit.

"I'm an arse." Simon gave an involuntary shudder.

"Yes, you are."

"You must hate me," he began. "Look, Mable, I needed time to think, to sort out shit." His eyes diverted to the ground, and his hand ruffled through his loose hair. "You know I care about you? More than you know … more than I made myself believe, and now things are getting complicated between us. I got scared." His eyes snapped back up and met mine dead-on.

"Is it Vanessa? Are you guys back together?" Maybe my insecurities were clouding my judgment, but I had a hard time buying it.

"Back? No." His face came across as a mix of confusion and irritation. "Nothing is going on between us, nor will there

132

ever be."

Not a word he was saying was making me feel that he was being legitimate. Did he think I was stupid? I'd never taken Simon for a big fat liar, and now I realized there was a side of him that I hadn't met before.

"There can't be anyone else when all I do is think about you, love. You've sent me over the edge ... That damn kiss and all its glories—just thinking about it makes me fucking crazy." He rubbed his forehead. "You force me to feel things I haven't felt in a long time ... We can't do this, right? Not if we want to continue to work together? I don't want to ruin what we have. God, I wish things could be different, but you don't know me, and the last thing I want to do is hurt you."

He had started it, but I wanted to finish it, have the last word.

"Listen, Simon, it was only a kiss ..." I shrugged, playing it cool, building up that wall as fast as possible before his words could continue to rip me apart. "I had too much wine, and I guess we've gotten to know each other enough that I feel very comfortable around you. I—just ... I don't know what I was thinking. It was an ending to a perfect evening." I watched him take a step back, allowing it to set in his mind.

"It meant nothing to you?" His voice came out tight.

"I'm sorry. I should have never done that." The words felt forced, and the center of my chest gotten heavy. "Can we forget about it?" I watched his eyes go dim. I only wished I knew what he was thinking. Then again, maybe I did.

"Okay ... if that's what you want," he said, in a tone that projected a hint of hurt. Did he expect me to fight for him? I wasn't going to beg; he was either in or he was out. I deserved someone who wanted me as much I wanted him, without making things complicated.

"So we're good? Because I don't want to lose you as a friend," I said. I was the one who had kissed him; why shouldn't

I dictate how this was to go down?

"No. Never. You will always have me," he said. I guess I had to own it, accept it for what it was. *I will always miss the mark, but at least I'm a cool girl, and cool girls don't give a shit.*

Rivalry off the Runway

There are three stages of a model's career: breakthrough, recognition, and, if you're lucky—success. Only a few mannequins achieve this, mind you. I can't pinpoint the exact moment where I can say I gained recognition, but after the *Elite* event, there was movement: people began to talk, and more designers were booking me. The photographs that were taken of me that evening were found in celebrity magazines. One photo of Julian and me was featured underneath the bold title: *Heir to Luxury Goods' Empire Dating Unknown Model*. I laughed at how ridiculous it was when Gloria first showed me the magazine. And it was more surprising to find a text message from Julian. *"Can it be true? Are we dating now? We make a charming couple. No?"*

Now I understood what Simon had said about the circus lights. Once you entered the tent, you were a willing participant, becoming a part of that circus. *It's a false illusion, making you think you're a lot more important than you really are.* Simon's words swirled in my mind. I felt guilty to admit it, but I liked the attention. To see my face in those glossy magazines, it was like a "screw you" to all the mean girls in high school who made me feel I was irrelevant. But still, I needed to stay grounded, not lose sight of who I was … to see fame as just another extension of my life.

I was in a cab on my way to the Ortiz fall-winter runway show with plenty of time to spare. *Simon would be so proud.* He had suggested that I text him when I arrive. Things were hunky-dory between us. I mean, I didn't want to lose him, because our friendship was important. We were accountable for our actions and our words. Even though it was a lot to swallow, together we made little sense. He had a demanding career, and mine had just begun to take up most of my time. *Like they say, it's not meant to be.*

The cab dropped me in front of Space 404, where the venue was being held. Bruno Ortiz, the designer, was more than happy for me to be part of his show, but his casting director and stylist were another story. A week before, I had come in for a last-minute fitting, and that's when they had put me in baggy clothes. I wasn't stupid; I knew they were trying to camouflage my body, so I didn't stand out from the rest. Since I had signed up with Amanie's agency, I had allowed my body to grow into its natural form. I had thighs, hips, and—*hello there, butt, I haven't seen you in a while.* So with my new physique, I didn't fit into the samples, and if the designers wanted me, they would have to accommodate my size. Not because it was me, but because I was Amanie's client, and she had established a good relationship with designers for years. Otherwise, they wouldn't have given me a second look. Simon had once said it might take a while before the industry matured in their ideas of what a model should be. To pioneer something that had never done before, there would always be a criticism. *But is this industry ready for someone like me? I will soon find out.*

Inside, I gave my name to the girl holding up a clipboard, and she sent me directly backstage. I was walking down the corridor, sending Simon a text, when I was body-checked into the wall.

"Watch where you're going, idiot," Vanessa said as she walked past me. I could have pulled her by her ponytail, swung my fist, but my father had taught me better. I was here to work, and I was a professional. I refused to play into her drama.

She had wrecked her integrity and I wouldn't allow her to destroy mine. It blew my mind that a guy like Simon would get involved with someone like her. *No wonder he has issues; she probably ruined him for anyone else.*

I turned the corner and walked into a large room filled with sounds of blow-dryers and chattering. There were a few tables lined up along the wall, made into several stations for the hairstylist and makeup artist, who were already at work. I glanced around the room, and all eyes were on me. I felt like I was coming out of left field, but luckily for me, I saw another familiar face, and my body relaxed.

"Hey there, cover girl." Noah kissed me in greeting. He was wearing a black T-shirt and dark denim pants. A backstage pass hung around his neck.

"Let's get you ready, shall we?" He pulled out a chair. This was the first time we'd seen each other in a while. We'd tried to get together sooner, but we couldn't get our schedules to sync. When I had the time, I was too exhausted, spending the time in bed with the covers over my head. I settled in Noah's chair, and he began his magic. From the corner of my eye, I caught Vanessa. She was in a white robe and sitting in a chair close by, staring me down. Vanessa whispered something to the blond model sitting next to her, and they both laughed. Shit, this was high school all over again.

"Don't get yourself worried about it, hon, she's just a jealous bitch." Noah caught my eyes in the mirror.

He's right. I shouldn't let it bother me, but it does. I had never offered her a reason to hate me, yet I gave her the power to manipulate my emotions. I wanted to despise her, I really did, but there was a part of me that felt sorry for Vanessa. She was a train wreck waiting to happen. I knew it, and the whole industry knew it: she was crazy and irrational, and it only made me wonder what had happened to make her that way. Would I feel the same about Simon if he had caused it? It would split my heart in two.

Noah separated my hair into sections, pinning them back with a silver clip. He started on the left side, so I removed my aid and placed it on the table in front of me. I was afraid Noah might yank them off while working on my hair.

"Why would she be jealous of me?" Vanessa was the third highest paid model. I doubted she had anything to envy.

"Maybe she sees you as a threat."

"A threat? Yeah, okay."

"Don't pretend you don't know." He gave me a level stare.

"It must be for my high-tech hearing aids." I laughed.

"For one, you're fresh blood, and her career is fading fast, but I imagine what burns her the most is that you're cute and cuddly with Simon,"

"We're friends." I played with the hem of my white T-shirt.

"No, darling, buddies don't lock lips just for the sake of being friends."

"What?" My eyes flashed upward. When I looked up in the mirror, Noah gave me a stare like, and I blushed.

"Simon?" I groaned, and he nodded. "Doesn't anyone keep anything to themselves?"

"Of course." He shrugged. "But that's not something you keep from your best friend."

"So what did he tell you?" I was hoping for more insight on Simon's part on that night.

"He's conflicted, but he cares for you. I can tell you that much." He smiled. Before I could ask him another question, one of the show's organizers came walking up.

"Can I steal her for a minute?" a girl with a clipboard said over my head.

"Okay, hon, I will pin the rest of your hair and finish up later. Come back and see me when you're done. Okay?"

Disappointed we couldn't continue the conversation, I followed the girl into the wardrobe area.

By the time I got my makeup and hair done, I realized that I had never placed my aid back in my left ear.

"It's not there?" Noah asked when I didn't find it on the table. "Well, that's strange, I saw you put it right here a minute ago." He bent down, looked under the table, but found nothing. I felt a hand on my waist and I flinched. My stomach was all twisted in knots, but looking into Simon's soft eyes seemed to have a calming effect on me.

He wore a dark gray pant and a matching vest, his crisp white shirt unbuttoned—the first two. He looked good, and I would have told him that, if I wasn't preoccupied with everything else.

"Hey, I wanted to wish you luck ... Are you okay?" My eyes dropped to his lips. With one of my aids lost, the surrounding commotion was making it tricky to understand what he was saying.

"What's the matter?" The crease between his brows deepened.

"I lost one of my hearing aids." I looked at him through my long false lashes.

"Oh shit. I found it." We both looked up at Noah. He was holding up a paper cup, trying to fish out something out of my coffee.

"Seriously? Who would do that?" I said in disbelief.

"Oh, I have a good idea, and it starts with a capital *V*."

Noah's eyes met Simon's, whose features seemed to have hardened.

"Do you think it still works?" Noah placed my hearing aid inside a tissue and handed it back.

"Probably not," I said. "It has to be dried before I can put new batteries in, to see if it works, but right now I don't have time." Out of the corner of my eye, I saw the woman with the clipboard coming around.

"They need you in the lineup," Simon said, fully aware I didn't catch what she was saying.

"What if I dry them with the blow-dryer, hon? Do you think it could work?

"It's worth a try, I guess," I said, watching Noah walk back to his spot.

"This is off to a good start." I gave Simon a weak smile.

"Your hands are cold." He warmed them between his.

"I will fall flat on my ass, I know it."

"You won't."

"But what if I do?"

"Don't miss a beat, love. Get up like nothing happened and go on. Make them think: wow—that Mable Harper walks like a pro."

"I don't feel so good." I diverted my eyes back to Noah.

"Hey, you got this," he said, forcing my chin up. "Listen, I will be at the end of the runway—just focus on me, okay?" Simon had been invited as a guest, not for work. It was difficult to focus on anything other than the fact that Simon had come to see me backstage. I felt a warm heat at the center of my chest.

"Sir, you're not supposed to be here," said the blonde dressed in black. Simon turned. "Oh, Mr. Rowe, the show is about to start—"

"I know, sorry. I'm going," he convinced her.

"Are you okay?" He looked at me for reassurance, and I nodded.

"Knock them dead, love, and I'll see you after the show?"

I nodded, and he kissed me on the cheek just before disappearing into the frenzied crowd.

The woman with the clipboard gathered us into a lineup. We all wore the same black strappy shoes. But otherwise, we were coordinated by the color of our outfits. I was in the second group of girls that was going out on stage, wearing gray chiffon. It was mundane to just stand there, but there was so much going on around us in the last twenty minutes before the show started. For one, there were makeup artists going around for the final touch-ups. And there were photographers, predominately men, all over the room, taking our pictures. Actually, they were always around us, even when we were getting dressed. The shit you have to tolerate.

"Chelsea, move aside. I need to check my girl," Bruno, the designer, waved off the makeup artist. He was going from one girl to another, making sure that the outfits were perfect. There was a magnetic allure about Bruno Ortiz, even for a man in his sixties. He looked so sophisticated in his blue velvet suit and black bowtie.

"Where's Vanessa? She's supposed to be in the lead." A girl wearing a headset rushed us by. Bruno just stood there silently; only a slightly-raised eyebrow indicated that he had caught that, too. His warm whiskey-colored eyes met mine as he repositioned the first button that had come undone of my ruffle dress. I glanced up and caught the model in front of me, swinging her hips rhythmically to some beat I couldn't quite make out.

"The show has started." He smiled and took a step back to get a better look at me before saying, "My little muse, you're hidden in the tall grass, and a wildflower should be seen."

"Willow," he called, and the girl that had just run by was quickly by his side.

"Yes, Mr. Ortiz."

"Mable will open the show," he said, matter-of-factly, and my eyes widened.

"But ... Vanessa," Willow said. Of course, Vanessa was MIA, but I spotted her through the crowd, off the shoulder where no one could see her, and she wasn't alone, either. I must have gotten the tail end of their spat, because she was trying to hold him back, and he gently removed her grip before walking away.

Simon.

"She was just over there a minute ago." I pointed in the direction I had seen her last. I could have minded my business, said nothing, but I wasn't one to take advantage of a situation for personal gain.

Bruno sighed, bringing my attention back to him. "I think we've given her enough chances. Bring my wildflower to the front, please." He winked at me and moved on to the next mannequin behind me.

I followed Willow to the front of the line. I could feel all eyes on me; the other models gawked as I walked past them. For once my scanty height was to be reckoned with, placing me in a position I could never have imagined. *When the show starts, I will be the first to set foot on that stage.* There was no time to be nervous. I had to stay focused and wipe my face of any emotion. A few minutes later, Bruno stood on a chair in front of us.

"You girls look fantastic! Enjoy yourselves ... Go out and rock it!"

Cheers and clapping echoed around the room. I had one last checkpoint to pass before going out. I was not ready, but I had no choice. There was no going back.

I began my walk behind a wall of white chiffon fabric suspended from the ceiling, pausing at the opening before venturing into the spotlight. I fixated ahead, walking in my four-inch heels and praying I didn't make a fool of myself. Chills ran up my body, like a rush I had never felt before. It could easily be addictive, this newfound high. The crowd was so big that I didn't see Simon or anyone else; the lights on my face were too bright. All that was visible was the front row, where all editors and buyers were hiding behind their white phones. But I didn't focus on them. Instead, I pointed my eyes ahead, making it down the runway, turning around and walking back up again. When I was back behind the scenes I rushed to get into another outfit, repeating the whole thing one more time. It was comforting, though, to know that Simon was somewhere out there.

After the show, the photographers took pictures of us together, of Bruno and me. He kissed my cheek and told me that we needed to work together again. I caught Simon across the crowd of people. He was being interviewed by the press. Our eyes met what felt like a thousand times—I smiled at him, he smiled back. We were parted by a sea of people, yet I had never felt a stronger pull. After I changed back into my clothing, he found me.

"You were awesome, love." He beamed, and it made me tingle. I didn't see him as Simon Rowe, the famous photographer, but as Simon, a friend I valued, even though I knew sometimes there were illogical emotions involved. Nothing more would come of it, but I was okay with that, because not having him in my corner was far worse.

"You're all right?"

"Exhausted, but what an exhilaration … I want to do it again," I said, and he laughed.

"Soon enough, little grasshopper, you'll get that chance."

He smiled. "Are you hungry?"

"Famished."

"Let's go. Gloria and your dad are waiting for us out in front." He slid an arm around my waist as we walked out the exit door. I hadn't seen Vanessa after the show, and I didn't care if she saw us together, because for the first time I felt he had chosen me over her.

"Oh wait, I forgot my bag." I stopped and spun around. "I'll meet you outside," I said over my shoulder, and headed back to Noah's spot to find my black satchel under the table.

When I looked up, I saw her. The mystery woman in Simon's studio. The woman in the Chanel suit. Even behind her big black sunglasses, I could have sworn she was looking directly at me.

Becoming or Unbecoming?

We left Heathrow airport by eight A.M., bound on a flight for Paris. I was sitting in first class, wondering when Gloria would stop talking about work. Usually I didn't mind, but winding down from fashion week, I wanted to talk about anything that wasn't work-related. Like how maple syrup on top of pancakes would be great right about now. I was starving and airline meals wouldn't cut it.

"There are only eighteen couture houses," Gloria said. I smiled because she was relentless in boring me with this useless trivia. "And they don't make any money on the shows."

"Wait, how can they not make money?"

"The shows are only to publicize their new collections. Initially, they only survive on their perfume and makeup products." Which made sense—why models made good money doing advertising campaigns for those sorts of companies.

Luckily for me, Amanie had kept me busy throughout fashion week. I was booked for a few shows in New York, London, and now Paris was my last stop before returning home. I was relieved I hadn't had the pleasure of crossing paths with Vanessa ever since the Ortiz show. *If she hated me before, she definitely despises me now.*

A short time later, I closed my magazine and glanced over at Gloria, who was now buried in her book. I took out my phone to check the time, and I was satisfied that we had twenty minutes before landing. I selected the photo gallery to look through the pictures of us: my dad, Gloria, Tracy, Noah, and Simon, celebrating my first runway show in New York. I couldn't even count how many times I had looked at them, especially the one of Simon and me, having his arm around me, kissing my forehead. It was an intimate moment between us, captured by someone who had taken my phone without my knowing. I suspected it was Noah.

"Simon is already in Paris," Gloria said without looking up from her book. "He's staying at the same hotel." Gloria discreetly glanced over my shoulder; she'd always been the nosy one.

"Oh really?" I tried to hide my smile. I suspected that much, especially after I had told him about Julian Gaspard. Julian wanted to show me the city on my second night in Paris. And when Simon went silent, and the humor left his eyes, then I knew he would be around.

"You already know that." Gloria studied me.

"No, why would I?" I tried to frown.

"What's going on between you two?" She closed her book and laid it down on her lap.

I wished I could answer that question, give her a straight answer, but I couldn't. I had no idea when it came to Simon. I only had an insight on my side of the wall, aware of my own emotions. I hadn't seen Simon in a week, but we texted each other often. Maybe too much for two people who claim to be only platonic?

"I ... honestly don't know." I placed my head against my seatback for a short second before rolling my head back at her. "I mean, I do ... and you're not going to like my answer." I had to find the courage to confess under Gloria's scrutinizing eyes. It needed to be said; the truth hovered between us, wanting nothing more than to set me free from the secret I'd been hiding, not only from her and Simon … but from myself. "I think I'm in love with him …"

"I know," Gloria lowered her eyes for a second. "I suspected that much. It's easy to see it when you guys are together. There's this magnitude of chemistry between the two of you."

I sighed, shaking my head. "You need more than good chemistry. It's obvious that something is holding him back."

"Yes, there is; he's afraid of hurting you." Gloria met my eyes.

"Is that what he told you?"

"We spoke about it, yes."

"I don't understand why he's talking about us to everyone? Instead of having this conversation with me?"

"He's tried, Mable." Gloria straightened her black-framed glasses.

"When?"

"That night at the *Elite* party."

"Hold on. Simon made it clear that even though he cares about me, he didn't want to get involved."

"Hmm, no—you didn't give him a chance to finish." Gloria's eyes softened, and I realized she was right; I had only assumed what he was saying.

"It's complicated, and Simon has his reasons, but you didn't give him the time to explain. You shot him down before he could."

"Tell me what?"

"That he's a widower." Gloria cleared her throat.

"What?" Now I was even more confused.

"His wife died two years ago, and it messed him up terribly." Her eyes watered.

147

"But I don't understand ..." The picture of him and Vanessa flashed across my mind. *It doesn't add up, because Vanessa is very much alive.*

"But Vanessa?"

"What about her?" Gloria shook her head. "Look, I should have told you this before, but I thought I never had a reason to. Anyways, it's making me cry just thinking about it, and you know I hate to cry in public. There's a lot you don't understand, and it's not my place to tell you. It has to come from Simon."

Good grief, this was driving me crazy. I leaned my head back against the seat, looking up at the ceiling. I could never imagine what it would be like, what Simon had gone through. I always felt he was trying to keep me at arm's length, and now I knew why.

A widower? If only I had let Simon finish talking that night. I had been insensitive, shutting him down—I had wanted to hurt him back. Was Gloria right, warning me to stay away? I realized now I was not what Simon needed. He was broken, and I could never be the one to fix him, because I needed fine-tuning myself.

"What should I do?" Simon and I cared for one another, even if we might never act on it ... It existed, and it was ours, but I didn't think I could live in the silence for much longer. Never taking that last final step, living with these big emotions and wondering if he felt the same way too.

"I don't know, but I will tell you what I said to him. You both need to sit down and figure out what you mean to each other."

"You're taking this rather well." I studied her for a minute. "Aren't you going to discourage me? That we're not right for each other?"

"No. I realize it now; I was wrong. Who am I to come in the way of love?" She paused. "I know for a fact he really cares about you. I mean not many people would have done what he did—for you."

"What are you talking about?"

"*Elite* never paid you for that cover."

"I don't understand. But I got paid for it." My brows crumpled together.

"No, honey, Simon gave you a personal check. Saying *Elite* paid him a lump sum, and he was paying your share through his account? No, none of it was true."

"But why would he do that?"

"What would you do for someone you love?" She raised her eyebrows.

"Mon cher, papa. We've landed and we're okay. I'll call you when I get settled in the hotel. XX Mable."

I texted my dad while I waited for my suitcase to arrive at the baggage claim. I was sure he had been tracking my flight sporadically, watching the little plane on the screen inch its way to its destination. We had spoken two days before, and he was in the kitchen cooking with Lauren. He sounded happy, almost rejuvenated, and it made me wonder if it was the trauma of a broken marriage that had been the culprit, holding him back from whatever joy life could offer. I had always wondered if love could feed a hungry heart, and now I knew: at least for my dad, it could.

After we had collected our luggage, we went through the glass sliding door, unaware that a black limo was waiting to bring us to our hotel, compliments of Mr. Gaspard. After the *Elite* cover party, Julian had somehow gotten my number from someone who knew someone, thinking it was my agent. So he said, but later I found out that Julian had already booked me for an upcoming spring campaign with Amanie way before he contacted me. And since he had me on the phone, he thought it wouldn't hurt to get to know each other.

Smooth.

He had disclosed to Amanie that he found my personality sophisticated beyond my years. An intellectual beauty was exactly what his business had been looking for. I allowed myself to imagine what it would be like to date someone like Julian, but my heart wouldn't have any of it, because it was already occupied by the Australian photographer.

Besides, with someone like Julian Gaspard, there were other women woven into his life. I knew that too. He was a man who manipulated things into his own favor, which made him dangerous for someone in my position. He could make or break my career. I couldn't say I wasn't flattered by the attention, and I needed the job, but it didn't mean I would sell myself out. I had to be smart about it, so I told him there was someone else in my life, and it seemed to have worked until I saw a driver holding out a sign with my name on it, standing in front of a long black shiny car. Only when I opened the door to our hotel room did I realize this might be more than a problem.

Julian Gaspard was a man that wasn't afraid of showing his true intentions, and he showed it then with big bouquets of roses displayed all around the room, and the mother of all bouquets affixed on the round table.

"Wow, this guy is something else," Gloria said, shoving her suitcase in the corner.

"Maybe they're for you?" I said, looking around the room.

"I wish Tracy could be this romantic."

"You find this romantic?" I passed a soft petal between my fingers.

"You don't?"

"Not really. Flowers die," I shrugged.

Our room at the Hotel Le Maurice was vast and beautiful, regal—fit for a princess. There were baskets filled with makeup

150

and clothing racks set up at the other end of the wall— all designer stuff that was sent to Gloria. This was a privilege that came with the job, that Gloria acquired by working hard and establishing healthy relationships in the industry.

"Wow, we have to work on your emo outlook on love," Gloria said, picking up her suitcase and rolling it into the bedroom next to the sitting room. My first intentions were not to read the card with my name on it, leaning against the tall crystal vase.

Nope.

I had only one desire: to walk across the room, open those French doors, and step out onto the gallery, losing myself in the brisk morning air.

I was in Paris.

Never in my wildest dreams had I thought this day would come. My life smelled and looked different. How else can I explain it? I was a long way from the girl who had come to New York to pursue a dream, and look at me now—I was even wearing nail polish! Gone were the days of vintage T-shirts— replaced with designer threads. This wasn't only my job, but it had become my lifestyle. I was given the possibility to travel around the world, and it opened my eyes to all sorts of new experiences. This new chapter of my life was exciting, but also terrifying, because I didn't want to get caught up in something I had no control over. There's a price to pay when you're the next money girl, and I had to find a balance between the paradoxes— the new and the real me. In my mind, they were already drawn up. I fabricated one for the other to survive. Funny, though; these days the only time I felt free enough to be myself was around Simon.

"You must have made quite an impression on him." Gloria smiled, waving the card out when I came back into the room.

"Geez, you're so nosy." I plucked the card out of her hand.

"When the richest, most eligible bachelor in France sends

my cousin flowers, how could I not?" she said. "Now what the hell are we going to do with all these roses?"

"Do I have to call him to thank him? As of next week, technically he will be my boss."

"I guess." Gloria's face said it all. This was not the situation I wanted to find myself in.

"Admit it … this is over the top. Like borderline creepy."

"If you feel uncomfortable with this attention then don't say anything to encourage him any further."

"Said the girl who was too quick to take up on a free ride," I said.

"I'm not going to refuse traveling in style while we are in Paris." She shrugged, leaving me to read the card to myself.

My dear Mable. I would have loved to show you my city and have the privilege of staring into your beautiful eyes. What can I do to change your mind? You know where to find me.
Julian.

I couldn't seem to shake off the feeling that there was something odd about Julian. I tossed the card into the air and watched it slowly descend to the ground.

"What are you thinking?" Gloria watched me from across the room.

"That it sucks to have the wrong guy chase after you." My shoulders went limp. I couldn't think of Julian, or anyone, for that matter, not when Simon occupied every inch of my brain. All I ever wanted was to be with Simon, more so since Gloria had told me about the personal check. I knew there was no end to what the man would do for me. He had been there pushing me along the way, making my dreams into a reality. Simon believed in me when I didn't. Now I allowed my stupid pride to keep him at bay.

"You know, Simon is not the kind of guy to shower a girl

with gifts. He isn't big on public displays of affection."

"I'm okay with that. I don't need Simon's money or gifts. This is not what I'm looking for." I lifted my hand to touch the ridiculous roses. "I should return the money."

"No—oh no. Simon can never find out I told you. He will never trust me with anything again."

"All I want from Simon is for him to be up-front with me." I sat down on the pink settee near the window.

"In all fairness, Mable, you should start with being honest with Simon if you expect that in return."

"Let's talk about something else, shall we?" I picked up the magazine on the coffee table and skimmed through it. *I know she's right, but I'm afraid of ruining things between Simon and me.* It's always fear that keeps us from the things we want.

"What are you wearing at the Jean-Pierre party tomorrow?" Gloria went through the rack of colorful clothing.

"I was thinking of wearing the maxi dress."

"Which one, the jersey knit?" Gloria made a funny face.

"Hey, what's wrong with it?"

She quickly pushed the clothing to one side. "Here, this is what you should be wearing." She pulled something off the rack and held it out: a beautiful emerald-green silk dress. "It's meant to be; it's in your size." Suddenly I had a fairy godmother. "Wear this, Mable, it will be such a shame if you don't. Do it … you will break hearts."

"Oh, I don't care—boys suck. All I want now is sleep," I mumbled, sliding farther into the settee and covering my face with the magazine.

"You're hopeless. I'm glad I've kept the bill," she murmured under her breath.

"What bill?"

"For your birthday gift. You won't be needing it since you've got the most eligible bachelors on your tail." She smiled.

"What did you get me?"

153

"A T-shirt that has a big cat on it with the words *Crazy Cat Lady Forever* written at the bottom."

I should have known better than to ask. This inside joke between us was getting old fast. "You got me a T-shirt for my birthday? You're a cheapskate," I teased.

"It cost me two hundred seventy-five dollars."

"What?"

"It's a Ronaldo."

"Shit, are you crazy? Do you know how many Nutella jars I can buy with that? Return it." I yawned. "But don't count the cat lady out just yet."

If He Wants to Play, Then Play We Must

"Mable?"

I caught him in the most compromising way, and it was not what I expected when I first knocked on the door of his hotel room. His hair was darker from the dampness, and a white towel hung nicely around his waist. Dewdrops of water slid off Simon's chest, and I couldn't help but smile. It was ironic, almost like something I might have daydreamed about, because God knew I had more fantasies about Simon than Walter Mitty had about life.

"For heaven's sake, put on a T-shirt or something." A fever washed over me, and the smell of fresh soap only put me further in hot water.

"Well, you didn't give me a chance." He grinned, enjoying the fact that I had found him like this.

Show-off.

"I came in from a run when I got your text. So, thinking I had time, I jumped in the shower."

I couldn't help but smile. *Shake it off ... Geez, woman, tell him why you're here.* "Sorry to barge in on you like this, but can I crash at your place for an hour?" I looked at him through my

155

eyelashes. "Gloria has a film crew in our room, taping a segment: what to wear for fashion week or—in your case, what not to wear …" I smirked, allowing my eyes to trail the length of him.

"Ha. You're a funny bird."

"Seriously, who knew you had this underneath?" I pointed my fingers leisurely at him. I had wanted to say something the last time he had removed his shirt, but I hadn't wanted to inflate his head. "And you're not even egotistical?"

"Not even vaguely." He placed a hand on his hip. *A good thing; I don't want that towel to go anywhere.*

"Why would I be? I've been rocking abs since the age of six—It's no big deal." He grinned.

"So are you going to let me in or what?" I leaned into the doorway, standing under his observing eyes, pretending not to be bothered by him. That was what I kept telling myself as the heat rose at the back of my neck.

"I'm not sure if I should. After what happened last time, I don't want you to take advantage of me." He began the verbal dance I knew too well, the kind that would get a reaction out of me.

I stifled a laugh. "Funny, I could have sworn you liked it."

"Trust me, Mable, liking it wasn't the problem."

So what was? I wanted to say, but the words couldn't find their way out. Now I knew it was possible Simon couldn't move away from what he had endured. I promised Gloria I wouldn't mention anything I knew about his wife—not that Gloria had told me much, but I would have to wait until he was ready to talk about it. That is—if he ever was.

"I'll try to contain myself, Mr. Rowe."

"Well, if you promise to try, then I guess I could let you in." He slid his arm down and moved off to the side, allowing me to venture farther into his room. The space was similar, but smaller than mine. The color scheme played on a soft red, the opposite of my room's green. Two Jansen Louis XV sofas flanked the center of the room, and a small round table with two chairs was in front of a large window. It seemed too delicate for a man like Simon.

"I thought of ordering us breakfast." He picked up the phone. "Tell me you didn't eat?"

In my room, I had had a sundried tomato with sausage, served with fresh fruit. But that was two hours ago.

"Not really." I flipped my hair to the side, trying to relax, keeping my eyes off where they shouldn't be. Instead, I plucked the magazine off the coffee table.

"So what would you like?"

"No, on second thought it's okay. I'm not really hungry—" *Not for food, anyway.*

"Mable." In a deeper voice, he continued. "I will not eat alone in front of you. Just stop being stubborn and tell me what you like, or I'm just going to order for you." He placed his mouth back on the receiver. "Yes hello, I would like to place an order ... Yes, room 201 ..."

"I'll have a crepe—No, wait, pancakes with strawberries and whipped cream on top, please?" I interrupted. I might as well, since he was offering. "Oh, coffee would be nice." I waved my fingers in the air to get his attention. "One more thing." I bit my lip. "Add a French toast to that ... with breakfast potatoes on the side. Would that be possible?" He looked at me in amazement. "I never told you this, but I have this syndrome, that I need to eat, like, all the time," I said, once he placed the receiver back down

"No worries. I like a bird who eats." Simon laughed.

"I'm going to put some clothes on before you get any ideas." He smiled boyishly, or I thought that was what he did. I was trying to avoid looking at him.

"Whatever makes you more comfortable," I said from the sofa, flipping through the pages of a travel magazine.

"For me? Or you?" he said from behind. I lifted my head

and quickly shifted in the settee. His eyes were a little darker.

"You think this is making me uncomfortable? Please, I'm a professional. I'm used to seeing half-naked men." I leisurely folded my arms on the peak of the sofa, resting my chin without batting an eye. "Oh wait, it came out wrong ... I mean ..."

"Yeah, I get it, but you've seen nothing like me before." The biggest grin appeared on his face. *If he wants to play, then play we must.*

"*Pssff,* sure I have." I smiled. "Besides, there's nothing sexier than a man with a great mind."

"Which I'm qualified for." He walked toward me.

"That would be debatable," I said, and he snorted a laugh. "Are you sure you're not egotistical?"

"You think you'd know me by now, Mable."

The thing with Simon was, it went beyond comfort. Our friendship wasn't a lie, but it wasn't the truth, either. Underneath, it was a host of other things ... We played around like children, splashing in the water but were afraid of getting wet. We watched the tide—hoping it wouldn't take us, though it was only a matter of time before it would. We both knew it. I wanted him as much as he wanted me, but there were consequences to getting the things you want. I thought we both believed it, or we would have dived in by now.

"Well then, if this doesn't bother you I'll just stay like this," he teased, leaning down closer.

The tide comes in.

"Sure, why not."

The tide goes out.

We always seemed to push those lines that held us in place, which kept us apart. We stayed where we were until a knock at the door broke the spell, and it was Simon who pulled away, making his way toward the door.

"Where are you going?" I laughed, knowing whoever was behind that door would get an eye full.

"What does it look like?"

"Like that?"

"Why not? You didn't seem to mind it." He winked, opening the door, and a man in a black uniform wheeled in our breakfast.

"Where would you like me to set it up, sir?" The man casually glanced at Simon, then back to me. He probably thought we were lovers.

"The table next to the window would be all right, mate," Simon said. It took the man a few seconds to empty the cart, placing everything on the round mahogany table.

"Thank you, sir," the man said after Simon tipped him. "Enjoy your meal." He walked out of the room.

"I better get dressed before I'm accused of indecent exposure." Simon headed off into the other room.

I smiled, but inside I was downhearted, wondering what would have happened if we weren't interrupted, but now that the food was there, my focus shifted to the French toast and strawberry pancakes that were begging to be eaten.

Moments later, Simon reappeared clothed, wearing a basic black T-shirt and faded five-pocket jeans. He took the seat in front of me, and I had one leg up to my chin. I felt his eyes on me as I buttered my bread, piling everything onto it.

"Wow, I'm glad you're not hungry," Simon smirked.

"I know, imagine if I was." I jiggled my eyebrows. He laughed, shaking his head in disbelief, and his eyes descended to his plate. It had been over a year since we first met, which was hard to believe, and I wondered how much more of Simon I didn't know. In many ways, he still was a real mystery to me.

"Okay, so what's the deal with you?"

"What?" He briefly looked up from his plate.

"How come you're single?" It amazed me I hadn't asked that question before. Then it occurred to me that he had never asked about my past relationships either. Or was he purposely avoiding the subject at all cost? Because if he had the right to know my history, I had the right to his. With Simon, that subject felt like it was off-limits.

"What sort of question is that?" He let out a low laugh.

"It's a fundamental question ... Just answer it," I mused. "You're single, right?" I was swimming, hoping I'd somehow get to the point. "And why is that? Do you have a weird fetish or something?" I asked.

"So what, I'm single. There's nothing to look into, Dr. Phil." He suspiciously constricted his eyes in my direction. "Wait a minute, what is it exactly you're trying to extort from me?"

That's the problem when you're friends with someone who has the same astrology sign. You can't pull a fast one without them knowing what you're up to. I wanted to open the conversation, stirring it right to the source—Vanessa or his deceased wife and, of course, me. *If three is a crowd, I wonder what they say about four.*

"I'm not trying anything," I said, not looking him in the eye. "You can't blame me for wondering. Look at you." I held out a hand. "You're hot and successful ... with abs of freaking steel." I took the napkin off my lap to wipe my mouth. "Good grief, for your apartment alone, I would date you."

"Might I remind you ... you had your chance, mate," he said, half-joking.

"Are you talking about when we first met? And you propositioned me to sleep with you?" I leaned in closer, continuing this proverbial two-step we had going between us. "Because that wasn't asking me out on a proper date."

"It wasn't like that ..." He cleared his throat and I shot him a look.

"You were trying to cover it up, but that's exactly what it was."

"Anyhow, maybe it was the whiskey talking," he replied.

"Or Richard," I said honestly. He did a double take.

"Richard?" he said, confused.

"What's short for Richard?" I held his gaze, and he finally got it.

He laughed. "Nah, yeah … Okay, maybe that too." He shifted in his chair. "Anyhow, it doesn't matter; you shot me down."

"You kinda did too," I pointed out, but he didn't respond. "Perhaps you should have taken your time and gotten to know me first … before making any propositions." I took a sip of my coffee.

"Look, I'm sorry if you took it the wrong way. Just to be clear, I wasn't looking for a one-night stand. Mable, I was interested in you—in every possible way," Simon said.

My stomach took a dip.

"So to answer your question, I'm single because I choose to be." He let out a sigh. "Why waste my time with anyone when I know what I want?"

"And what is it you want?" I asked, taking another bite of my crepe.

"You know the answer, Mable. So stop acting like you don't." He jerked his eyes away, and the silence just hung there for a moment before he continued. Maybe he wanted me to say something, but I wasn't going to come out of the woods unless he called for me. No more shades. I wanted it in bright colors.

"In all honesty—" He pushed his unfinished plate to the side and leaned in closer. "I spend a stupid amount of time on airplanes. I'm a crazy workaholic. I need to have at least twenty projects going on, and that doesn't leave me much time for anything else." Message received—loud and clear.

"Yeah, but don't you ever get lonely?" I knew that I did.

"I find it's easier being just me and my shadow. What's the point? To get involved in something just to pass the time? Besides, I'm never alone. I have Captain, and … you."

"Me?"

In his eyes, I caught a hint of something, some sort of truth that was wearing him down. I felt it coming, and I knew it wouldn't be long before he let me in to see what was behind that wall. "Wow—the cat comes before me?"

"Don't get jealous. That feline has been in my life longer." He grinned. "I'm happy you're in my life, and I appreciate someone who has something of substance to say, even though she lacks good taste in music and is a horrible liar."

"Ah, I don't lie."

He gave me a knowing look. *What does he know? I think I'm a fantastic liar.*

"Pass me the croissant, please?" It didn't look like I was anywhere near to cracking him open. "Oh, and the Nutella ... merci beaucoup."

"What about you?" Simon asked.

"Why I'm single? Ha, where do I start?" I held out my cup to Simon, who poured the hot coffee in.

"My love life is ... like a madwoman's breakfast." I attempted to say it in an Australian accent, but it came out sounding more like Patchy the Pirate. When his laugh quieted down, I continued. "I think my expectation of love tends to be big, which makes guys run for the hills. I don't know, maybe I'm not lovable."

He made a noise that came deep from his throat, and I looked up to meet his eyes. "Can I be frank with you?" he asked.

"I prefer the Simon of five minutes ago," I replied, watching the sides of his lips go up.

"That could be arranged." He gave me a sexy grin before putting his fork down and looking me in the eyes. "Let's be serious for a moment. I think you should stop blaming yourself. It's not your fault she left, you know."

"I know," I said, spreading the Nutella inside my croissant. I could feel his eyes watching me.

"No, I don't think you do." He sat farther back in his chair, his face basking in the sunlight.

"It never worked out because you wasted your time with boys. When you needed was a man. A man who means what he says and says what he means. Someone who will remind you every day what an incredible woman you are. There you have it; that's just my opinion." He pulled the plate back in front of him and continued to eat.

"Sure," I murmured. "They're all lining up at my front door." I waved my fork over my shoulder. "I was never the kind of girl that had a long list of criteria for the kind of man I wanted in my life. I just want someone simple. Someone to see me for who I am—is that too much to ask?"

"No, it's not. Trust me, he's not that far from your reach."

I swallowed everything whole. *Here's to hoping.* He observed me from across the table like he was summing me up.

"You're fun, witty, and I adore you. Just for your legs alone, I would date you." Simon smiled from across the table, and my heart did a flip.

"Anyway, how did this become about me?" I asked.

"You started it." He poured more coffee into his cup. After a short moment, he asked, "Is Julian taking you out?" He diverted his eyes back to his plate.

"No ... well." I cleared my throat. "I don't know. I haven't given him an answer just yet." I smiled. *Liar, liar.*

"How come?" I caught his eyes as they came back up to meet mine, a visible sign of annoyance.

"Well, you of all people should know to never get involved with people you work with. Right?"

Touché. I pushed his words back to him, but what I should have said was, *I'm in love with you ... idiot*! But, as usual, I chose silence over admission.

"Right."

"But lucky for him, I have no problem with that," I said. If I wished for a reaction, I sure got it.

"What?" He chewed his food slower. "You have me confused, so let me get this straight. Are you or are you not seeing him tonight?" he said, without taking his eyes off me.

"No, I don't think I'm going to." *I'm toying with him. Is it wrong that I like it?*

"Smart girl. Anyhow, you'll only be the flavor of the week, you know that, right?" His shoulders relaxed.

"Too bad, though, French men have this … je ne sais quoi? A way to seduce a woman." I brought my cup to my lips and watched him nervously twitch in his seat. "When I arrived, I found my room filled with red roses. You should see it … it's insane." I tried not to make it obvious that I was observing him under my lashes.

"Yeah?" His eyebrows came together, and his jaw tightened.

That's it? All right, I'll press on. "He texted a dozen times just this morning," I said. It was actually only once, but who cared about the minor details?

"Huh." He looked down at his plate, tossing around the chunks of scrambled eggs. *What is going on in that head of yours, Mr. Rowe?* I wished I knew.

"Julian keeps insisting on taking me out, and I'm running out of excuses for what to tell him."

"It's easy. Just *say—no.*"

I ignored him and continued to talk. "On second thought, maybe I should just go out with him." I leaned back in my chair. "It's not like I have anything else going on in my life."

His dark eyes snapped up to meet mine. He rushed forward, pulling me into his arms, his warm lips on mine, dominating. A few things from the table crashed to the floor as he pulled me harder up against his chest. I wondered if he felt my heart pounding wildly inside me.

"Stay with me," he said, in a hushed voice I would have

missed it if his lips weren't right up against my ear.

"What?" My body softened under his touch, melting faster than wax from a flame.

"You still want to see Paris?" Simon asked.

"Yes."

"So stay back a day … We'll go home together on Wednesday." His voice was silky. It wasn't what he said—it was what he didn't that got my attention.

"With you … here?"

"Sure, there's enough room in here for both of us … I want you with me," he said, without hesitation. I had nothing booked for the following days, so that wasn't the problem. The problem was that there were hundreds of big elephants dancing in the room, and one of them was taunting me, wearing my Forever Cat Lady T-shirt. *I can't think right now.* My brain was buzzing with such good feelings that I was overlooking one good reason not to go along.

"Yeah … okay …" He left me breathless, yearning for more. I only had two things on my mind. One—why did he have to be such a good kisser? Two—why wasn't he still kissing me?

"Okay," he reconfirmed.

I wasn't entirely sure what I had agreed to. But, then again, we didn't have to say it out loud. We both wanted it, this passion, this tension that existed between us, and it hung in the silence. Suppressing it only intensified it more.

"Promise me you'll never go near Julian alone. Always bring someone with you."

"What? Why?" I stepped back

"I don't trust that guy … Tell Julian you're with someone else," he said, still holding on, as if, if he let go, he would lose me. "The only thing—don't tell him it's me," he said. *Here we go with the two-step again.*

"Wait a minute … not that it's any of Julian's business, but why not?" I asked. I knew what I wanted, but I wondered if it was clouding my judgment. Simon wanted me to stay—to spend the night with him? I wasn't stupid. *I can see when I'm only wanted for one thing.*

"Look, the reason is—" he began.

"Oh, I get it. You want no one to know—for this to get out? After spending time between the sheets—we would be done, right?" It became clear. *He's no better than anyone else, and it's devastating.*

"No, no, no, that's not what this is about—" His face went from pleasant to complete and utter confusion, and I pushed out of his arms, adding more space between us.

"So what is it then? I'm not something you can have fun with and throw away when it doesn't serve your purposes. I deserve more respect than that, Simon."

With a kink in his brow, he said, "Can you calm down and let me explain? You have it all wrong—" He stopped me from stepping on a piece of broken fine china. Picking it up, he placed it back on the once perfectly-set table we had started off with, now in disarray—like us.

"You once said you cared about me. I thought I could trust you, but I guess I was wrong." I made my way to the front door.

"Mable, I am the only one who's been looking out for you, so don't you dare twist this up. You don't understand what I'm thinking or feeling because if you did, you wouldn't be acting like this."

If I wasn't blinded by rage, I would have said, *tell me, then—tell me what I mean to you? Because I can't take this foolish game anymore.* But instead, in the heat of the moment, I went with, "Oh yeah, and how am I acting, Simon ... hmm?" I paused in my steps, turning just enough to look at him.

"Like a crazy person. I said one thing, and you spun out on it. Making up things in your head. I'm not the villain here, and yet you keep making me out to be one."

"I shouldn't have come. This was a mistake." I had had

enough, wanting to get far away from him.

"Where are you going?" He kept right up with me. "I'm sorry, okay? Whatever I said to offend you, just give me a second to clear things up."

"Please, I have no time for this right now …" Exasperated, I let out a long breath when Simon put himself between me and the door.

"You're stubborn, you know that?" he said, after a failed attempt to pull me into his arms, a last attempt to disarm me.

"Well, I warned you," I replied. There might have been a moment of truce, but then I thought what an idiot I was to believe that Simon was different. Inside, the storm brewed back up again … *Someone with substance … blah, blah, blah …* Please, what bullshit, and I had played right into it. Men will say anything to get what they want.

"Move out of the way, Simon. You will make me late for the show." His eyes searched my face just before turning from the door. As I reached for the knob, his voice stopped me.

"Hey, I wasn't planning on you choosing me. You're the one who wanted this, and now you're walking away?"

"Stupid me, I thought you chose me too." I gave a quick side-glance, and with a swift movement, I opened the door and walked through, not waiting for his response. When the door closed behind me, everything went out of focus.

Reap What You Sow

Simon

Gloria was the first person I saw when I got out of the elevator. She was on her phone, pacing the length of the hotel lobby. That was typical for Gloria, but it was her face, whiter than my shirt, that had me worried.

At first, I thought it had to do with Mable, because I hadn't seen her since early yesterday. After our fight, Mable had been keeping her distance. She believed the worst of me—this happened, when you weren't completely honest with someone you cared about. I had acted out at the wrong time, out of jealousy, because every man had his breaking point, and Mable was mine.

There was so much more to my story, and honestly, I couldn't bring myself to speak the words without reliving the pain—but then again, the pain never went away. It only subsided enough to make life somewhat bearable. In the past two years, I'd fought hard to keep my emotions under the water, away from the light. So I'd immersed myself in work; it was the only thing that kept me afloat. Everyone close to me understood that it wasn't something easy for me to open up about—the loss—without sending me into a downward spiral. Then Mable had come into my life—or had I come into hers?

That night we met, I wasn't supposed to be there, but something changed when I stopped at a red light on my way to the *Nylon* party. That was when I first saw Mable at the intersection, passing us primitive blokes as we took in the sight of her. But there was something peculiar about Mable. She never once glanced in my direction, and then her head came up like someone had called her name. And it made me wonder about a belief there is: that two people who are meant to be together feel this unexplained force when they are around each other. I had felt it, and it had only made me wonder: did she feel it too? When she got onto the sidewalk, some moron in a yellow Bugatti hollered the kind of shit that made us look like a bunch of Neanderthals. She walked away, but not before she flipped him the bird. She had me, there and then.

I thought I was in my right mind, and it wasn't something I was in the habit of doing—but after that interaction, I wanted to make sure she made it safely to where she was heading off. Maybe she had a boyfriend, and I should have minded my business, but I wanted to stay in the belief that something amazing was about to happen. If I lost sight, I would never find her again. It seemed inevitable; Mable lit the fire in me that demands pursuit, and so I followed.

"Hey, is everything okay?" I walked over to Gloria when she got off the phone.

"No. Tracy's mom is in the hospital." Gloria was staring at me, but her mind was elsewhere. "She took a nasty tumble."

"Will she be okay?"

"Honestly, I don't know. The woman is eighty-five years old—everything at this point is critical." She put her hand on her forehead, and her sequined sleeve caught the light, sparkling like a million diamonds.

"What should I do? I'm so far away, and Tracy needs me right now." I knew Gloria, and it was very typical for her to get lost in a glass of water.

"Look, it's straightforward—you will go back up and pack your things. I'll find out about the next available flight."

"What about the party? And Mable was looking forward to tonight ..."

"Where is Mable?" I glanced around.

"She's upstairs getting ready. I want her to go to the party without me. Can you make sure of that? Take care of my cousin while I'm gone?" she said, as I walked her back to the elevator. "You owe me a favor, remember?" She cast me concerned eyes, and I was disappointed she had to ask.

Didn't Gloria realize what lengths I would go for Mable? But then again, Mable was the kind of girl that never needed to be taken care of by anyone. She had paid back her father and the agency every penny she had borrowed from them. No, Mable wasn't the kind of girl that wanted to be saved; she was capable of saving herself. That was why I found Mable so refreshing. She was the only person who expected nothing from me, and I would bend backward for her if needed. For her, I would.

———————

"I never bought into that, the whole Cinderella thing. The girl waiting for the dude to save her, and they live happily ever after," Mable said, standing in the middle of a shoot we had worked on last month. Her lips were painted red and the gloss cake on her face made her looked like a manufactured doll. I watched her struggle with the stupid dress, kicking out the layered tulle from underneath, trying to move around the fairytale set, which I had had the crew build for this project.

"It's a bunch of crap to feed young girls. There's no such

thing as fairy-tale endings," Mable said. I waited for the makeup artist to add the final touches before we shot

When the makeup artist removed herself from the set, I started shooting a few frames for a test run.

Chick che ... flash.

"Well, let me rephrase it. I don't trust that happiness comes easily. It takes hard work and choosing the right decisions after making a couple of shitty ones, and maybe then you'll get a happy ever after."

"Huh, interesting ... I never thought about it that way. Maybe there's still hope for us." The words came out the way they should have, but I could see in her eyes that she didn't trust their meaning—maybe I didn't either.

"I can't believe you're making me wear this—I'm pulling such a sweat." She held on to the plastic wig with her gloved hand. "Noah, it's not staying on." She giggled as it toppled over.

I loved the sound of her laughter.

Chick che ... flash.

"So you know, I'm keeping this." She meant the synthetic yellow do-up with the painted blue headband. The whole theme of this editorial was what happened after Cinderella came back from her honeymoon, and so Mable was playing the part of the cinder girl who had metamorphosed into a princess. Not my idea—the magazine's.

"And what are you going to do with it?" I smiled.

"Burn it," she said flat out.

"I see someone didn't have their brekky this morning," I said, watching Noah readjusting the headpiece.

Chick che ... flash.

"Why couldn't Cinderella be a girl who took charge of her own destiny? Just ditch her evil stepfamily and be determined to live a meaningful life? Who knows what she could have been instead of a princess ... Maybe a buccaneer."

"A pirate?" I mused.

"The captain of a large vessel." Her eyes shone brightly. "She'd run a tight ship."

"If she's anything like you, sure." Over the months I had come to notice a sudden change in Mable, something that wasn't there before. It was as if she'd realized she could trust herself.

"She'll eventually return, though," she continued, "There's always something that brings you back home." Her words lived within me, and I allowed them to sit there for a moment. I'd been all over the world, lived in three different countries. It was easy to uproot myself, and in all honesty, it didn't bother me. For a short moment Rachael had been my home, where the heart had once lived, but now that was gone.

Chick che ... flash.

Home ... It was a word I had lost sight of, and it would be difficult to define it these days, but something had come over me where all I could think was that the answer might have been staring me in the face.

"And what of the prince?" Now I was curious to know.

"That's where my version takes an interesting twist."

Chick che ... flash.

"Cinderella hears about this boring ball that's happening, and when she sees the prince for the first time, standing there, looking so miserable, she knows she has to save him. So she walks right up and taps him on the shoulder and says, 'Dude, you know, we could turn this night around. But first I want to know: are you in?'"

Something mischievous flashed across her eyes, and I suddenly laughed. She was having fun at my expense. Well, maybe I deserved it.

"Seriously, you guys should just get on with it," Noah said, coming from behind Mable after repositioning her headpiece for the last time. "It's just disgusting to watch you two." He huffed before walking away.

"What's his problem?" Mable flashed an amused look. It

172

happened so often that I forgot that we had a large entourage. I guessed she had that effect on me: simply made everyone else disappear.

"So now, how does this story end?" I asked, watching her contemplate it for a moment before a smile reappeared.

"They go back to the ship, and she has him scrub the deck floors. Only then does she know if he's a keeper." Mable winked.

"Shit. Poor fella, he never knew what hit him." I couldn't help but laugh. She had me owned with everything she said, the way she thought, the way she could get a chuckle out of me, at all unimportant things, silly things. But it was the best time— only with Mable. I think that was the moment I realized something had shifted: the day she made me think about home again.

"Simon?" Gloria's voice pulled me back, and I realized what I needed to do.

"Don't worry about Mable, I'll take care of her even though she hates me right now." I halted in my steps, wondering if Mable told Gloria what happened between us.

"No, she doesn't hate you—" Gloria turned around, gave me a side smile. "But you want my opinion?"

"I have a feeling you're going to give it—no matter what I say."

"I shouldn't have to tell you how to live your life, but I can't refrain myself any longer. You deserve to be happy. It's time to face your issues and move on. Mable won't wait forever, you know?" I watched Gloria disappear behind the elevator doors.

I didn't know what to say; it was never easy to be transparent with anyone. I wasn't a man who wore my emotions, but that needed to change. The question stirred in my mind: had I suffered enough? I wasn't sure if an eternity would be sufficient. I couldn't dredge all the pain up at that moment, not when the next elevator doors opened, and there she was, looking like a Greek goddess. Mable stiffened at the sight of me.

When she had composed herself, she walked out of the elevator and the fabric of her dress flowed behind her, exposing her beautiful legs.

"So? What do you think?" She spun around, and it made me smile.

The thing about Mable was that you couldn't stay mad, not at her—not at the world. She was a good example of the fact that, even though she'd been through a lot, it wasn't going to get her down and, if it did—not for long. And maybe that was why she faced everything with empathy. She saw the world in another light; it only made me want to love her even more. That was why I was hesitant to tell her what I had been through. I knew she would feel for me, and I was not ready to let anyone in, to share the pain. I couldn't do that to her.

"Wow, lost for words, that's a first, Simon Rowe," she said, trying to put the awkwardness behind us. I was in trouble. Not even heaven could help me. "You don't like the dress?" Her brows knitted together.

Christ, what's not to like about the strapless, long emerald number that caressed her curves perfectly?

When she'd come into my hotel room the day before, all I kept thinking was of her beautiful neck and how badly I wanted to kiss it. The tension had been building between us for weeks. Well, I knew how it went—the heart wants what it can't have. At first I had to question my motives. Was I acting out of jealousy? Yeah, of course. But I also wanted to protect her from Julian. I was too damn stubborn to admit that, not only did I care for her, but I loved her, too. My emotions went beyond spending time between the sheets, like I'd been accused of. There is a path that leads down to desiring someone and wanting intimacy. Over several months we had kind of drifted back and forth like the tide, pushing ourselves far enough until we had to go back. It was fear holding me in place. I know that now.

"No, what's not to like? It's very … breathable." I shot her a look of amusement.

"It's not that revealing." She tapped my arm with her black clutch purse.

"You look beautiful." I said. Mable smiled, like she was satisfied with my answer.

"And you look sharp. No tie?"

"Nah, I hate wearing ties, they make me feel restricted. But it doesn't mean I don't like to use them." I was messing with her, and the side of her mouth slightly rose.

"Maybe one day you'll show me what exactly you use them for?" She tapped my chest, walking past me. I was relieved that she was willing to let it go, and I hoped that, when the moment was right, she would give me a chance to explain.

"Where's Gloria?" Mable slightly turned back.

"She went up."

"Back to our room—why?"

"There's an emergency. Tracy's mom is in the hospital."

"Oh no, what happened?"

"She fell."

"Maybe I should go and see what I can do to help."

"Gloria wants us to go on without her."

"I feel kind of bad … to go now."

"I know, me too. I'll tell you what, why don't you go up, and I'll find a place to get us some coffee."

"No, go to the party. I'll stay with Gloria until she leaves for the airport, so there's no reason why both of us should stay behind."

"I'd like to stick around, if you don't mind? Gloria was always there for me."

"Are you sure?" Mable said, looking me over.

"Nah, yeah, you know me. I hate these events … I wouldn't have fun anyway." Not without Mable, that's for sure. I was toast, wasn't I? The moment my eyes saw her face. It was as though I'd dreamed her up. Mable was the kind of girl a man will always be haunted by. The way she had wrapped her arms around me, sitting behind me on my motorcycle. I was hooked. All I had wanted to do after that day was to claim that sweet mouth of hers. I hungered to taste … again, even now.

"Okay." She made her way toward the elevators. It hurt to watch her walk away, because there was no reason for me to believe she'd come walking back.

"You go ahead. I'll be up soon," I said. She nodded, standing between the open elevators. Her eyes never left mine until she allowed herself to disappear behind the metal doors. I wondered how I was going to start the conversation. *Maybe I should start by telling her that, when she's around, the darkness leaves me.*

Butterfly Effect

Mable

Simon loaded the Louis Vuitton suitcase into the cab as I pulled Gloria in for an embrace. "Send Tracy our love. Tell her we're praying for her mom's speedy recovery."

"I will," Gloria said, shifting her attention to Simon, who was now standing beside me.

"Keep us posted, will you?" Simon said. They had formed a bond in the years they'd worked together. And it warmed my heart to know how much he cared about my cousin.

"Yes, I will." Gloria tapped him on his chest before sliding into the cab, and Simon closed the door. We both stood there like a couple of statues, watching the taxi drive into the night. The air was awkward between us—the way I'd left him so abruptly. I wanted to be mad at him, I really did, but the urge to kiss him was much stronger.

"So what now?" I asked. With Gloria gone, it almost felt like there was no parental supervision.

"We can still make it to the party if you like." He looked down at his watch.

"Oh, I don't know … I was looking forward to rubbing elbows with designers and movie stars, but this whole thing with Tracy's mom—kind of bummed me out."

"Yeah, me too." Simon had his hands deep in his pockets, looking gorgeous in his suit. It was such a waste that we wouldn't be going anywhere.

"I think I'll call it a night," I said, standing there under his liquefying stare.

"I …" He exhaled before continuing. "Look, the reason I never wanted Julian to know you're with me was because it will alter his decision in hiring you for his next ad campaign."

"Why would it?"

"We had an altercation a while back."

"What kind of altercation?"

He hesitated before saying, "The kind that involved my fist with his face." He scratched his temple.

"No! Why?"

"He was taking advantage of a friend. It's a long story. I was trying to tell you this guy is a creep. But I didn't want to come right out with it because then I would sound like a fucking jealous moron."

"Were you?"

"A fucking moron?" His lips went up slightly. "Only when I'm around you."

Oh.

"I don't understand why." He swallowed hard. "It's just you never needed me the way I wanted you … I'm afraid of losing you."

"But you won't." I blinked.

"You say that, but it's all speculation," Simon said.

I look at him until I couldn't anymore. "Why is it so complicated … between you and me?"

He looked up at the sky like he was searching for some answer. "How do you feel about gyros?" he said as our eyes met.

"I know a place close by."

———————————

"Look at us! All dolled up eating our gyros on the streets of Paris. I can't think of anything so romantic," I said.

We had begun this adventure down the street listening to the sounds of the city playing our soundtrack, and suddenly I had the urge to lose myself in a night that seemed so electrifying. Surrender myself to a man I had fallen so hard for.

"Is it romance you wanted?" Simon's eyes questioned me. "Because you don't seem to mind it when I feed you." He smiled, wiping his hands with his napkin, then tossing it in a nearby trash can.

"How did you eat so fast?" I wasn't doing a good job with my gyro. It was falling apart every time I took a bite of it.

Simon gave me a side-glance. "Hold on, you have tzatziki sauce all over your face."

"Do I?" I laughed. I felt comfortable around Simon, enough that I didn't need to impress him. *That's the beauty of our relationship, or whatever it may be.*

"Yeah." He stopped, giving me the once-over. "How on earth did you even get it in your hair?" He grinned, getting closer. "Look at you—you're a mess." I snorted out a laugh, and it made us laugh even more.

"You're a hell of a messy eater, Mable Harper." He tried his best to clean it off.

"Oh, that's not true."

"I give up." He sighed, handing me a napkin. "You got some … uh … um—on your …" He winced, scratching his temple. I followed his gaze.

"Are you staring at my breasts?" I threw a piece of bread at him.

"It's kind of hard; you have them out in the open." He laughed. "Christ, I can't look anywhere without seeing them."

"Don't get excited; they're not that big. It's all tape and contouring," I said, watching Simon take off his jacket and drape it over my shoulders in a protective matter. I didn't know if I wanted to be annoyed or to appreciate the gesture, but since I was feeling cold, I allowed it.

"Nah, yeah, I'm more of a butt than a boob guy." He chuckled to himself. "I can't believe I just said that." I watched him roll up his white sleeved shirt. *Simon does this all the time. How does he know I find it sexy?*

"Maybe we should have changed into something more comfortable before we started this little venture."

"Are you freaking kidding me? I'm wearing this Tabitha Daz dress to bed. Tomorrow I have to return this to its rightful owner, and I'll be back to plain old Cinderella." I took another bite, and whatever remained of the gyro toppled onto the sidewalk. We both looked at the ground, and then I glanced up at Simon. I knew he wanted to laugh, but he did a good job containing himself.

"No worries love … Come, we'll get you another one." He spun in the direction we had just come from, holding out his arm for me.

"No, I give up. It's getting late and I'd better get my butt to bed. No pun intended." I shot him a wink, throwing the wrapper in the trash can nearby.

"All right, Cinderella, let's get you back home before you turn into a pumpkin."

———

"Would you like to come up to my room?" Simon half-whispered, slightly turning in the crowded elevator. "We could share a bottle of wine and sit out in the gallery?"

"Why would I want to do that?" I lowered my eyes.

"Because my room has a better view? And I would like to talk to you about something … if you give me a chance."

His eyes softened, enough to sway me. *We needed to talk or let it go once and for all.*

"All right, but only because you have the best view of the city," I said. "And you have to order us something to eat."

"Sure, anything." He nodded "Anything you want."

We walked down the corridor with my hand in his. Inside his room, I made my way out to his gallery while Simon ordered a bottle of wine from downstairs. As I sat on the black iron chair, taking in the view, I wondered how this conversation would go.

"Okay, so here's the thing—the kitchen is closed downstairs, but the concierge was nice enough to go across the street and bring me back this," Simon said, coming out fifteen minutes later with a bottle of wine in one hand and a platter in the other. "I got us an assortment of cheese and stuff." He set it down in front of me.

The platter looked appetizing, and I grabbed the square piece closest to me. The taste differed from anything I'd eaten before.

"This is not cheese." I chewed, allowing the flavor roll on my palate.

"That looks like fois gras."

"A—What?"

"Fat liver." Simon filled the glasses with wine.

"It's either goose or duck …" he continued. "What's the matter?" He laughed.

"Even I have my limits." I discreetly disposed of it in my napkin.

"I guess you do." He handed me my glass. "Here's to surviving your first fashion week."

"I'll drink to that." I touched my glass to his.

"You've come a long way, and I know I never told you this, but I'm proud of you." Simon smiled, sitting across from me. "What's the matter?"

He caught it like I was an open book. His words were heartrending, and I was trying to understand this emotion that ran through me.

"Sometimes it's just too much … The paparazzi, the parties—I guess the gist of it. I thought this was what I wanted, but yet … I should be happy."

"Remember when I told you about the lights?" He placed his glass down. "Sure, I think it's a struggle, and the longer you stay in this business, the more difficult it is to remain unchanged. But there are ways around it, to stay grounded."

"Hmm … like the man who volunteers his time," I said, and his eyes matched mine. "Who uses his photography to raise money for charities and adopted a rescue cat named Captain." I hid my smile behind my glass. "And you thought I didn't know? It's interesting the things you learn on a Friday night with a couple of mojitos and Noah."

"Okay, so I lied. Captain wasn't a gift from my sister." Simon realized that it was silly to lie about it. "I thought you might think I'm a weirdo if I told you I set out to get a cat." *He's mistaking my silence for something else.* "Look, she was in an unfortunate predicament. Either I took her home, or they would euthanize her. So I couldn't let it happen."

"I think that's sweet … A man who wants to save the world because he doesn't know how to save himself."

He diverted his eyes away from mine, and I realized I was onto something.

"What else do you know about me?" he asked.

"Not enough, I suppose," I said matter-of-factly.

He played with the glass in his hands. "Everyone has a different definition of success; mine is to help others. Otherwise, what's the point?" he said, and I realized—that had been the reason he was so willing to help me. Was I a cause for him? My stomach twisted in knots.

He continued, "You have to do everything for the right reasons. Or at least try, I suppose."

"That's admirable ... You're making me feel bad." I turned my eyes to the lights of the city.

"Why?"

"Because I feel like my reasons are selfish," I said, looking him straight in the eye. "I'm doing it for the free breadsticks." I giggled. "I'm insensitive. I'm sorry. It's amazing what you're doing, and I'm just trying to be funny. Good grief, that wasn't funny." I placed my glass on the table.

"You're trying to be playful because you're hiding how sad you are."

"You think so?" I hadn't realized that about myself. "Here I was thinking I'm broken..."

"Nah, people who are broken never admit to it."

I noticed how quiet he got. I sat there, watching him focus on a spot in the skyline. I couldn't help wondering if he was thinking of her, his wife. I hadn't given her any thought until now. I couldn't say I was resentful ... She was his wife, someone he had promised to spend the rest of his life with; it was tragic. I wanted to know more, about her and their time together. Would he ever give me that privilege?

"Simon." I drew his attention back. "I wanted to tell you, I changed my ticket," I said, placing my glass on the table.

"Really? So we'll leave on Wednesday together?" His eyes lit up, declaring the word *together* like it was a promise. *I know I've made stupid decisions in the past, but this doesn't feel like one.*

"You know what this dress is missing?" I said, smoothing out the luxurious fabric with my hands.

"What?"

"Pockets—so I could carry stuff." I peered down at my

green chiffon dress.

"In your case, it might be a good thing." He gave me a half smile, referencing my stolen purse.

"Anyway, it's better I don't; they would probably be a bunch of dirty tissue and gum wrappers." I stared at him. He looked so handsome.

"Men are lucky. They have all these secret compartments in their suit jackets."

Simon opened one side of his coat to reveal two pockets on the side. I had felt something in them when I gave it back earlier.

"What's in there, anyway?" I asked.

"You want to know, detective?"

"Sure, well, you know what they say—you can learn a lot about a man by the content in his pockets."

"Is that true?" His eyebrows peaked.

"It could be."

He gave me a curious look, and for whatever reason, he emptied his pockets. Simon laid the items in front of me, but what caught my eye was a gold ring with a blue stone setting. With a gentleness, he placed it on the table, and when he did, the wind picked up. I told myself it was pure coincidence, but the hair on the back of my neck went up, anyway.

"So what does this tell you about me?" He leaned back in his chair.

"Well for one, you missed a hell of a party." I held up the invitation. "Which I can't understand. Why would you ditch it to come and hang out with a total dork like me?"

"Dork? No. Don't feel bad for me. I got to spend time with a real looker and—God, she's far better company, more than those smug and superficial people there tonight." He held up his hands. "Look what I would be missing. It's a beautiful night under the stars; there's no better place I'd rather be than here with you. Right now, this is the real icing on the cake." He caught me staring, and I felt the heat rise in my cheeks, and my eyes diverted back to the items on the table.

"Okay next ... a wallet." My hand went to the next object. "Thank you very much, I think I'll hold on to this." I winked, pretending to slip it into my dress.

"Don't make me come and get it."

"You wouldn't dare." I giggled as I opened his leather wallet.

"To take back what's mine? Try me." He smiled wickedly. I didn't doubt him, not one bit. I had already seen his license; that was where I'd found out that Walter was his middle name. He had two credit cards, and on the other side of a slot, a picture of a boy and a taller girl in front of a Christmas tree.

"Who are these cuties?" I held the photo out for him to see.

"My sister's kids. My nephew Liam, who's six, and Abby is eight." I liked that he carried a picture of them. I smiled to myself. I thought he would make a great father one day.

"You must be close?"

"I try to see them as much as possible. A bunch of great kids. The house could get rowdy with the three of us."

"I could imagine." I smiled, but the tenderness faded when my eyes set sights on the next item. The key to the Pandora box. My fingers hesitated to touch the cold metal because of the energy it carried. I held my breath, because I knew what was coming next. I watched Simon leaning in, folding his arms across the table, his eyes focusing on the ring.

"It belonged to your wife?"

He nodded, the shade of blue of his eyes darkening with every breath. "It's Racheal's wedding band ... She died two years ago." He looked away, leaving the ring where it lay, but I had no intention of picking it up. It was almost sacred, undeserving of my fingerprints, and instead, I reached out my hand to him.

"Simon, I'm sorry."

I hated when people said that, but I did anyway. It's not a

stupid response, but loss is a personal injury. You can imagine what it's like, but you can never feel the pain for someone else. My heart sank as I continued to see the grief that thrived in his eyes, and he didn't turn away from me this time. Simon needed me to witness the hurt he'd been holding on to for so long. Maybe he wanted me to watch him fall apart; perhaps he thought I was the cure. The only thing was—I wasn't. He was broken, and I had no glue. With me, he would only shortchange himself.

"She was the girl you met on the bus in Nepal?" I asked because I'd been thinking about it for a while, piecing together everything I knew about Simon.

"Yes. She offered to show me the city, and it changed everything." He averted his eyes to the night sky.

"It seems like a start to a perfect love story."

"Yep, it was for a while." He picked the pack of cigarettes off the table and walked over to stand near the railing. I noticed one thing: Simon smoked a lot when he was anxious.

"The truth is, I can't stand myself … It's all my fault. If I had known what impact I would have had on her life, I would never have approached her that day."

"You blame yourself?"

"I do." He looked out to the open air, then continued. "It wasn't always perfect. Maybe we married too young, but we wanted to be together. After a while, work picked up, and over time, it was hard to blur the line between my job and my personal life, and Racheal gave me a lot of heat for it. I didn't know I could be that kind of person. Like my father, you know? A workaholic. I tried for her sake to get it together. But I failed." He inhaled his cigarette and allowed it to disperse through his lips before speaking again. "Because love should come first, right?"

"You didn't fail her, Simon." I wanted him to understand there was no judgment, only that it was important that he talk about it.

"But I did, don't you see? I set the whole thing in motion, but I never thought I wouldn't have time to make things right … It just tears me apart."

"What happened to Racheal?" I swallowed hard, and my eyes blurred with tears, because I knew what was coming next.

Pull the Past into the light

Simon

"Hmm, smells great." I walked into the white kitchen of our West Village apartment to find Racheal cooking up a storm, wearing her lavender cotton pants and a matching top that fell off the shoulders, exposing her white porcelain skin. "But I thought we were going out for breakfast?" I said to her.

"Yeah, but do you realize we haven't had brunch together in our new home, like never? I thought this would be nice." Racheal brought two plates from the counter, placing them on the small wooden table by the window.

She was right. I was out the door before the sun came up. Making my way to the studio or catching a flight to some location while Racheal lay asleep in our bed. We never had the luxury of starting our mornings together. Racheal was in no hurry, since the custom jewelry shop she owned across town only opened at ten. Now, looking back, she might have felt neglected, but Racheal already knew what she would get into when she married a freelance photographer. My job kept me away from *our life together. Every time I came home from a project, I thought I'd have time to spend a few days with my wife. Then I'd get a call for another job, and I'd be off on the next flight out. I took them because I never knew when the next one was coming. I kept telling myself: "a small sacrifice of quality time, but one day it will be all worth the big payoff. When we're ready to start a family, I will ease off with the rush of work, choose my projects according to my family life." Someone once told me the meaning of real success is to have success in all parts of life. Love, family, work. I was already failing, because the most important things were taking a back seat. I'd been so tied down with my ambitions that I hadn't realized what was important to her, what should have been important to me. How we forget the simple things.*

"Yes, it's perfect." I smiled, kissing her on the top of her head before taking my place at the table.

Those olive eyes gazed at me like I'd just gotten home, but I'd been home for three days. She was happy, and knowing that pleased me. We'd gotten married over a year ago in Lancaster, Pennsylvania, where her family was from. We said our vows on an old farm with a pristine view of the countryside. My parents came over from Stralia and my sister from New York; the rest of the guests were mostly her family, whom I had never met before. Racheal was worried we would get rain, but it never came. It was a perfect day.

"So, what are we doing today?" she asked, moving her long black braid to the side.

"Whatever you want. I'm all yours,"

"Oh, whatever I want?" A teasing smile tugged at her pink lips. "Maybe I'll drag you to the museum."

"As you wish. I don't care where you take me. You know what I'll be thinking." I smiled boyishly at her.

"Well, then, maybe we should stay home."

Before I answered, my phone chimed from the counter.

I knew taking a few weeks off meant I would be losing jobs, but I had to, for Racheal.

"Baby, you promised me you were going to shut that thing off." She placed her fork down and stared at me.

"I know. Don't get mad." I got up and reach for my phone. I recognized the number; it was my agent Adeline.

"Don't you dare answer it, Simon Rowe."

"It's Adeline. It might be important ... just let me see what she wants, and I'll shut it off, I promise." She didn't look at me.

"Hello." One word to seal my fate. When I first told Adeline I was taking time off, she thought I was crazy. After a few years of getting one or maybe two jobs a month, things had begun to turn around.

"Simon, I told you this day would come, and now you have to hit the ground running," she'd said to me once. And Adeline had kept me running for quite some time. There are moments I stepped back and couldn't believe I was doing what I loved for a living. But I also loved Racheal. And finding the balance was not so easy.

"Simon, before you hang up, just listen." Her raspy voice came through the phone. "I got a job for you. It's the biggest you've ever had, and the most significant amount of money ever offered."

"Adeline, you're going to get me into so much trouble." I looked up at Racheal's face—too late—I was already in the doghouse.

"Please, if you do this job, Racheal could gain a substantial shoe collection—What does she like? Hermes, Gucci, Versace? I'll send a carrier over this afternoon." Adeline thought she knew all women, but Racheal wasn't like that. She didn't care for the designer stuff. She was a good person who loved animals, was a vegan, and had a profound talent for jewelry making. Sometimes it made me wonder if that was all I knew about her.

"I'm going to regret asking, but what's the job?" I looked up at the seat Racheal had been sitting in, now empty.

"It's to shoot Crystal Z in her L.A. home for Elegant Home magazine."

I closed my eyes and breathed in deeply. I would be turning down a lifetime opportunity.

"For when?" I hoped it would be after my probation.

"Tomorrow ... I mean, it's two days, Simon. Your wife will understand." She had no idea.

"Look, can I call you back?"

"Listen, hon, I know this is last minute, but you got to let me know, or else I have to pass this on to another photographer."

"Adeline, just give me twenty minutes." I hung up the phone, feeling like I would crumble up. Racheal emerged, this time with a change of clothes.

"Come back and sit with me. Aren't you going to finish breakfast?"

"No." She wrapped her arms around her chest.

"Racheal ... Racheal, I didn't accept the offer."

"You told her you're going to call her back." She walked past me. I figured she would have been listening to my conversation.

"Yes, because I wanted to discuss this with you before officially turning her down."

"What's there to talk about? Looks like you already decided." She took her running shoes from the front closet.

"I didn't say yes to anything ... if you don't want me to—" I was talking, but she was already tuning me out.

"All I asked was for two weeks ... To have you all to myself. I should have known. The first opportunity comes along, you would drop me."

"I'm not choosing work over you. The bills stacking up is what's worrying me." I knitted my brows together.

"I wouldn't have asked my sister to replace me at the store if I knew this was going to happen," she said, tightening her laces with force. As if they were around my neck.

"*Yep, ah ... that alone was a big mistake,*" I said under my breath.

"*What did you say?*" She shot me a stare.

"*Do I have to remind you? The last time, she stole money from the cash register.*"

"*She was going to replace it before I found out; she was just borrowing it.*"

"*Oh, that's what we're calling it now? But she never replaced the money.*"

"*You leave my sister out of this. This is about you breaking your promise.*"

I wanted to put it behind us, but the reality was there was more than my work coming between our marriage. There was the jewelry shop. A business failing to make money, sucking our account dry. My job was the one thing keeping us afloat. No, I didn't dare to press that button.

"*Racheal, let's look at this seriously. We could use the money, and I'll be back in two days—*"

"*I don't care. You've made a promise, and now you're breaking it.*" So much for a happy wife. I sometimes felt she resented me for my profession and the success I was having with it.

"*Why can't you be happy for me? I'm doing this for us, for our future ...*"

"*No, you're doing this for yourself and this big dream of yours.*" Racheal stood up and threw her hands in the air.

"*Of course I want to be recognized for what I do, for what I love. Who wouldn't want that? God knows I work my arse off enough for it.*"

"*Simon, I know how this is going to be. You're on your way to becoming a bright star, and I'll be the one left behind,*" she said. She plugged her ears with her headphones, just before she walked out the door.

Deafening silence.

I called Adeline, told her I wouldn't be taking the job, and waited for Racheal to come back from her run.

I wasn't sure how much time passed after that, but the sounds of glass and metal impacting just outside the window jolted me out of my chair.

A woman's scream ... The kind you hear in movies, the kind that pierces through your heart, had me out the door, barefoot. I got to the front steps, when I paused, feeling disbelief over what I was seeing. A car had come up the curb, close to the front steps of my building. A few people ran to see if the driver was okay.

He seemed so, if not entirely fine.

"Call the ambulance," someone shouted, but I already had the number on my phone.

"There's someone underneath the car." I caught a glimpse of a white running shoe, laces still tied, lying there a few feet from where I stood.

Then I knew. Nothing can prepare you for moments like these. When you're about to walk into your worst nightmare. No time to process what was going on, no time for panic.

Just action.

I remember little about what happened next, but I was told later I lifted the car up enough for two bystanders to pull her out. They later called it superhero strength in the local newspaper. It' was ironic, because I didn't feel like a hero ... superheroes are supposed to save people, and I couldn't do that.

"Simon," Racheal moaned. I was too afraid to look, worried what I would see, so I focused on her face.

"Am I okay?"

"You're okay, baby, you're going to be okay." I kept my voice calm. If there were a lie I wanted both of us to believe in, this would be the one.

"Somebody help!" I yelled out. She moaned again, and my eyes found hers. An urgency ran through me.

Keep her eyes open.

"Simon ... it hurts." Her eyes wanted to close.

"No, no, no, you got to stay awake, Racheal! Look at me, you have to stay with me." My voice cracked, getting more desperate. "I will get you all fixed up ... baby. I promise everything will be okay." Fix you—something endearing my mom would say to me as a child when I would get a scratch, but this wasn't a scratch, this wasn't something I could fix ... But God, I wanted to.

"Simon, I can't see you." There was panic in her voice; her eyes were wide open.

"Racheal, I'm here, I'm here, baby ... God, I don't know what to do ... what do I do?" I looked up, and all I could see was a wall of legs.

"Racheal ..." I cradled her in my arms.

"Simon ... stand up, I can't see you ..." She was fading. The sirens were far in the distance, but Racheal was fading ...

"Shit, baby, no, no, no, somebody help!"

"Simon," a soft voice called out, and I flinched at the touch. Her sweet fragrance brought me back from the other side. I looked down to find Mable standing in front of me.

"Simon, it's not your fault," she said, and I broke in two. "You didn't cause it to happen; it was a freak accident ... The car was hit by another van."

Mable brought her hands to my face, leveling my eyes to hers. Now I could see why it was so easy to open up. Her nonjudgmental demeanor lowered my walls ... allowing her in.

My arms went around her waist, pulling Mable closer. There was more to the story, but honestly, I couldn't bring myself to dredge it all up from my mind and say it out loud. Maybe I wanted to spare Mable the full details, but after Racheal had died in my arms on the street where we lived, where we were supposed to build a future together, the paramedics finally arrived. But it was too late. Racheal had no chance. They did what they had to do, and then they were off, refusing to bring her to the hospital, leaving me to stand there on the streets with a couple of firemen and police officers, while my wife's cold body waited under a sheet for hours for the morgue to pick up her remains. It was hellish. A hellish nightmare no one should go through.

"It's all right, I'm here," she whispered, and suddenly the world seemed smaller. We stood there, quietly staring into the darkness, speckles of lights scattered below and above us. With Mable still in my arms, I was reminded that I still had the capacity to connect with another human being, and it felt amazing. *Why do I feel bothered by it? Will the guilt ever go away?*

"I never told you this before, but that night we met was the anniversary of Racheal's death. You seemed to give that day a new meaning. I'm glad you're here, but at the same time, I'm afraid that you are." I looked down.

"I'm not here trying to take your wife's place. But you have to understand something. I believe Racheal loved you, and she wouldn't want you to torture yourself the way you have. She would want you to remember the good times with no regrets, and that's what's worth holding on to."

I leaned closer, wanting her to take the friction off my lips, and she welcomed it. At first our kisses were full of restraint and tenderness, but then they quickly evolved into hunger and yearning for something more. I hated that I wanted her in the way I did; maybe I shouldn't have at that moment … But it felt right.

"Wait …" she said, out of breath, taking a step back and putting space between us. "I think we need to take a breather … literally." She smiled. "I should go …" Mable pulled away farther, gazing into my confused eyes.

"Don't go …"

"Yeah, it's late …"

"Stay."

She inhales deeply. "Please don't ask me to. If I stay, it will only confuse things between us. I think you're not entirely sure what I mean to you, and our emotions are running high … I don't want this to be about a moment to lose ourselves, a quick fix … a way to dull the pain." I saw the havoc in her eyes, causing chaos in my heart. "I don't want to be your distraction, Simon. I want to be your reason."

She was doing the right thing, putting a stop to something we might regret later. *Because I know when we start nothing will stop us.*

"Get some rest, and I'll see you in the morning. You promised you would show me the city," she said, and I brushed her hair away from her face.

"Of course." I didn't expect it to be simple, but I knew what we had was worth taking our time. "You'll be by around nine?" I asked, watching her pick her handbag off the table.

"Make it ten-*ish*? A girl needs her beauty rest." She gave me a side smile, then came back and kissed me on the cheek. My heart faltered.

"Hey, I'm not going anywhere, and I hate leaving you like this … but it's for the best," she whispered before she moved away from me, and I watched her go past the French doors. She didn't look back, because if she had, she would have seen me with a clear focus. I was ready for what came next.

Almost.

Find Better Glue

L ast night's episode replayed a thousand times in my head as I lay in bed, allowing the morning light to claim the walls of my room. Mable's words were affixed in my mind ... *I don't need to think about what she means to me, I already know.* I just wasn't ready to say it out loud, because there was a vulnerability that came with the truth. To discover that the love of my life might not have been Racheal alone? Where did that leave Racheal's legacy? Or Mable? After Racheal died, I had shut the door, so sure I locked it, but Mable had come in anyway. The pain would always be there, living within the walls of my heart until my last breath, but I didn't feel tragic anymore. I felt hopeful.

If I had any doubts, they were all gone when I opened the door to find Mable standing in her beige fitted coat, her blue scarf nicely wrapped around her neck. She was a far cry from the girl I'd first met, but Mable Harper could never fool me. I knew her like I knew every beat of my heart. When she looked at me, she made me feel like there was only us in the world. I leaned on the door because I knew what was going to happen if I let her in. *I should tell her, this is a mistake, that I don't want it to go any*

197

further, but that would be a lie.

"G'day, mate," she said, like a burst of sunshine.

I laughed. "That's pretty cliché. I don't know anyone who says that ... Maybe a few do. But I think you're cute, so I'll let this one slide." Why did everything look so different this morning? Like something had finally lifted off my shoulders. "You're sure you want to come in?" I said, hoping that she had better judgment, the heart to turn me away.

"Let me in, Simon." Her words were sharp, with enough power to allow the walls to come undone.

"I'll put your stuff in the room," I said, looking around. "Where's your luggage?"

"I kept my room for the rest of the trip, if you don't mind."

"No, not at all." I was thinking that, after last night, she had had a change of heart, and my chest felt heavy. "What should we see first, the Eiffel Tower?"

"No."

"The Louvre?"

"Nope," she replied.

"Then where?"

"Can we go off the beaten path? I want to discover the city organically. Go wherever our feet lead us." She smiled, playfully bouncing with each step she took toward me.

There was something very comfortable about Mable that I found interesting. I thought at first it had to be forced—*she can't always be this enthusiastic.* But then, getting to know her, I had realized she was vivacious, not because she was trying to be fake—she was coping. Mable was a good reminder we could live with our mental suffering, that out of pain other things flourished: friendship and even love ... As long as we were alive, we have the right to be happy. It was something I'd forgotten until this beautiful wonder came into my life.

"Sure, I'll take you wherever you want to go." I beamed. "Just let me get my camera."

—————

"I can't believe you don't like chocolate." Mable looked at me like I was an alien. "There's something seriously wrong with you."

She slid another morsel between her lips, and my eyes couldn't help but linger there. I wanted to kiss her again, but I wasn't sure if she wanted me to. *After last night, I feel like we're nowhere near where we should be.*

"Yeah, nah—there are plenty of things wrong with me," I said.

"Sure, you might be broken in a few places, but so is everybody. You need to find better glue," Mable said, glowing under the sun.

It took a lot to let go and to be myself, the man I had long forgotten, the one I thought I'd long ago buried with Racheal; now I realized he was very much alive. I'd been doing things wrong, especially in those early days. I used alcohol, women, and even work to escape. Those were the only glues I thought to use, thinking it would miraculously put me back together, making my guilt disappear. I knew now I needed to do a better job. Needed to find the better glue to hold me together, and perhaps I might have found it in Mable.

She held out the paper bag I had purchased at the chocolatier.

"Sweets are not my thing." I shook my head, realizing how persistent she could be.

"So why did you buy all these chocolates?"

"Because I know how grumpy you get when you don't eat, and I need something to hold you over until lunch." She snorted a laugh. "Besides, you're so indecisive."

"*Pff*—me? Indecisive? Well, I guess it takes one to know one." She smiled. "Okay, open your mouth." She slid her hand into the paper bag.

"Why?"

"Because you're going to have at least one."

"I told you—"

"But these are not your ordinary chocolates. Now open wide." Mable said, pulling one out and shoving it into my mouth.

"Good, right?"

"Shit, does this have peanut butter in it?" I allowed the chocolate to melt in my mouth.

"I don't know?" She looked confused. "Maybe."

"I'm allergic to peanuts," I said.

"Oh my God, what?"

When I saw the look on her face, I knew I had to take back my words. "I'm kidding. I'm just joking."

"Why would you do that?" She shoved me hard and walked away. "You scared the shit out of me."

"Mable, I'm sorry." She came back. "I was just messing with you," I said with a laugh.

"Don't talk to me. You're a fucking asshole, Simon Rowe."

Yeah, she might have been right. Mable was furious, and it only made me want her more. I bent down and picked up the bag of chocolates she had dropped and ran to catch up with her, but the look on her face said it all. I would have to beg for forgiveness …

Maybe macarons would help. Just maybe.

After supper, we walked along the canal. I took out my camera, capturing a few shots of Mable walking up the bridge ahead of me. The sun had gone down, and the night brought in the chill, but somehow we couldn't be bothered by it, because our minds were somewhere else. I thought about tomorrow. We would leave this place and my time with Mable would end. I was gutted. When she got to the high point, she turned and stared, like a woman who longs to be embraced by a man.

Chick che … flash.

I knew it wasn't for the camera.

Chick che … flash.

It was for me.

As a photographer, I know when my subject gives me something. Without words, it's given. Its natural what transpires between us, and I'm entirely bewitched. All my nerve endings ignite and pass through me like an electromotive force. The world comes to a standstill, like everything around her goes out of focus—only Mable never is. And at that moment something came over me, and all I could think was this: how much I wanted to leave my fingerprints on her curves.

"Are you just going to stand there and stare?" she said. The breeze blew her hair around.

When I didn't answer, she smiled and continued on. This journey … The path I'd been following had left me broken and alone, but it had also led me right to this moment—where I was supposed to be. And I knew this, but it was fear that paralyzed me. I knew what love could do once you let it in because—the moment you let your guard down, settled and happy—life would twist that road, bringing disruption and loss along with it. Nothing lasts forever, even love, but yet the heart continues to whisper.

When we reached the end of the bridge, I found Mable looking up. "Simon, stop, you're missing it all." She took the camera from my hands.

"What?"

"This moment, life as it is … Aren't you tired of living behind that thing? I don't know about you, but I'm played out in front of it. No more until we leave, all right?" I watched her take a few steps back.

"Look around you." She held her arms out, my camera still in her hand. "Wherever we are … whatever street this is … it's just so breathtaking … Paris is just beautiful." She twirled around.

"It's not as gorgeous as you," I murmured, making Mable stop and stare. A smile grew as she walked over toward me.

"You think I'm beautiful?" she said. The heat traveled to my face and everywhere else. "Tell me … again."

"You know I hate repeating myself," I said, peering down at her.

"Say it, because I want to memorize your lips when you do." Her bright eyes trailed down to my mouth. I desired to enter another dimension that only dwelled in us. Where no past, no pain could exist. That was what it was like to be in the presence of a wildflower. It always made me feel like a clean slate might be possible.

"Not unless you give me back my camera," I said. She gave it a thought before answering.

"Nope, forget about it." She was about to walk away, but I pulled her back into my arms.

"I can't believe how gorgeous you are. I don't know, being here with you should be easy … It frightens me."

"What are you afraid of?" She looked at me with those eyes that went through my core.

"Losing you," I said.

"You keep saying that, but I'm here waiting for you, Simon," she whispered. I leaned in and claimed what my lips hungered for. Then, for the first time, I felt something I hadn't felt in a while.

Alive.

Make Me Feel

Mable

Simon was quiet. He said little after he kissed me. After he abruptly pulled away.

He disconnected ...

I thought it would be clear what he wanted, what made him happy, but when his vibrant eyes found mine in the back seat of the dark cab, en route to our hotel, I understood it wasn't as simple as that. We would never be two straight lines, hoping one day we'd find ourselves aligned. No, we were like the ocean, with waves that depended not only on timing but on the endless procession of physics. We crashed together with an equal hunger for love, but the same turn of rushing water tore us apart with the turbulence of grief. One thing was for sure: after this feverish night, either way, nothing would be left unchanged.

When we walked into Simon's room, I watched him remove his coat, then place his camera on the surface of the hotel desk. I stood there wondering what would happen next—talk? But I had had enough of talking—was sick and tired of this red light, green light we were playing. I wanted to remove the lines, let it go further than we'd ever been. He'd started something; his lips had enslaved me like a drug. *If this should be the only and last time we'd touch, I will forever chase the memory of it.*

There was a short pause before he turned around, and when he did, he found me leaning against the wall close to the entrance. If Simon had had any insight into my demeanor, he would have realized that I was not sure of myself, or what to do next.

"I'm sorry. I shouldn't have done that."

"Done what?" I flashed him a small smile.

"Kissed you … again," he said, rubbing the back of his neck.

"Yes, you should, and more often. You're a hell of a good kisser," I said, and he chuckled. *There's nothing subtle here, so why try to make things delicate?* "Good gracious, I don't think I've ever been kissed like that." I glanced back at him.

All this time there'd been a strong connection between us that seemed to grow. The desire we found in each other—now it was clear, all revealed every time we kissed. We could continue, pretending there was nothing, but what would be the point? It would be easier for me to ignore a big hole in my living room floor than to ignore the magnitude of the attraction we felt for each other.

"Come here," he urged, leaning back on his desk. When I got close enough, he brushed the strands of hair from my face. "You should always be kissed like that … but only by me." His voice came out huskily, his eyes matching mine.

"I have no problem with that."

"Mable, I don't want you to think this is the reason I invited you to stay with me." He inhaled a deep breath. "I don't want you to do anything you don't feel comfortable with."

I liked the way he was looking out for me, trying to protect me even from himself.

"We're both adults, Simon. I think we know what's coming

next."

"Is it that obvious that I want you?" He searched my face.

"Yeah … Isn't that what started this?" I smiled. "Our friendship is built on the founding fact that you wanted me."

"And you didn't want me?" He knits his eyebrows together.

"No …" I teasingly pushed away from his grasp.

"Liar." He drew me closer.

"Well, not at first," I lied, pulling away from his grasp. I slid off my jacket and set it on the settee across the room. I wanted Simon like every kid wants candy when they see it. But as I got to know Simon, it had become less of a matter of wanting, and become entirely something else. I was in love with my best friend.

"Hmm … as I recall, it started because I bailed your arse out of a jam." He lightly pushed off his desk and began making his way toward me, his eyes never leaving mine.

"My ass, you say? You got that part right." I beamed. His lips went up at the sides, and now he was standing tall before me. I saw it in his eyes; he was as nervous as I was. There was a lot at stake, especially because we both wanted to cross that line but didn't want to destroy what we had already built. Then, for those reasons alone, we were in the perfect place to take this forward.

"I had this vivid dream about you last night," he began.

My heart started to beat faster, and my legs felt a little unsteady. "Really?" My eyes widened. "What was it about?"

"I can't believe I'm telling you this …"

"Was I any good?" I pressed on, amused by his sudden bashfulness.

"I … it's just that I can't get you off my mind."

"So then don't."

"God, I have this thirst for you … But there are still things you don't know about me. What I'm trying to say is you deserve so much more."

He might be right, but I don't care. There was nothing to derail, not when you gathered enough momentum.

He continued. "I will let you down. I always disappoint the people I care about." He was inches away from my face, and I could smell the sweet scents of mint and grapefruit. He stood there without touching me, allowing me to cling with anticipation. His eyes begged me, like an undisclosed warning … *Caution: proceed at your own risk.*

"You can't disappoint me if I know what I'm getting into. We both know we don't have time for each other with the lives we lead. So don't overthink it. Let's make whatever time we have here not more than it is—we're just two people enjoying each other's company." I shrugged. I was okay with no strings attached. Without any reservations, I was attracted to Simon and felt safe when I was around him. I was here because I wanted to be. There was a spark that started inside me, and I would have done or said anything to keep the fire going, even if it meant that, after tonight, we owed nothing to each other. I wanted to live in the moment; there was no sacrifice in that.

"So where do we go from here?" His voice was low, and my breath was picking up the pace.

"That depends on you … What do you want, Simon?"

"You." He licked his lips and his eyes grew darker, providing many feelings throughout my body, as though, if he didn't touch me now, I would die.

"I want your curves, your touch … your mouth on mine."

The inflection of his tone ran right through me. With his fingers, he loosened my blue scarf and let it slip to the floor. I could feel his warm breath on my face and my heart's rhythm picked up the pace. He lowered his face, kissing me slowly, but soon becoming intrusive, inducing hunger within me. His hands trailed the length of my body. I knew what he wanted from me, what we both wanted from each other … to lose ourselves.

"Are you sure this is what you want?" he whispered, as a

last attempt to put a wedge between us. *I know he thinks I can't handle this, and his concern for me only spikes my desire for him even more.* Is it a crime to wish for a moment you may later regret? I didn't want to think about grief. I wanted what we had now.

"Just stop … stop giving me any more reasons to like you." I smiled between kisses, and he lightly laughed.

"I promise … I won't give you any more reasons. From here on out you're responsible for your own actions. I will not be accountable for any more increased likes on my part." His hands went through my hair.

"Great, now stop talking and … more …" I said, out of breath, allowing his lips to caress the curve of my neck. His touch was addictive, causing a wave of euphoric sensation that ran throughout my body.

"God, Mable, why do I get the feeling you're going to kill me." His kisses went beyond my neck, and I surrendered to my senses.

"I promise I'll go easy on you." One by one I allowed my fingers to play with the buttons of his shirt, pushing it off his shoulders, letting it fall. We kissed as we slowly paced ourselves toward the bedroom, removing each piece of clothing one at a time, allowing it to fall wherever it may. No shirt, no pants, my silk underwear lying casually on the floor, everything was removed until there was just skin.

"You're so soft," he murmured as we lay in the unmade bed, burning for each other and hoping we survived it enough to do it all over again. Hopefully, we'd make it out alive.

"I want every inch of you," he whispered as his kisses trailed the length of me. "God, you're so beautiful."

"Don't stop," I said in a hushed tone, as the water washed over us, pulling us out to the ocean, and I didn't care if my feet never touched the sand again.

Love Slow

Simon

Even before I opened my eyes, I could feel the warmth of her body pressed up against mine, like we were two pieces of a puzzle. We had spaces that needed to be filled, and every edge and curve came together so beautifully. It made me wonder if she had been the only piece I ever needed. I had given myself many reasons to justify what we did last night, but there was only one I hoped for. She was the elixir for my soul, a new breath of life. The love that once had shattered me had now put me back together. I wasn't sure if I could be affected like this again. As it turned out, she had the magic, touched me in places I thought no one could ever reach. Mable was everything … and it made what we had thrilling and terrifying all at the same time.

I opened my eyes and found her lovely face pushed up against the pillow beside me. The morning sun caught the highlights of her golden hair, making her seem less real. I allowed my fingers to brush the strands away from her face. No, she wasn't a hallucination. And when her eyes fluttered opened, it sent sweltering heat throughout my body.

"Good morning, love."

"Good morning." She gave me a lazy smile and reached over for something on the nightstand. Mable sat up, placing her hearing aids back in her ears; at some point in the evening, she must have removed them. "How are you feeling?" she asked, reading my mind.

There had been other women after Racheal. In those early days of grief, my life had been headed in a spiral, because once I got rolling in the sheets, it felt impossible to stop. I wanted to forget what I had lost, lose myself within them. That's all it ever was. That's not what it had been last night with Mable. With her, I wanted to gain everything, and I knew what we had was irreplaceable.

"Otherworldly, fantastic." I pull her down next to me.

"Yeah, me too." She blushes.

My hand trailed down to her neck, allowing my fingers to play with the silver chain that hung around it.

"It used to belong to my mother," she said. "I don't know why I wear it, because there are times I resent her." Her eyes diverted to the ceiling. "I remember the day she left, the way my dad begged her to stay … It was heartbreaking to watch, but I couldn't turn away. It's like that moment in my life had cemented itself most depressingly. No matter what I do in my life, it seems to be overshadowed by that memory." Mable's doleful eyes found mine.

"Well, time forces us to move forward, and memories hold us back. I believe when we love someone so much, and they leave us … all that love, it gets stuck inside us, and after a while, it seems as though we haunt them instead," I said, tracing the outline with my fingers from her shoulders to the curve of her hips. "Memories exist only for the sole purpose of showing us a life lived right or wrong. But it doesn't mean we should have that book open all the time. Sometimes it's okay to leave it on the top shelf."

"What do we do? A couple of broken people?"

"Together we'll find better glue." I repeated her words back to her.

"I was high on chocolate, what the hell do I know?" Mable laughed.

"You made perfect sense. I mean, you don't always." A smile spread across my face and Mable gasped, pushing me farther away, but I didn't move, only drew her closer.

"For the first time in a long time, I feel like everything's right with the world." I nuzzled my face in the crook of her neck, and she squirmed underneath me. "You, me, here ... nothing else could be more perfect." I saw a shadow fall over her eyes. "Do you have any regrets?" I asked.

"Yes, I do."

"What?" I pulled back to get a better look at her face.

"I regret ... that we have a plane to catch in nine hours, and I don't want to leave this bed."

"It doesn't have to end," I said, knowing what I wanted, more of this, more than inside a bedroom ... maybe even to venture out and hope for a future ... together.

"No?" she said.

I slipped my fingers through her silky hair and kissed her tenderly. First her lips, then her neck, and when I did, she closed her eyes and swayed her body closer. Like a feline, she gently rubbed up against me, igniting new desires.

"What are we now?" she whispered seductively. "Is this friendship ... with benefits?"

In my heart, I knew that wasn't true. No strings attached? Not possible, when they were already affixed to Mable, every single strand knotted.

"Mable, I've been thinking. Am I the only crazy one who believes that this could work?"

"What are you saying?" She fluttered her eyes open. "You

want to be together—for this to be more?"

"Yeah, don't say you never thought about it,"

"I did … I do, it's just, I thought—" She looked at me with clear eyes. "You don't get involved with people you work with,"

"Well, it's too late for that, love. You're my only exception." Her eyes were bright, drawing me in. "No matter what you put between us, we'll always find a way around it. Why fight it? I hope this is something we both want." I braced my head in my hands, casting my eyes down at her. "Want to be my Aphrodite?"

"You don't want me to be your Aphrodite, Simon. She was nothing but trouble for Adonis."

"Christ, hopefully you'll be worth the trouble." I gazed reluctantly. "What I have with you, I've never had with anyone. I'm trying to work out my regrets in my head and my heart. That I have to give myself permission to move on. I feel deeply for you, Mable, I really do. And if you accept me for all I am … that I might never get my shit together, but I will try for you. Please let me prove myself to be the man you need me to be."

She climbed on top of me, her hands on my bare chest. I wondered if she could feel my heart beating under her palms, the rhythm already altered … It beat only for her. I glanced up at Mable. She was like a mirage; I wasn't sure if I could trust my vision. *Her hair disheveled and her face bare, this is how she looks her best. She's so beautiful, my muse.*

My Aphrodite.

"I'm in love with you." I wasn't sure if I was truly ready to say it out loud, but around Mable, I didn't want to hold anything back, not anymore. Love was a reality you chose to be a part of, and I needed to know if Mable was ready to be part of mine.

"*Oh*, you don't love me. You love this, what we do," she said, trying to hide her eyes, and I knew it was fear that kept them away from me. Mable was scared I would hurt her, but I never intended to do so.

"I may be slightly damaged, Mable, but never mistake me for a confused man." I lightly pulled her wrists to get her to look back at me. When she refused, I rolled her on her back, gently pinning her underneath me.

"Yes, I love what we do on these white sheets. I only hope to worship your body like it was my holy place. I don't know how you did it, but you've made me into a believer. And I swear to you it's love that pulls me into your temple ... Never doubt it—my devotion to you," I whispered in her ear.

I looked back at her face, and I knew she believed me.

"After what I've lost, what I've been through ... This is far beyond I ever thought I would do again—fall in love. But now I don't think I could do without it—do without you, Mable. I want to be yours."

She exhaled. "See, when you say crazy things like that, it only makes me..." She put her hand on her face, hiding her eyes from me. "Shit, I'm in trouble."

"I like causing you trouble." I kissed the back of her wrist. "So we'll keep seeing each other, and no one else," I whispered.

"I don't want to see anyone else, because I love you, too." She brought her hand down and stared, causing an uncontrollable rush over me.

"You have me smiling ear to ear, love." I playfully pulled her closer, kissing her deeply. We pushed boundaries that maybe we shouldn't have crossed. We remained in this space so we didn't get hurt, but it hurt the same to be silent—it benefited no one. I would take a chance, because Mable was worth it.

Light a match, and there we were.

There was nothing better than this, the thrill of knowing how alone we were together in that room. Unknown to the rest of the world that right now we were making magic. I didn't know what would happen beyond those doors. I couldn't predict the limitations of tomorrow, but, at least for now, Mable was mine, and that was all that mattered.

Take the Back Seat

Mable

I got a text from Simon, which had me thinking. It had been three days since I had seen him, and at the very least I had wanted was to hear his voice. But I wondered if my past insecurities were causing my sudden affliction. When I read his text message, all my concerns took a back seat.

Christ, what a morning I'm having. Only makes me miss your eyes and sweet lips like crazy.

I never thought I could be this kind of person, giddy and lovesick. Good grief, I was such a cheeseball.

Are you at work? I wrote. He would be, since it was nine in the morning in L.A.

Yes, and it's going to be a long day, a lot of drama going on the set. I'm regretting I agreed to this project. I should be there with you.

Then he added that I should send him a sexy picture of myself to ease his pain.

Poor baby.

I wasn't able to make it work, since I was sitting in a

restaurant, in a crowded room. My eyes glanced up, scouting the sea of people who were already digging into their lunch. A broad smile came across my face, and I knew exactly what he needed to get him through his day. So I found a random picture of a sweet old lady on the internet and pressed send.

Wow, I definitely need a shower after this, he replied moments later, and I laughed to myself.

"Is that Mr. Rowe?" Tracy glanced over my shoulder, catching me off guard. "I was wondering why you had a freakishly big smile on your face," she said, coming around the table and sitting in the chair in front of me. Tracy had called me last night saying she needed to talk about something. It was not unusual that we went out together without Gloria, but I hadn't the faintest idea of what it could be about. I sent Simon a text saying that I would call him later, and I put my phone on the table.

"So I take it things are going well? Gloria said she'd never seen Simon so happy." Tracy moved her chair in. She was wearing her business attire, a blue shirt underneath her fitted suit jacket, which I made a note to borrow sometime.

"Everything is great,"

"Hmm, *but?*" Tracy was good at seeing through people. Maybe it was a talent she cultivated over time with her line of work.

"No, there's no *buts* ... it's just that we've been together for two months, and I've only seen him a few times."

"But you knew what you were getting yourself into with Simon, right?"

I loved Tracy, the way she got everything into perspective. There was no muss or fuss with her; she always told it how it was.

"I knew our crazy schedules would be an issue. I'm not going to whine. It's just that I miss him." I waved my hand in the air. "Anyway, he'll be back Friday."

"It's hard, I get it. You can't help falling for who you fall for, but no relationship is perfect. I work fifty plus hours a week at the firm, Gloria is constantly on location. But you have to find a way to make it work. Love has to be bigger than yourself, and at the end of the day you've got to think there's no one else you'd rather run to." Tracy studied me for a slight fraction of a second. "This is all new to you, Mable. The relationship, the job. You have a lot on your plate right now. Just don't lose sight of what's important."

"It's just been so bizarre. This time last year I had nothing going on, my love life was a flatline—it's all or nothing." I reached for the menu.

"What you have to remember is that real love can't be jeopardized. Love may bend, but it will never break. Never let your pride come before true love—that's what my mother always told me."

"How is your mom doing?" I asked.

"She's better now and back in her residential home." Tracy's eyes focused across the room before they returned to mine. "It's hard for her, you know, being alone. She has a couple of friends, but after my father died ... I don't know, it got me thinking."

"About what?"

"Making it official. I mean, I know that's what Gloria wants—what we want. So what are we waiting for?"

"Are you thinking of proposing?"

"Yes. I'm going to." Tracy slightly lowered her menu.

"*Really*? Oh my God, that's great." I reached out to her. "We will officially be family!"

"I need your opinion." Tracy unzipped her purse. "Gloria doesn't think I have any taste for jewelry." She pulled out a teal box and handed it to me.

I opened the case to find a pear-shaped diamond ring. "Good grief, it's gorgeous!"

"You think she'll love it?"

"Of course she will. If she turns you down, then I'll marry you." I closed the box and handed it back to her.

"No offense, but you're not my type." Tracy smiled at me.

"Why wouldn't I be your type? I'm everyone's type, I'm fun and—"

"You're all over the place. You forget we once lived together?" She picked up her menu, and I rolled my eyes.

"Geez, you leave one dish in the sink and suddenly you're pegged as a sloppy moppy," I said.

"Sloppy moppy? You and Gloria are definitely two peas in a pod." She shook her head.

With Tracy, everything in her life had to have a place and time, which was okay, but I couldn't live like that. Maybe that was why Simon and I went well together. We allowed the waves to take us where they would. We weren't too pretentious about the small details.

"When are you planning on asking?"

"Well, I was thinking this Friday," Tracy replied.

"Her surprise birthday party? In front of everyone? Wow, you're courageous. That's a lot of pressure."

"Tell me about it. But I figure Gloria won't see it coming."

I smiled, knowing better. Gloria couldn't be surprised. She always found a way to somehow ruin it. I had to keep my distance from her until Friday.

"Hey, I wanted to ask—are you still getting those calls in the middle of the night?"

"Oh, are you talking about the creepy heavy breathing? They stopped suddenly."

"Did you think about getting another number?" Tracy asked.

"Ugh, it's such a hassle. If I change my number, then I have to call everyone with the new one. I'm not afraid, it's just some asshole trying to have fun with me."

"I don't know … Now you're in the public eye, it could be some crazed fan." Her eyebrows knitted together. "Have you told Simon about it?"

"No. Simon has a lot on his plate with work, and I don't want to worry him. Anyway, it's three days now. They must have gotten bored with me."

My phone dinged, and I coolly glanced over at it. Simon had shot me another message. He told me he'd call me after work and added that he couldn't stop looking at my picture.

You're sure one beautiful woman.

Lol, the old lady pic?

No, the one I took of you in my bed the other day while you were sleeping.

I must have blushed, because I felt Tracy's eyes over me.

"Jesus, you guys can't get enough of each other. I bet Simon is great in bed," Tracy said with a sideways smile, putting her menu down. "Creative people usually are." She shot me a knowing look.

I smiled and shook my head. I knew she was trying to get some gossip out of me, but I divulged none. What was it about people? As soon as they knew you were in a new relationship, they wanted to know everything about your sex life. But I was never one to kiss and tell.

Home

S imon caught a flight back to New York that arrived at nine in the morning, but I didn't rush to see him. Instead, I took my sweet time, waking up later than usual, and when I came back to my apartment with my morning coffee, I installed my new blue drapes in the living room. I was aware I was stalling for time, trying to distract myself. It wasn't that I didn't want to see Simon—I wanted to catapult myself to his front door. I felt alive when he was around, and when he wasn't, I ached for him. Honestly, it scared me, wanting Simon so madly. When someone you love becomes your all, there's a danger that, if they leave, they'll take everything with them. And what are you left with? Hopefully, a jar of Nutella ... a big one. I felt like I needed to create some distance and remind myself that there was *me* before *us*. Besides, it was always good to let a man wait around for you. It gave him time to reflect on how much he missed you.

After I stepped off the ladder, I looked up and admired my handiwork. My little apartment was coming along, feeling homier with each moment and dollar I had to spare decorating it. Thanks to Amanie, I could keep more of my earnings, which had allowed me to rent this little place. There was a knock at the door, and I smiled. I didn't need to guess who was on the other side.

I opened the door and found him standing there, lost in his thoughts. It almost took him a minute to realize I was in front of him.

"Simon, is everything okay?" I asked, observing the lack of brightness in his skin. His eyes met mine, and there was something in them that should have had me concerned. But, like a light switch that was flicked up, Simon's face returned to its natural glow when he looked at me.

"Yeah. Nah, I was just thinking about something for work." He shrugged it off, and I closed the door behind him.

Simon's mind was always spinning. If he wasn't shooting, he was researching for his next project, ripping out images from magazines or snapping away at something he could use later for inspiration. Sometimes he had his assistant pin those images on a board, to generate his artistic flow when he worked on a project. I knew how he ticked—that's mainly the reason we worked great side by side. But we agreed that, when we were together, we focused on us and whatever normal couples did. I sometimes wondered if I was his only reason to disconnect from that part of his life.

"How was L.A.?"

"Shitty, and I don't want to talk about it because I'm here in my happy place."

I thought I sensed a tone of guilt, but when I turned around, I discovered a look of yearning flashing in his eyes, and he reached for me.

"I thought we were supposed to meet later at the restaurant?" I giggled at the way he was staring at me, like I was fresh meat to a predator.

"I couldn't wait. Every minute is like torture when I don't see you." He brushed his fingers across my jaw; his eyes took me in like he was memorizing every inch of my features. "I don't want to lose you—ever." Simon's expression became serious.

"No, you won't. What's going on, Simon?"

He searched my face like he was trying to understand it himself. "I'm okay. I'm just exhausted." He moved my hair from my neck and kissed it, melting me like butter.

"Hold on—wait." I sighed. "You're going to make us late." I took his arms off my waist and stepped back. He tried again to take hold of me, and I moved farther from his reach.

"What's the matter?" His smile sagged a little, a brief look of something in his eyes. Confusion?

"We have Gloria's surprise party to go to, remember? And I'm running out of time to get ready."

I left to go, but he grabbed hold of my hand and kissed the inside of my wrist. As his lips went up the length of my arm, he pulled me closer. His eyes always had a way of disarming me. I knew Tracy would reprimand us for being late.

"You don't need to. You already look beautiful." He began to kiss the crook of my neck, and it sent me wild again.

"Yeah ... I reek of sweat ... And I'm not wearing a sports bra and sweatpants to the party."

"Hmm." Of course, this wouldn't bother him. I gently pushed away.

"Simon, I'm serious. I'm going to get cleaned up."

"Is that an invitation?"

"No." I laughed, unraveling from his arms. Again.

"I thought you would be excited to see me." His brows knitted together. "I'm a little disappointed not to have found you at my home this morning."

When we first started seeing each other, I was surprised by how reluctant he was to make me a key to his apartment, but he had never asked me to officially move in with him. But then, the more I thought about it, I realized that he probably wasn't ready for a big step like that.

"Of course I'm excited. I had stuff to do first." I refused to be the psycho clinging girlfriend type, even though, deep down, she was raging to come out.

"What's more important than wanting to see your amazing boyfriend?" He playfully arched a brow.

"Simon, I'm not going to be at your disposal every time you need me," I said.

"Sure you will."

I rolled my eyes as I moved away from him. "Nope, sorry, but you're going to have to get used to the fact that I'm a girl who can't easily be pinned down."

"Pinning down is exactly what I had in mind." He smiled wickedly, taking a step closer toward me.

"I'm serious." I giggled.

"So am I."

"Stop right there." I held up my hand to prevent him from coming closer.

He sighed. "I don't understand why you're acting like this. I only want to give you a kiss." Simon flashed those innocent eyes, but there was nothing innocent about Simon Rowe.

"No, you don't. I see right through you. Why is it that men rush when they think they're going to get laid?" I said. I knew that, once he'd gotten home from the airport and saw that I wasn't there, he'd come straight to my apartment.

"On the contrary." He raised his eyebrows. "We're more patient when we know we will." He gave me one of his charming smiles.

"I don't have time for this," I said, placing my hands on my hips. "And it's a big deal tonight. Tracy is going to propose, so we can't be late." I noticed his attire; he was already dressed for the occasion. A cute white button-down cotton shirt and a pair of black dress pants.

"All right," he said, with defeat in his eyes. "Go on, get

ready. I'll be a good boy and wait out here," he said, but he still followed me toward the bathroom. Just before I closed the door, he leaned in the doorway.

"Can I at least get a kiss hello?" He tried one last attempt, but, unluckily for him, I was not buying it.

"Nope." I closed the door. I smiled when I heard a deflated sigh coming from the other side, footsteps leading away from the door.

"Nice curtains." His voice boomed over the noise of the running water. "Are they the reason you're not in my bed this morning, tangled in my sheets?" He continued. "I feel lucky about getting up in the morning with you there next to me. Having your beautiful eyes meet mine and your sweet smile to coax me—getting me back in." I didn't hear him moving around anymore. "Shit, I should have said something to you, that I was ready to have you there indefinitely." Simon's voice went low, but not enough that I couldn't catch it.

I caught my reflection in the mirror and allowed my hair to fall down on my shoulders. I was anxious to give Simon my full potential, because somewhere in the back of my mind I knew he would get bored and leave. They always did. But what I had never considered was that Simon felt the same way. He, too, had insecurities about our relationship, and was, in fact, normal. Maybe there was nothing to be afraid of, because every time we were away from each other, it only solidified our love. This connection just grew stronger, and it made me believe that this was where we were supposed to be, and it was only fear that kept those walls up. I hadn't had a clear view before … I had wanted to love, but I was only opening that door an inch at a time. Love demands for the door to be swung open, the rush … That's the only way it comes in—it needs to take hold of you. Love shouldn't be feared or denied for the sake of not getting hurt, but reckoned with. Yes, romantic love is risky, but I would have lost out on so much more without Simon. I was having the time of my life, and whatever it was worth was more than heartbreak could ever bring.

I opened the door with such force that Simon glanced up from the sofa. I loved it when he looked at me like that— like he could fulfill every desire in me.

"I need you," I whispered. He jumped over the back of the couch and came for me. With one motion he scooped me up and I wrapped my arms and legs around him, stumbling further into my white bathroom.

"I missed you ... my sexy little bird." He held me tight and kissed me like he was about to lose me. "I'm so glad to be home."

"Home?" I asked. He gazed at my face lovingly, brushing the hair away.

"Wherever you are, that's where my heart lives."

"Gloria, do you remember when we first met ... sitting next to each other on the plane? You were freaked out because you lost your bracelet, and I found it wedged between the seats. I never told you this, but at that moment I thought—" Tracy began, and Simon and I watched attentively from across the table. Thanks to me, we had made it just in time before Gloria arrived at the restaurant.

"This girl is a total mess," Gloria added, and everyone laughed.

"Yes ... maybe a little." Tracy smiled. "But my first initial thought was ... I didn't know you, but I had this amazing feeling that I wanted you in my life. You're magic to me ... So here we are a few years later, in front of friends and family." Tracy pulled herself up to stand beside Gloria. "Baby, I've been dreaming about this day since the moment I first gazed into your panic-stricken face …" Tracy said, and Gloria let out a little laugh. "But I realized that, even though I found your bracelet, you were the one who came to my rescue." Gloria put her hand to her face as Tracy pulled the ring out of her pocket and knelt. "Will you marry me?"

"Oh, my gosh." Gloria laughed tearfully. "Yes … a million times yes." They kissed, and everyone clapped and cheered. I felt Simon's hand tighten around mine. He had been acting so strange since his trip back from L.A., and it made me wonder if Tracy's proposal had gotten him thinking, because he acted more affectionately throughout the night, I almost felt I could have read his mind.

Simon and I came out of the restaurant, with the breeze at our backs. It was only the first week of August, but the air had changed, whispering that fall was not far behind. We turned the corner, continuing down the street, with the light poles illuminating our path as we made our way to Simon's car.

"I'm so happy for them," I said, and Simon wrapped an arm around me, nestling me closer to his side.

"Me too."

"They looked so happy, didn't they?"

"Gloria knew," he rumbled.

"What? No—I thought so at first, but—"

"Okay, right, didn't you see the look on her face when we yelled out surprise? I know what Gloria's shock face looks like, and that wasn't it."

"And how would you know?"

"I've seen it before, and it's not pretty." He shrugged. "It looks like this." He showed me, and I laughed. I wondered about the things he'd done to surprise Gloria. Like the time that Simon had told her that he was paying me out of his own pockets. Even though Simon was strong-minded and opinionated, I liked that fact he always strived to do what was fair. The more things I discovered, the more I fell in love.

"Maybe you're right." I leaned my head onto his shoulder.

"If I would have known, I wouldn't have parked so bloody far."

"What's your rush? It's such a beautiful night for a walk." I pulled my shawl closer.

He flashed me a seductive smile. "I wanted to finish what we started back at your apartment." He kissed the top of my head.

"Making up for lost time?"

"You know it." His eyes glanced down the street before meeting mine again. "Have you ever thought about the future … about us?"

"As in moving in together?" My eyebrows peaked, figuring it was what he said earlier.

"Hmmm." He moved his head side to side. "I was thinking about something more."

I figured I'd seen something in his eyes when Tracy got up from the table to give a speech back at the restaurant. It was emotional to witness something as beautiful as two people who were meant to be together. It solidified your faith in love and the possibility that it existed for anyone who wanted it.

"Marriage?" I almost felt stupid saying it out loud, because it would be the last thing he would have on his mind. Right?

"Hey, don't panic …" He looked me over. Maybe he saw the sudden hesitation in my eyes. After all, I was still too young to be thinking about marriage.

"Are you serious? I'm just surprised you thought that far along," I said.

"Sure, why not? I'm happy being with you, and I can't help thinking about wanting more. We could elope … just you and me. We'll ride to Vegas." Simon always thought ahead, and this pleased me, knowing he was a man who realized his goals and knew what he wanted. This made me want it more with him. But there was an underlying feeling I couldn't ignore. Maybe it was too fast.

"On your motorcycle, from New York to Vegas?" I frowned. *That's so like him, but is it me?*

"Yeah, sure."

"That's a long stretch."

"It'd take roughly about thirty-nine hours." He caught me squinting my face. "Come on, it will be fun. We'll make stops. Look at it this way. It will be part of our honeymoon on the way back."

I appreciated his enthusiasm, but I didn't picture myself on the open road for that long.

"No relatives? Oh, that will not go well with our parents."

"We could have a small party for our rellies when we come back."

"Wow, you really thought about it." I glanced up at him.

"I don't know, it was just an idea." He cleared his throat. "One day, maybe."

"One day," I said, hopeful.

"Look." He suddenly halted, placing his hand on my chin. "I don't want you to get weird on me … whether it's in two months or years from now … I don't care. I need you to know I want to be part of your future, whatever it may be," he said, seeing through my demeanor.

This conversation was making me uneasy, but not for the reasons he thought. It was because I didn't wish for my mind and heart to commit to an idea, only to later be disappointed. We were fresh; our roots hadn't taken their place just yet. Anything could change at any time. We knew that more than anybody. I kissed him with no reservation, making him understand I was his, and whether it was on paper or not, it didn't matter to me.

"How about we take a last-of-the-season road trip this weekend?" He pulled back, taking my hand in his, and we continued on our path. I enjoyed hopping on the back of his bike, wrapping my arms around him, feeling the rush of excitement and the weightlessness as we cut through the open air. I wasn't thrilled about the prospect of riding across the country, though.

"Where do you want to go?" I asked, wondering what other crazy ideas he had in his head.

"Well, my sister has invited us up to her house in the Hamptons. She's been driving me crazy, and she really wants to meet you—but only if you want. No pressure."

"I'm okay with that." I glanced at him. "I'm excited to meet your sister and her family. Don't get me wrong, I want to merge our lives together, Simon. I just want to make sure it's at a pace we're both comfortable with."

"I know." He nodded and kissed the back of my hand. "I know you love me."

"More than anything," I reassured him.

"So the only thing we have to figure out tonight is—your place or mine?"

"Mine,"

"Okay, but I have an early day tomorrow," I stopped talking when Simon suddenly halted in his tracks, and my eyes followed his gaze.

"Bloody hell!"

Parked between two cars was a black two-door sedan with the words "*Asshole, you should never have fucked with me*" spray-painted on the hood of the vehicle. It took a second to realize it was Simon's car.

Women of Vision

We were outside on the red carpet when Bruno placed his arm around my waist. He tilted his head closer to my face as we posed for the camera.

"And so my wildflower becomes the rose," he whispered close to my ear. I didn't know if that statement held any actual value. Even as my feet glided across the plush red carpet of the Gala Fashion for a Cause, I was not sure what I had done to deserve this sudden attention. A sea of men in black suits rolled out in front of us, and hundreds of lights flashed sporadically, setting off this seizure-like episode inside me. I realized that this person standing there was not even me. The real me would be at home, watching this on TV in her fuzzy sock slippers, eating a container of ice cream.

After Bruno had placed me at the front of the line a year ago, he had chosen me to represent his designer label, Ortiz. I was his ambassador for most of his perfume ads. I guess you can say I became more than his muse, I appreciated the camaraderie between us. This industry had brought amazing people into my life, yet, on the flip side, it had also brought more insecurities. Looking in, it was so easy to be seduced by the glitz and glamour, but when you got behind it, you'd be surprised by what you'd find.

The other day I had been in a cab driving through Times Square when it stopped at a red light. I looked out the window, and there she was in print, in the process of being plastered on the side of a building. It was on a big billboard where millions of people would see it for weeks at a time. For most struggling models, this would mean you had arrived. I should have been mad with excitement, but all I remember was feeling sick to my stomach because—there I was, put on the highest shelf, and it could only mean one thing ... unnecessary and hateful criticism that would range across everything, from my hair to my weight—or the fact that I was hard of hearing. Because who could imagine someone like me would get this far? I was tormented by adults all the time, and it baffled me. Did people think I didn't read the comments? Didn't they realize that I was human too?

Flash, flash, flash.

Up top ...

Mable, over here ...

Flash, flash, flash.

Like the riddle of the tree that falls in the forest, did I exist if I didn't have the public's attention? Fame was a privilege that could be taken away. I was a realist; I knew at some point this would end and they would stop hiring me for not being young and beautiful. And then what?

"I think I will never get used to the attention," I said to Bruno as we moved on to the next row of photographers.

"Well, darling, it's either you're somebody or nobody ... you're somebody, so use this to your advantage."

This success wasn't overnight, but progressive. I'd sought fame out—I wanted it—but it wasn't what I imagined it would be. The lights were attractive, but get close enough and you'd be scrutinized by them.

"When you've been around a long time like me in this business, you get to meet lots of people. I think modeling is fun for the first couple of years. You fly around and get to wear designer clothing. If you're good at what you're doing, then eventually you get to be overpaid to do so little. But at some point reality sets in, because nothing is what it seems in this business. Be smart about it; find your purpose besides modeling. You're a smart girl. I'm sure you'll figure it out." Bruno winked at me.

I loved our chats, and Bruno's advice had already been put to use. I'd been working on other things that were more fulfilling. I intended on keeping my identity rooted. *They will see me bend, but I won't break ... only focus on what's important; then maybe I have a chance for survival under the lights.*

After the photo calls were the interviews, and the past few weeks I'd done tons of them. I understood it was part of the game; the only thing was that they all appeared to ask the same irrelevant questions.

What would be the best piece in your wardrobe?
Does the world care?
What outfit do you regret wearing?
Really?
What do you wear to bed?
Nothing, except Chanel No. 5 ... kidding. I didn't say that Marilyn had.

Was this what the world wanted to know? What was inside my purse? Thankfully, tonight it was not about me; it was about raising money and awareness for a cause I held close to my heart. And, like Bruno had said, I had to use this attention and gear it into something relevant. My newfound fame would allow me to talk about things of high value that should matter in the spotlight. That was something I'd been working on.

I made it up the stairs to the extended platform where Christopher Leon waited for me to be interviewed. He spoke to most of the guests before they went inside the reception area. Christopher was the editor at large for *Blind Item* magazine. He had been a permanent fixture on the front row of every fashion show in the past twenty years. This was the sixth time we'd met on the red carpet.

"Look at you." We kissed hello on each cheek. I knew the camera was rolling and this would be shown on *Entertainment Weekly*.

"What a magnificent dress. Who are you wearing?"

"This gown was designed by my dear friend Bruno Ortiz," I said, adjusting the fabric. The garment had a high slit and rolls of feathers all sewn at the base of the dress.

"Beautiful! And those shoes."

"Thank you," I said, as if I'd made or bought them.

"Is the dress comfortable? Because it doesn't look like it," Christopher asked.

"Very much so; it appears deceptively heavy, but it's quite light and easy to maneuver."

"Yes, I've been watching you from up here, moving around with such grace and elegance. Well, you look gorgeous. You own it."

"Thank you." I felt uncomfortable with the compliments, but this was work.

"Okay, so now I want to talk about—you."

"All right." I smiled. *This should be good.*

"You are the first model to be hard of hearing to grace any magazine cover. How does that make you feel? What kind of message do you want to send out to the girls who want to follow in your footsteps?"

"Am I the first? Well, I'm aware of how the industry works and the distortion of what beauty is. Yes, I talk funny; no, I'm not the ideal model, but for me, I don't view myself as being different—this is who I am. I want the girls out there to feel beautiful no matter what the world pressures them to be. I wish for them to embrace their differences ... because that's what makes us unique. I believe little girls shouldn't have a limitation on their dreams because they don't fit the norm ... mold the norm so that it fits you," I said.

"You're also a global ambassador for Humanity Matters Worldwide, and you work in close collaboration with organizations that promote gender equality and the empowerment of women ... Woo, that's a lot to swallow! You've been busy, Miss Harper." He looked up from his cue card.

"Yes, modeling had given me a voice, and I intend to use it."

"Well, I'm looking forward to what you're going to do next. Enjoy. Have fun tonight."

And the camera cut off. I came back down and found Bruno at the bottom of the steps waiting for me.

"Bruno ... who is that woman with the dark sunglasses?" I recognized her, but I didn't know what she did or what her name was. We had crossed paths before but never actually talked. It almost felt like she was trying to avoid me, and I wondered why.

"My dear, you don't know who Elaine Furstenberg is?" Bruno looked at me like I had two heads.

"No," I said as he laughed at my confused stare.

"The editor-in-chief of *Elite* and the artistic director for *Most* magazine. How is it you've been in this industry this long without meeting her?"

"I guess ... I never got the opportunity."

"You were never introduced?"

"No, never."

"Well, in all fairness, she is a difficult person to come by. I will have to present her to you later."

The night that had ended with us discovering Simon's car marked with graffiti had stirred some uncertainty in me. I trusted him, but somewhere in the back of my mind, I couldn't shake off that feeling. What if I was wrong?

When I suggested we call the cops, Simon was too eager to brush it off as probably some jerk fooling around. He said there would be no point—they wouldn't find them anyhow. That night we went back to my place, and he was quiet for the rest of the evening. That was what had me thinking his behavior was off. If it was some random jerk playing with spray paint, why would they choose those words? Maybe I was overthinking it, but perhaps I wasn't.

Tonight we could have made our first appearance as a couple, but we had both agreed that our work and personal life should be kept separate. We didn't need the paparazzi to distort our relationship into something ugly and dramatic like they usually did. But inside the gala, no paparazzi were allowed past the red carpet, and guests posting on social media had been prohibited. I guessed we could have been seen together inside, in a platonic nature. But I hadn't seen him all day. I imagined that, like me, he had been pulled right, left, and center. When I got away from the entourage, I went out into the hotel lobby and searched my phone for any missed messages, disappointed there were none.

I looked up when I felt like I was being watched.

"Hello." I smiled at the bright eyes that caught mine. I almost didn't recognize Simon with his hair so short. So unexpected.

"You look hot," he said.

"Hot?" I frowned. "Please don't let that be your best pickup line. You will say something more substantial if you're trying to win my attention, sir."

"Huh, alright … you're incredibly smart." He continued to

walk toward me.

"Hmm … keep it coming." I bobbed my head from side to side.

"And beautiful."

I sighed and moved around him. "Nice try, but your time is up."

"Hold on, I'm not done yet."

"Oh, I think we are."

"You want to know what I thought when I first saw you?"

I turned. If he was trying to get my attention, he had finally piqued it.

"That I was the most incredible woman you'd ever seen." I smiled.

"Yes, but there's more." He smiled, placing his hands in his suit pockets. "I told myself if I could get within three feet from you, then I'll know."

"Know what?"

"That you're just right … that there was something legitimate about you. Back at the Little Orange, you thought you made a bad impression because you talked funny, but that's not why I reacted the way I did. It's because I saw you with the most accurate eyes … I felt this wanting … this knowing that I would desire nothing more in life than I did you." He was being emotional. "I knew you were the kind of person to make me feel like the world is my oyster."

"You're just saying that."

"Bloody oath, I mean every word." He got close, dangerously close. I could almost taste his breath.

"I should warn you, I'm unavailable." I glanced around to see if we were within anyone's eyesight.

"It's no surprise, lucky fellow … but it makes no difference to me."

I laughed. "It should. He's a big guy."

"Let him come. I'm not afraid." His eyes shone like the

light, and I couldn't help but be turned on by it.

"Yes, you should, and he won't be happy if he sees me speaking to you." I looked at him through my eyelashes.

"I'll take my chances." His eyes trailed down to my lips. "I really want to be alone with you." His voice came out huskily, making my cheeks burn.

"Are you trying to get me into trouble?"

"Would it be wrong if I said I did?" He flashed a coy smile. "Forget about him. Meet me upstairs on the rooftop in five minutes … That is, if you're feeling a little adventurous."

"What if someone should see us together?"

"Let them." He turned and left me, and I watched him disappear around the corner before I followed. I found him waiting for me inside the elevator, and I took my place beside him. Quietly we stood there, without touching or even looking at each other. Only when the doors opened did I allow him to walk out first, but I didn't get far before he dragged me into his arms and kissed me like there might be no tomorrow.

"We probably shouldn't be doing this here." I smiled between kisses.

"You're right, but how am I supposed to keep my hands to myself when you're near? I can't wait to get home and get you out of this fucking thing." He tried to maneuver around my long train, but somehow part of my dress kept getting in the way. I laughed at his transgression. Then my hands went to his freshly cut hair.

"Is this the surprise you texted me about? You cut off your locks." His hair seemed darker now that it was short.

"I thought it was time for a change. You don't like it?" He searched my face.

"I do. It's just different." I smiled. The wind picked up, and I realized we were standing outside. This high up, the view of the city was always beautiful, especially at night. It almost felt magical.

"I thought tonight would be easy, but I'm having a hard time," Simon pulled out his pack of cigarettes from the inside pocket of his tuxedo.

"With what?"

"Not having you by my side. At least that would have kept the vultures away."

"Don't tell me you're jealous?" My smile widened.

"Damn right. I don't want some bonehead near my girl." He fished out a cigarette and lit it.

"Jason was just saying hello," I reassured him. I appreciated that Simon wasn't possessive. He has his insecurities, sure, like I did, but he was always in check with his emotions and never would act out unless he was forced.

"His hand on your lower back had me concerned." He knitted his brows together.

"You're cute, you know that? But you've got nothing to worry about."

"Yeah?"

"I'm yours," I said, and his smile widened, like I'd shown him a magic trick.

"I like it that you're mine." Simon grabbed my hand and pulled me closer.

"We've got to get back," I whispered. "They're going to serve dinner."

"Let them wait."

"No, we can't. The guests paid thirty-three thousand a ticket for me to sit at their table. We need this money to drill boreholes in villages."

Simon cast an adoring look over me.

"What are you thinking?" I asked.

"How lucky I am. To have met someone who feels equally passionate about the things I do." He kissed me.

Simon and Amanie had opened my eyes to things I didn't realize were happening in the world. They sparked this fire—

inspired me to want to make a change. I'd signed up for Humanity Matters, and they were sending me on a learning mission in a few months. When they first asked me, there was no hesitation; I was on board. I would need to experience firsthand and see with my own eyes what was going on. So I had made sure Amanie was not to book me with any new projects. I was going to Rwanda, or maybe somewhere in India, but one thing was for sure: I wanted to be a strong advocate, bring light to the issues that girls living in poverty faced every day.

"This is a good sacrifice on your part not to have me by your side tonight," I mused.

"Who's sitting at your table?"

"Who's sitting at yours?" I mimicked his tone, and he laughed.

"I asked you first."

"Oh, I don't know, we'll soon find out." I cast my eyes away from his. I knew Julian Gaspard was the one who'd paid for the whole table. *Simon won't be happy, but we'll get through tonight somehow.* I kissed him and turned to go back down.

"Mable."

"Yes, darling."

"We're going together—to the after-party." He didn't ask; he demanded.

"I thought …"

"I had a change of heart. I want you by my side."

I'd thought he would never ask.

Hell Breaks Loose

Simon

When we arrived at the after-party, we didn't stop to pose in front of the cameras that ambushed the invitees as they came. Mable, wearing a short black cocktail dress, dashed right inside the club, and I followed her, not far behind. This was killing me; we couldn't be ourselves and instead were keeping a low profile. I knew this day would come, when the world would take notice of the woman I loved, and that worried me. They would soon want in, into her life, and I felt anxious that I wouldn't be able to protect her from it.

Maybe it was my fault that she found herself in this predicament. I had led her down this path, but there was only so far I could go, because the spotlight only had room for one. *Is it wrong I want to keep her all to myself?* Maybe it was, but with me, she could be any version of herself, no matter how small or big her insecurities. *I will always love her for who she is.* Love sometimes can be made to feel like a competition, with no one to adjudicate who wins or loses. And so we remained where we remained—no rules—only to anticipate what would happen next.

"Don't you dare think you can maneuver yourself out of this." She laid the magazine flat out on my desk.

"Huh?" I glanced up at the sharpness of her voice. "What am I looking at?"

"Take a good hard look, Simon. I think you owe me an explanation," Mable said, flustered.

There's a catch-22 to living under the lights: it could work in your favor, and it could also give you a ninety-degree burn. You couldn't take your pick on which way it would go— only hope you weren't the deer caught in the headlights. As a photographer, your job was more than to take good shots that told a story. It was about reflecting something most profound. It was my lens that disclosed life in a pure light, the way it was or the way we desired it to be. And then there was the ugly— paparazzi, their lenses distorting the truth. They were not artists; they were turds hiding in the shadows. Paired up with trashy magazines, they would take everything out of context if it made a juicy story that would sell their publication.

"Simon, aren't you going to explain?" Mable looked at me as if I'd done the most horrible thing—maybe I had.

I took a second to process what she was showing me, and then I saw it. Shit ... There you had it. Now I was the deer in the headlights. I was not totally fucked, at least ... not after I explained to her about the picture.

Disappointment set in, and I didn't know if I could ever forgive myself, that I had been deceitful to the woman who I loved with every fiber in me. Not that I was trying to get away with her not knowing, but I had thought it would be best. There it was, slapped hard on the glass window, like a bird that hadn't seen it coming. I had a legitimate explanation—I did—on why Vanessa and I were on the front cover of a celebrity gossip rag. It was not what it seemed. It never is, under the lights.

"So." Her voice was steady, but I had known her long enough to know she was talented at holding back. She picked the copy up, studying every detail. "I will give you the benefit of the doubt, Simon, because I know you wouldn't do anything to hurt me." She raised her eyebrows. "But you need to tell me what this is." Some of her green rollers had come loose. Noah was prepping her for a shoot we were to start in an hour. "Is this true? Is this her apartment you're coming out of?"

"I promise you, it's nothing to worry about. Can we talk about it after?"

"After what? So you can come up with a better excuse to cover up the possibility that you've done something to hurt us? I won't make a scene in front of everyone ... I want to know ... Simon, what's this about?"

Her glassy eyes pegged me, and my stomach twisted in knots. I had never meant for this to happen. At the moment I had thought I was doing the right thing.

"You think I'm cheating on you?" I came closer, and she moved away.

"I don't know, you tell me." She glanced at me briefly before looking away, the magazine half-crumpled in her hand. "Apparently, Vanessa gave the interview herself ..." She vigorously flipped through the pages, trying to find the article.

"Can you let me see it, please?" I wanted to tell her to relax, but I had a hard time doing that myself. She stuck the glossy paper hard to my chest and walked further away. I didn't need to look at the picture. I know it was of us coming out of Vanessa's apartment, but what the picture didn't show was that three of her friends, two males and a female, had followed us right out after that picture was taken. What I didn't expect to find next to that one was one of Mable and me on the rooftop that night at the Gala Fashion Show. The caption read: *Vanessa slams cheating Simon.* Then a smaller caption was underneath: *"I thought we had a future together. This is the worst betrayal. I will never forgive him."*

I either wanted to laugh out loud or cry. Only Vanessa could mastermind this. I'd been helping her out, and this was the thanks I got. This was easy to feed to the press. No one knew Mable and I were dating except close friends and family … and, of course, Vanessa. She'd been trying to sabotage everything in my life since she found out Mable and I were together. Now Vanessa was trying to destroy the thing that mattered the most.

"You know this is pure rubbish, right?" I looked back at Mable.

"What, you're going to tell me you were Photoshopped in?" Her tone was crude, but it had every reason to be.

"No, I was there … It's definitely me," I replied, feeling myself deflate.

"When was this taken?" She swallowed hard.

"In Los Angeles, a few months back."

She closed her eyes like I had just confirmed what she suspected. "I thought you were on location for a shoot."

"No, I wasn't." My voice came out hoarse, and I tossed the magazine on the desk.

"You lied to me?"

Her voice didn't come out as anger, but as a disappointment.

"Did you sleep with her?" She asked me like I'd known she would. The light in her eyes diminished with each second, and my heart plunged. *This is my fault. I created this.* I wanted to come clean, but somehow I thought things were better left unsaid … unknown. For me, it was an unfinished business I had to take care of.

"You know I love you—only you—and I would do nothing to jeopardize what we have."

"But yet you went behind my back … visiting an old girlfriend? What is she to you? Why does she have this pull on you?"

"I'll tell you everything you need to know. Just sit down."

"No, I'll stand, if that's okay with you." Mable wrapped her arms around herself as I leaned into my desk.

"Vanessa Todd—she's my sister-in-law ... or was."

"What?"

"Racheal and Vanessa are sisters ... identical twins," I said.

"Your wife Racheal?" And when I nodded, she settled down in the chair behind her. I could sense the wheels turning in her head.

"Oh God, don't tell me you cheated on Racheal with Vanessa?"

"No. No, I would never—I thought you knew me better."

"You lied to me. I never thought you'd do that either," she responded coldly, and her eyes avoided mine. She was furious, and I wouldn't hold it against her if she despised me.

"Look, Vanessa had always been a mess, and after Racheal died, it only escalated. She was the only one who understood what I was going through. And we hung out a little more than usual. Then one night she kissed me and I kissed her back. She looked like Racheal, but it didn't feel right, so I stopped it from going any further. I swear. We were never together—nor ever will be, but Vanessa never accepted that fact. That time I flew to L.A. because she agreed to check herself into rehab if I was the one to bring her there. I told Vanessa that this was the last time I would help her out. After that, Vanessa needed to stay out of my life. But she never kept her word, checking herself out and following me back to New York. I should have known better. I don't know what I was thinking."

"Why didn't you tell me? Didn't you trust me enough I would understand? I thought we were a team; we would have worked through it together." She stood up abruptly.

"I didn't want to involve you in my past because Vanessa is not your problem. After my wife's death, I felt like I owed Racheal to look out for her sister. It's the least I could do. I know this puts you in the wrong light."

"You mean my integrity?" She sarcastically laughed. "All

my efforts to advocate for my charities—have you any idea what I look like now? I will be criticized as the other girl who broke up a relationship … one that never existed." Her eyes lit up like it had just hit her. "I don't think my career will recover from this."

"I could fix this." I quickly added.

"How are you going to do that? Get her to confess? She'll never do that; she hates my guts." Mable threw her arms up. "Vanessa was out to get me from the start, and you have been covering it up. Vanessa was the one who vandalized your car— and the calls on my phone in the middle of the night—you knew all of it."

I couldn't look her in the eyes.

"This magazine sent this morning—it was Vanessa—wasn't it? You knew what she was capable of, and you never let me in on it because you thought … I don't know what you thought." Her voice got louder with every word.

"I was doing it to protect you. I thought I could take care of it on my own."

"No—you're selfish, Simon."

"I made a mistake—okay. It's one stupid mistake, and I don't want it to come between us."

"You chose Vanessa over me," she said under her breath. "I can't believe I took this long to realize it. It's always been her."

"What? No." It came out sharp. "I chose no one over you. It's just you—only you."

She got up, regarding me for a moment, and something happened behind her eyes. The anger that was there a second before faded away, replaced with sadness.

"I'm not someone who will tell you what you want to hear. I love you, and that's why I have to be transparent and give you the facts—you're a mess, Simon. You're struggling with guilt, and you think the solution is to help everyone you can because you don't know how to save yourself, but it doesn't work like that. You're going to have to come to terms with the fact that there was nothing you could have done to change things. Trying to save Vanessa will not bring Racheal back. Cut the cord, because she will take you down with her."

Mable was right. I'd been trying to make things right through Vanessa. Nothing I ever did would change the past, but I couldn't help but want to try.

"Can you ever forgive me?"

Her voice became bold. "I honestly don't know. Maybe with time … but how can I trust you again?"

"Where are you going?" Mable was making her way out of my office.

"I can't … I can't think when I'm around you." She shook her head.

"Mable."

I tried to get her to look at me, but she only placed her face in her hands before looking up again. "No—Simon, I'm *so* pissed at you. I think we need space, you know—to breathe." She took one step back and regained her composure, holding on to her tears because she was too proud to give me that privilege.

"Okay," I said, and she took her final step toward the door.

"I hope you can forgive yourself, because this will eat you up if you continue like this. I care too much, and that's why I can't watch you crash and burn." She spoke softly. "I can't be around when that happens."

Then I watched Mable disappear through the doorway, and most likely from my life.

A year,
plus one
month later

If life Hands You Paper, Origami the Heck Out of It

Mable

There are days I wished I could go back to the beginning, when life was simpler, but then I would never have learned about myself like I did in the past two years. There would have been a trade-off at some point, and I wouldn't imagine giving those best parts up. I thought about this and other things as I made my way back to New York City. Fresh off a plane, I ran out of the taxicab and scaled up the concrete stairs like my life depended on it. Because it did.

It had been twenty hours since I'd first gotten the call. I knew something was off by the sound of Gloria's voice. It was uneven, and it cracked when she asked me what I was doing. Somehow it seemed like she didn't care. Now I knew: she was trying to muster up the courage to tell me. I recognized that tone, the kind when someone was about to deliver the worst blow of your life. And just like it should have, those few words after would finish my already ailing heart.

Come home.

New York hadn't been my home for the longest time. I had

been living in Italy for the past five months.

He had a stroke.

What was he doing in New York?

My phone made a *thunk* on the neutral Tabriz carpet, never giving Gloria a chance to give me the details. It's devastating enough to be miles away from the ones you love when something like this happens, and the thought of the possibility of losing him scared me.

I had come to Italy to take refuge from the limelight for a couple of weeks. If only I'd stuck to the plan. I had been living in a beautiful seventeenth-century villa in the Lombardy region, overlooking Lake Como, with a man I thought I was in love with. After spending time at Bruno's villa, I had fallen madly in love with the countryside, so much so that Julian had purchased a property in the area. It seemed right at the time. I guess loneliness and heartache were the culprits, sweeping me away with the idea that this would fill the void. But no matter how hard I tried, I wasn't ready to move on. *Maybe I never will be, not from Simon.*

When I became too emotional to function, it was Julian who put me in his luxury car and helped book the first flight out of Milan. He showed me kindness even though I was the one who had dropped the bomb in his lap, days before I had to rush back to New York. *Boy—oh boy, I sure know how to make a mess out of things.* I only hoped Julian could forgive me someday, but I could never deny myself the truth: there was only one person who could make me happy, and unfortunately, Julian wasn't him.

I walked through the glass door, rushing towards the first desk I saw. "Hi, I'm looking for my father … Charlie Harper … He was admitted … I don't know, I think last night." I forced the words out of my mouth, leaning on the counter for support.

"Third floor." As the words came out, my feet moved.

"Ma'am?" The voice got smaller.

I pressed the up button, as if the elevator would open immediately. The door to the left was the first to open. When I walked inside, a familiar scent struck me … mint and sweet grapefruit? The smell reminded my heart of something long lost. *Just when I think I'm over feeling broken, something reminds me of Simon.* I guessed I was fooling myself to think I'm immune to the past. No one is. The only difference was how you dealt with it, and I wasn't sure if I was coping well or just accepting it. Maybe that was the reason I almost made the biggest mistake of my life. A way to keep my distance from the past—Simon.

I'd been struggling for a while with something, and I'd told no one, not even Gloria. After I broke it off with Simon, I threw myself more into charity work and did fewer modeling jobs. Humanity Matters sent me on a mission to Rwanda. I thought it was a good idea, but the thing was, I didn't go there alone. There was another humanitarian worker that made the same trip, someone close to my heart. I guessed I wasn't the only one who needed time away from the light, the kind that brought us together and ripped us apart with the same hand.

The doors opened, and I found Gloria standing at the end of the hallway next to a man with a white coat. They glanced my way when I approached them.

"Mable." Gloria's hair was poorly tied, and the dark circles under her eyes made me think she'd been here from the start, standing in my place as I made my way back.

"Dr. Evans, this is my uncle's daughter, Mable Harper." Her eyes found me and they displayed the same amount of anxiety. She had every right to be devastated, since my dad was more than an uncle to her.

"How is he doing?" I asked the doctor, well into his fifties, sporting a pair of silver glasses.

"Your father experienced a mild stroke. He's stable now, and we're running further tests to determine the cause for it, and once we do, then we can work on preventing it from happening again," he said.

"Can I see him?"

"You can, once he's back in his room. As soon as I get any news, I'll be sure to give you any updates."

After the doctor left, I turned to Gloria, and she asked, "Did you know he was here?"

"No … I had no idea," I gazed into her bloodshot eyes. "You mean, he wasn't here to see you?" I asked, trying to put the pieces of the puzzle together.

"No … I don't understand … Why would he be in New York and not tell us?" Gloria's eyebrows crashed together. I was thinking back to the last conversation I had had with my father, which was last Monday. He was at home in Montreal, doing well, considering Lauren had broken things off several months earlier, but he never mentioned that he was planning a trip to New York.

"I can answer that question."

I took a second to recognize that tonality. I turned, and there she was, the woman with the dark glasses in a bouclé suit.

"Charlie was in town to see me."

"You?" I wondered why I had never realized it before, but then again, I had had no reason to suspect it until now. What seemed like a ghost from the past was standing before me in the flesh.

"Elaine?—how do you know my uncle?" Gloria asked, but I already knew the answer.

Gloria wouldn't have recognized her. She was a child herself when she took off for the hills. Elaine had changed her name and gotten enough work done to alter her attributes. No, she looked nothing like the old photographs, or any of my memories of her. She removed her dark sunglasses and adjusted her tailored jacket, then slowly raised her eyes to mine. It was almost like watching a broken glass shatter in reverse, each small piece placed back together. No one could ever forget their mother's eyes.

"Hello, Mable." Her voice was soft. "Can we go somewhere to talk?"

Elaine glanced at Gloria before returning her tawny eyes back to mine. I refused to go anywhere, but I needed to know what her part was in this, and where she had been all this time. Elaine, or I should say Joyce, must have been here in New York, building an impressive career while back at home my father and I were picking up the pieces.

"I ... I'm going to go find Tracy and Simon." Gloria touched my arm to get my attention.

I could sense Gloria felt just as awkward about this as I did. Then it hit me—was Simon here? But she walked away before I could even ask. To be honest, I couldn't deal with Simon right now. I had so much on my plate. Elaine Furstenberg, the editor of the most prominent printed magazine on Earth, also my mother? A hell of a lot to swallow.

We made our way to the cafeteria, but I didn't acknowledge her existence and kept listening to the sounds of heels clicking on the linoleum floor behind me. I found an empty chair in the corner, and Elaine took her place across from me.

"You had a long flight ... you must be tired. Did you want something to eat?" She looked around, then focused back on me. For a woman wearing a ten-thousand-dollar suit, cafeteria food probably didn't live up to her standards. *This is all too strange. What is she even doing here, now, back in my life?*

"Ha, don't bother pulling the motherly act on me." I glared at her, sliding up my cotton sleeves, revealing a stack of silver bracelets that Simon had gotten me for my birthday when we were together. "You lost that privilege long ago." There was heartbreak knocking at the door, and my heart wanted to take refuge under the bed.

Her eyes softened. She looked so different from the woman behind the dark lenses, the one I had first seen in Simon's studio.

Something told me she was not as stern and obdurate as she first appeared. Maybe I had her wrong. Had she any regrets? I hoped so, or else I was wasting my time. Then I realized something. Perhaps we had more in common than I hated to admit. She hid in the back of those sunglasses the way I had hid behind Julian Gaspard those past seven months. We were both running from reality. I knew what mine was; what was hers?

"What I want to know is … Why is my father here—why are you?" I said sharply.

Elaine breathed in, holding it for a moment. "It started at your first runway show. I was so sure Charlie wouldn't have recognized me … so much time has passed, but he did." She looked down, playing with the tips of her black glasses. I could have asked her what they talked about, but then again, it was none of my business what transpired between them.

"A short time after that, he showed up at my home in Greenwich Village. And we talked and realized that the feelings we thought were gone were in fact still there. So we kept in touch."

"How adorable." I laughed sarcastically. "Okay, so?" I wanted her to wrap it up because my stomach was curdling. "How did this all happen? Were you there when he had his stroke?"

"We had gone out for dinner, and your father started not to feel well."

"You mean you guys were on a date? You've got to be kidding me." I sat far back in my chair. What was my dad thinking?

"I wouldn't call it a date; I've known your father since the age of fourteen. But yes, we were together when it happened," she said. I guessed that, if he had been alone that night, who knew what the outcome would have been? *But it still doesn't change the fact that I don't approve of this.*

"I can't believe my father would keep this from me," I

murmured.

"It's not his fault. I asked him to. We agreed to keep it quiet for a while until we were sure what we were doing," she said, and I let out a laugh. Kids are supposed to hide things from their parents, not the other way around.

"This is nuts. What do you think will come out of it?"

"I know this is all confusing to you, Mable," Elaine said.

"To be honest, I don't know what to feel right now. You disappeared out of my life, and now you're trying to weasel your way back in? By getting through my dad to get to me? So what … so you can do it to us all over again and leave? You don't have the privilege to do that—not again."

"You don't understand, Mable. It's so easy to sit there and judge when you don't know the facts." She used a calm tonality when she spoke. "Your father and I have a long history," she said.

I didn't think I knew anyone who would be bothered by the prospect of their parents getting back together, but my father deserved better. So did I.

"Oh my God, this is unbelievable." I rubbed my eyes. I tried hard to hate this woman. Whatever biological attachment we had, she was just a stranger. "You're just going to hurt him again, and honestly I don't want you around him, or—us."

Her shoulders dropped, and her eyes saddened. But what else could I say but the truth?

"I can't blame you … You were too small to understand what actually happened. You think it was easy for me to leave you?"

"The truth? You left because of my disability. You couldn't deal with the fact I was such a disappointment to you." I cast a frown in her direction. I knew I was getting ahead of myself, assuming the worst. But it was a long time coming, and the hurt was spilling out of me like Niagara Falls. No walls could hold back these emotions.

She made a noise in the back of her throat. "See how wrong you are. It's easy to jump to conclusions. I guess you get that from your father," She squared her shoulders. "I left because of my issues."

"What?"

She took a deep breath. "Do you remember how it was to be around me? How erratic I was one moment, and lifeless the next?"

"To be honest, I don't remember much." I was so young when she left, and the older I got, the more I forgot things about the past. The only fact I recalled was that I wanted my mother.

"After I left, I sought help for my issues. I was just all over the place and couldn't understand why."

"I'm not following you." I slightly shook my head.

"I have Bipolar II disorder," she said, and I tried to grasp what she was telling me.

"But look at you … You seem fine, and you've got this great career," I said in frustration. *How do I know she's not lying?* "You're Elaine Furstenberg, the editor-in-chief of the biggest magazine in print."

She gave a vibrant smile and leaned in closer. "Anyone with any kind of physical or mental restrictions are capable of accomplishing so much more. Our setbacks don't define us unless we allow it." She brushed her bangs out of her eyes. "I'm on the right medication that works for me. I have my good days and bad days, but I've been dealing with it the best I can. What else can I do?"

"But Joyce—Elaine, no matter what issues you have, we would have gotten through it together as a family."

"Maybe." Elaine's lips went thin. "I left because you're worth more to me than anything else. Things at the time seemed screwed up beyond repair. I thought you and your father would be better off without me. So I came to New York and got a job working at a magazine, writing gossip columns. That's when I change my name … A way to start with a clean slate," she said.

"It makes me sad when you say that, because all I ever wanted was my mother … all those milestones … all those times I needed you … you were never there," I said, and she diverted her eyes down to her hands.

"No amount of *sorry* will change the fact I wasn't the mother you deserve. If I could revise the past, believe me, I would. With all that happening, nothing altered that I loved you—but I somehow knew you'd be all right." She paused. "Now I can only hope to move forward, have you and your father in my next chapters."

Being left by my mother had been traumatic, but what else could I do? Life would never hand me a Nutella jar with a spoon and say, "Hey, knock yourself out." Take it or leave it—this was my life. Life is what you get and what you make out of it. If I stayed in a place of resentment, then it meant I wasn't progressing.

Maybe she was right; it was time to turn a new leaf, but I couldn't help but wonder what this version of Joyce would have had in common with my father. *My dad is beige, and this woman is Chanel.* I feared that he would get hurt and I would be forced to hate my mother again. But it was not my choice to make; it was my dad's, and right now my primary focus was for him to be healthy again.

"Look, I'm not telling you this because I want pity, or to make my illness an excuse to make everything okay—because it's not. I made a terrible mistake, and I had to live with that. And your father did a fantastic job raising you without me. Maybe I have no right saying this, but I'm proud of what you've become. You're the most beautiful thing I've ever seen."

As I stared, I felt like I was six again, and my heart wanted to forget everything, but my mind had some doubt. *How many chances do we get in life?* If I turned her away, she might never come back.

"Give me some time," I said.

"Whatever it takes, I'm not going anywhere—not this time."

"Elaine Furstenberg ..." I said it like I might wake up from a dream. "Wait a minute." Then I realize. "Did you know it was me? Your daughter? When you put me on the cover of *Elite* magazine?"

"I did," she said, and my heart dropped.

"But now I feel cheated. I believed the editor chose me, but now—knowing it was my mother—" I shook my head. "I didn't earn it. I'm a complete fraud."

She sighed. "Understand something, Mable. Simon took amazing pictures of you, and any editor would have been crazy to pass them up." She paused. "Do you know we sold five hundred thousand copies of that March issue, and the dress you wore on the cover was sold out? No, Mable. I wouldn't be where I am if I gave people a free pass. I don't care if you were the Queen of England. If the pictures are shit, you're not getting on my cover or in my magazine."

"Okay, but you never thought to reach out to me?" I asked.

"Honestly, I didn't know how. I thought you hated me."

"Well, you're not far off, but maybe with time, I could learn to forgive you," I said, leaning back in my chair. "Huh, five hundred thousand copies. Wow. And I never got paid for that cover." I crossed my arms like I was a teenager.

She slid on her dark shades. "Don't you know you shouldn't do anything before getting it in writing? Don't take offense, but business is business, darling. I gave you a better opportunity than a couple thousand dollars would have provided you. I opened the door, and the rest you did yourself, like I knew you would."

Whatever You Do, Make It Count

Simon

I inserted several coins into the vending machine and pressed A2, but then I realized too late that what I had wanted was A3. So now I was stuck with something I didn't want—story of my life. My mind had been preoccupied since Gloria called me last night and told me that Mable's father was in the hospital. No hesitation. I had to come. When you looked at the logistics of it, I had no business being there, because I would be the last person on earth Mable would want to see in the middle of her crisis, but I had come for support if she needed it. Even though she was a former lover, I still cared for her. People who share the past are forever engraved in the heart. No matter how hard you try, you can never erase the memory of it. What I experienced with Mable, the love we had shared, was something that most people never experienced in a lifetime, and that was why I couldn't just tell her "I wish you the best" and get on with my life. Our story, whatever version it might have taken, whatever it may have been, it was not over, and perhaps it would never be. In the time we were together, I'd gained something of higher value than just the privilege of loving her. I had changed somehow, the way I saw myself, and it was Mable who made me realize I was done licking my old wounds. I had somehow come to this place of reconciliation. It took a lot of soul-searching, but I was finally able to move on. I didn't do or say anything that had caused Racheal's death. Whatever I was struggling with didn't have a part in the tragic outcome.

I loved my wife. I had to believe that. I had stayed in an unhappy marriage because, if I hadn't, it would have ripped her apart. Don't we put people we love before ourselves? Above our own happiness? When I lost Racheal, I kept waking up, thinking it was all a nightmare. And just when I thought I'd be forever living life in black, Mable had come strolling in, and the world suddenly switched to color again. Losing someone is gut-wrenching, but never finding love again would have been the saddest of all. What I felt for Mable would never overshadow what I had with Racheal, because I had learned that there are many loves, and the depths can vary for each person in our life. Regardless, I had found love again, and now I was moving on. If I had never let Mable into my life, I might have never concluded that on my own. I trusted that Mable was my soul mate, but I also believed soul mates were not someone you spend a lifetime with. They come slowly into your life, and before your eyes, they change it for the better just before they sneak out the back door. That was what made them more special than anyone else. I would forever be grateful, but I was left to wonder why I hadn't fought harder … and Mable would always be labeled as the one that got away.

Shortly after Mable confronted me about being in L.A. with Vanessa, she realized she didn't want to continue the relationship. I was heartbroken, but I had to respect what she wanted.

She went right; I went left.

I'd kept myself busy with work, but the pain of not having

Mable beside me didn't go away. I guessed it was necessary for people to feel broken up because it only made things more meaningful. I'd earned that pain, felt deeply for another, and for me, a life with zero meaning was not a life well lived.

There was stuff between us left unsaid, but I had gotten closure when I saw her in Africa five months ago. We were both sent from Humanity Matters on a mission to Rwanda. The organization was there to help drill a borehole in a rural community, and we wanted to be a part of that. Initially, the plan was to do it together, before everything blew up in my face. I was relieved to find out that Mable didn't opt out, which was a good sign that she didn't hate my guts. I was man enough to own up to it even though at the time I felt I had done nothing wrong. I should have never hidden it from Mable, made her think I didn't trust enough for her to understand. I was an idiot; the fear of losing her was what had cost me the most important thing in my life. Yet I needed to forgive myself for that, too, because Mable was the one who showed me you can't slosh around in regret. Regret was nothing more than being a goldfish in a bowl with nowhere to go. I had to accept it for what it was if I wanted to move forward, and I was ready.

I had arrived in Rwanda a day before Mable, and I could have sworn I felt her presence before I caught sight. I found her outside, standing next to a black Jeep, sliding on a gray backpack. My eyes drank her up like a man who was lost out in the desert, suspecting what was in front of him a mirage, but she wasn't a ghost … just my Aphrodite. She wore a baseball cap, and only a tail of her golden braid came around her left shoulder. The last time we had spoken, she had asked me to give her some space, but yet here I was, walking straight for Mable, shortening the air between us. I couldn't help it. It was like a natural reflex. The heart never forgets home. Mable had said something to her driver before slightly turning, and I caught her attention. She took a step back and considered me. I didn't know how long we stood there, looking at each other in silence, like we wanted to read each other's minds.

What was she longing for? What was I?

"I hope you will make yourself useful this week," I spoke out, inching up closer until she was looking up at me.

"Uh-huh. But you should worry about yourself, Mr. Rowe." She narrowed her eyes. "What are you doing here, gawking, when you should be out there working?" Her eyes were lit up like two bright stars. I didn't realize how much I had missed looking into them until now.

"Gawking?" I stifled a laugh. "Don't think because you're a girl, I will go easy on you. We've got a lot of work ahead of us."

"Oh, I wouldn't imagine it any other way." She flaunted a bicep that peeked from her green T-shirt. The words Humanity Matters Rwanda *were printed across her chest.*

"That's impressive, but you think you can keep up with me?" I knew what to expect, since this was my third mission trip, and it was Mable's first. This was nowhere near the lifestyle or comforts she was used to, because we were to eat and sleep like everyone else in this community. But, knowing Mable, she wouldn't have it any other way.

"You know I can, Walter." She coyly cast a look before walking away.

"Hey ... I thought I told you what I'd do if you called me by my middle name."

"Oh, I remember." She slightly turned and flashed a knowing smile—a smile only meant for me. And there it was, like nothing had changed—only she wasn't mine. I didn't know how many times I had to remind myself that. But I had come to realize

that no matter, how much we loved each other, we couldn't seem to repair what was broken between us. Then again, maybe we were too stubborn to admit that we wanted things to go back the way they were.

We had spent two weeks together. We were never alone except for the few days before Mable left. I took her on a road trip to see Lake Kivu, wanting to get shots of the scenery and possibly to talk.

"Um? What do you mean—exploding lake?" She cast a worrisome look from the passenger seat.

"Yeah, it's susceptible to underwater eruptions because of the volcanoes and the anaerobic bacteria in the water. But I promise you it's perfectly safe." I grinned.

"Okay, sure, why don't you endanger my life." She pushed strands of hair away from her face.

"No worries, love. They extract the methane gas from the lake and use it as a power source that provides electricity in the region, so it elevates the possibility of explosions happening."

"Geez ... that sounds reassuring." She lifted her sunglasses to the top of her head.

"Trust me, I would never put you in any danger. I would protect you with my life."

"I know," she murmured, looking far off in the distance.

I placed one hand on the outside of the Jeep door, the other on the steering wheel. That way I could contain my fingers from going anywhere they shouldn't, like her knee or her thigh. She was wearing a pair of navy-blue linen shorts, but I couldn't stop imagining touching her soft skin again.

"Pretty cool," she said, looking out the open window. "I can't believe I'm here. It's so strange, isn't it?" She shifted in her seat to get a good look at me.

"What is?"

"You and me ... together ... again."

"When I first found out we would make this trip together, it

crossed my mind it would be awkward, but being around you—this thing between us is the most natural thing I ever felt," I said, giving her a quick glance. "It's good to be us, for a little while." I was relieved that my eyes hid behind my aviator sunglasses, shielding her from the downcast air behind them.

"What's next for you? After this, I mean?" she asked, playing with the hem of her white cotton shirt. "Back to New York?"

"New York? Nah, you know me. I feel like I outgrew the city. Especially when you come back from a place like this, witnessing a paradise attached with a horrific history. It changes me every time I leave this place. You know, Rwanda goes beyond gorillas or genocide. These people are the simplest kind you'll ever meet, so inspiring. They have so little, and yet they find joy in the simplest things and draw hope from the darkest shadows. It puts your whole life into perspective." My gaze flicked down at Mable as more strands of hair came loose from her messy bun. "I'm thinking ..." I watched her from the corner of my eyes, hanging on to every word. "I'm going to stay back."

"You're considering ... living here?" Her voice went up at the end.

"Yeah, nah ... Yeah, maybe ... just for a while. Besides, I have nothing waiting for me in New York," I said, not wishing it to be hurtful. But honestly, I didn't see the point in going back without Mable. It was hard living in the same city knowing she'd never come back. When I had Mable, I had everything.

So what do you do when you lose everything? I figured this was a good way to distance myself—a clean slate, even if it would only be for a short time.

"What about your sister? Or work?" She kept her tone level, but her body language disclosed something else. She didn't seem too pleased with my answer, and it made me wonder if she still felt something for me. I had hoped my intuition was accurate.

"Yeah ... my sister ... sure, but you know she has her family, and I can fly to see them anytime. My job, well, I can be wherever I need to be," I said, and her expression dropped. "I'm working on a project right now, collaborating with Humanity Matters on the world's most troubled areas and the issues the people face today."

She turned away from me, gazing out the side window. "Troubled areas?" Her voice came out uneasily, the same way my sister's had when I had first mentioned it to her. "Will you be putting yourself in any danger, Simon?" I felt her eyes on me, but I kept mine on the twisting road ahead.

"Hmm ... possibly." I twitched in my seat. "But I won't be traveling alone. There will be a guide and a journalist who's a friend of mine."

"Now you're making me worry ... Where exactly are you planning to go?" I loved that her tone was assertive.

"There's nothing to worry about." I glanced over, and from the looks of it, she didn't believe a word.

"Simon ... Foreigners are kidnapped all the time and held for ransom. The majority don't make it out alive ... And what about the airstrikes? Why would you put yourself at risk ... put your family and me through something like that?"

"Don't forget I've done this before."

"No. Not like this—it's just freaking dangerous." Her voice came out louder. I hated that I had caused her some stress, but it was my life.

"Look, to be honest, I haven't quite mapped things out just yet. I can't jump into a project without getting a feeling of my surroundings and the subjects I'll be covering."

"And you'll be covering war?"

"I don't know yet."

"I know you, Simon."

"Relax. Right now I'll start here and work my way around. Maybe I'll be covering the effects of war; mostly I'll shoot the

refugee camps." I watched her sit there quietly. "Someone needs to tell their story, Mable."

"But at what cost? Your life? You have a suitable career waiting for you in New York," she said, but deep down I knew she understood, or else she wouldn't be here, far from her cocooned life. Mable didn't want me to do this because she had a set of alternative motives, and I couldn't love her more for it.

"Mable, the people in the camps don't want to live in those kinds of conditions, but they have no choice. They are trying to flee their homes because they are not extremists. They're decent people who just strive for the same things we all want out of life: a roof over our heads and for our family to be safe. And yet they go on days and days with nothing to feed their children. I have no kids, but I could imagine it's absolute fucking heartbreaking as a parent to watch your kids starve to death. Nobody should have to go through that." I watched as her eyes turned down. I knew she was trying hard to get me. "I need to be there."

"And what do you think pictures will do?" Mable asked.

"I'm hoping it will get the attention of lawmakers, get people proactive. It isn't right for me to just stand back and do nothing. These people deserve for the world to know their stories."

"I know. I know—okay." Her voice came out in a somber tone. "You have to do this. It only reinforces what I always believed you were—a man with a good heart. God, I love that heart ... But it also means you give too much—help too much, and that's what gets you into trouble, Simon."

She shut her eyes to bar me from her pain. I was expecting at some point for Vanessa to come into the light, like some barricade that had stood between us all these months. When she reopened her eyes, I saw it. That was the sad part about love: it broke you into small pieces, but no matter what, those pieces would always be bound to something else, preventing you from becoming whole again.

"I want you safe because ... God, I don't know what I'll do if I ever lose you," Mable whispered.

My stomach dropped. "You still care about me?"

She sighed before continuing. "You know I do. You're my friend."

I didn't know what kind of answer I expected, but something about the word friend *had me rattled. I didn't let it show.*

"What about you? Are you going home after this?" I asked, after we shared a long moment of silence between us.

"Um, well I'm embarrassed to tell you after what you said. I'm headed to Italy after this."

"Italy?"

"Bruno has invited me to stay at his house ... on Lake Como."

"Lucky you."

"When you say it like that ... it sounds condescending," she said, annoyed.

"Look, I didn't mean it to sound like anything ..." I wasn't jealous. It was known that Bruno Ortiz had a partner who was also his business associate, Jonathan Riley. Maybe it came out sounding a little funny, because somewhere down deep I had hoped she would stay back a while longer. Stay with me, but I had no plausible reason for that idea to even cross my mind. She had moved on and had every right to.

"To be honest, I feel guilty staying in some mansion for two weeks, after leaving from here."

"You shouldn't feel guilty. Life is not about having more or less than anyone else. It's about having empathy toward others, and if you should have a little more on your plate, then share it, and if you have slightly less—than share it too. My dad once told me that in life you have to be of use to someone," I said. She looked at me with interest, and I thought, God, she's beautiful. *"I guess when you're young, you think you're entitled to something—but the world owes us nothing. And so when we*

allow ourselves to only take—that's when things get ugly. I'm not worried about you, Mable. You're here doing your part in trying to make someone else's life better. That's how the world should work, but unfortunately, it doesn't always turn out that way."

"Maybe you're right."

"I'm always right." I flashed her a coy smile.

"Oh yeah, I forgot that about you."

"What's that?"

"Your occasional cockiness," she said.

I laughed. "Have you missed me?"

She didn't hesitate before answering. "Always. I miss talking to you. You have a way of making me feel ... ordinary." She smiled.

But she wasn't ordinary, not to me.

"So I guess ... it will be awhile before we see each other," I said.

"It seems like it." Her voice was heavy with dolefulness.

I glanced at her, but she slid down her sunglasses as though she didn't want me to witness what her eyes were saying. I read her well, and she knew that. Yeah—I was going to fucking miss her too.

After an hour, we made our way to the town of Kibuye, an area that had seen horrific brutality firsthand, and there on top of the hill we came to Saint Jean Catholic Church, which was also Kibuye's genocide memorial for the people who had died. I watched Mable as she stood in front of a display of the skulls of some of the victims, just underneath the words Never Again *in bold purple letters.*

"Are you religious, Simon?" She looked up at me. It was funny; we had never spoken about our views on religion. I guessed we were too busy creating our own divinity.

"Religious? Not really ... More spiritual than anything else, I guess. I'm curious about other religions, cultures, but that's the

extent of it." I brushed her hair behind her ear. "But when you see something like this, it makes you wonder whether beliefs lie, or if they hold any truth to anything." I cast my eyes around. "They all came here to take refuge from the violence, thinking they were safe. How does a house of worship become an extermination center? Children ... women and men ... they had no chance," I said, and her eyes caught mine.

"You feel it, don't you? In the air ... the sadness," she said. "It's so heartbreaking. How can anyone be capable of such a thing?"

"Only men can be made into monsters," I told her.

We continued our road trip through Rwanda's countryside, with the window down, passing the breathtaking view of the green slopes. Mable peered her head out of the open window, allowing the air to brush her face. When she settled further into her seat, she flashed me a smile, the first since we'd gotten back into the Jeep. She had been silent after we left the memorial.

"What?" I felt her eyes burning into my skin.

"Am I making you feel uncomfortable?" At some point she had lost her elastic; her hair was picking up air. Christ, she was beautiful.

"Nah ... You make me feel many things, but uneasy is never one of them." I cast a quick glance, and she shook her head, but at least she was still smiling. "What are you thinking?"

She was quiet, and my inquiring mind wanted to know. I glanced in her direction, then back on the road.

"Oh, you don't want to know," Mable said.

"Huh." I flashed her a knowing grin.

"No ..." She lifted her pointer finger into the air. "Get your head out of the gutter, Mr. Rowe," she said, reading my mind.

"It's always been terrific in the sheets with us; I wouldn't blame you if you were," I said.

Mable shook her head at me, her lips expressing amusement. She knew I was right.

"I know now why I've been avoiding you," Mable said, and I glanced back. She was now looking out her window.

"Have you've been avoiding me?" I frowned.

"Intentionally, yes. Haven't you noticed? I've stopped going to functions because I thought you might be there." She sighed. "I didn't have the heart to face you."

"But you followed through with this trip knowing I was here? And I'm offended, by the way," I said.

"Honestly, I thought for sure you weren't coming."

"You've been misinformed. Where have you been getting your information?" I looked in the rear-view mirror before casting my eyes back on the road.

"Noah ... I thought he was looking out for my best interests."

"Ah ..." Maybe he was.

"I should have known. Noah had been broken up over us," Mable said.

"He's not the only one," I replied.

I looked at Mable, settling her head back—her eyes never leaving me. "What I meant to say was ... It's so hard to look at you and not think about the past and how we were. And having to let it go. It hurts."

"We don't have to let it go," I suddenly said. "When I look at you, I feel nothing has changed, like you're still mine."

"Don't say that, Simon."

"No, I do. I need to tell you ... All I know from that day with that fucking rag magazine. Nothing was the same between us. I was there, ready to do anything for you, for us. Where did you go?"

"It didn't work out the way we thought it would."

I couldn't sympathize with her words, so I pulled the Jeep off the shoulder, and the car jerked. Mable's eyes widened.

"That's bullshit ... Tell me you don't love me anymore. Tell me why you can't be with me."

She was taken aback, and her eyes watered. "I ... I love you, Simon, but—"

That was all I needed to hear to reach my limit. I leaned in, allowing my lips to do the talking. I tasted her salty lips, the scent of her skin. Christ, I missed this interaction, us— intertwined. Not knowing where she started, where I ended. It took the slightest fraction of a second for her to follow through, then her hands were in my hair, around my neck ... pulling me closer.

"Tell me you don't want this," I whispered between kisses.

"Simon."

"I need you, Mable."

"I can't ..."

"Why?"

"Because ... I'm with someone else."

It came out a little less than a whisper. I would have missed it if I wasn't practically on top of her.

"What was that?" I slowly eased my way back into my seat. It was like someone had just stabbed me in the gut. My eyes never left hers—her face flushed with heat, my heart muddled in a new ache. What did you expect? *A voice from within taunted. She had moved on. I didn't fight for her. Instead, I watched her walk away without giving her a good reason to stay.*

She closed her eyes like she was trying to gather up the courage to continue. "I'm with Julian."

"Why?" I said.

"What do you mean ... why?" She softly laughed through her tears.

I wanted to wipe every single tear away. I loved her, and it was tearing me apart ... Were her tears for me—for us?

"It just happened. We worked on a campaign together last month. And, well, one thing led to another." She diverted her eyes away from me.

I closed my eyes for a moment, letting it all sink in. I had seen it coming; I always knew Julian had a thing for her, ever since that night at the Plaza. I had watched them together through the crowd. It wasn't difficult to see he was already taken by her, not only by her beauty, but by who she was. Her eyes had a magic to stop the world from moving, making you feel you're the center of the universe, her smile radiating such a glow, making you believe in what it all could be. Who couldn't love the sun?

"Mable. I said this once ... Julian has a terrible reputation. You don't know what you're getting yourself into. He'll only hurt you." Her eyebrows were tangled in a disapproving manner. She may not have liked what I have to say, but her eyes—I saw it. Mable knew she was with the wrong guy.

"Maybe he will, but I'm not yours to worry about, Simon."

"You're right, I'm not," I interjected. "But I do anyway."

Mable was the first to break away from our gaze. "Look, Simon, I'm not trying to hurt you ... or wanting to throw this in your face." I sighed, rubbing my eyes. "It's just ... It was never only about Vanessa or the fact that you lied ... Yeah, at first I was furious, and if I'm honest, I was mad with jealousy. Vanessa was ruthless with me. Me, the woman you were supposed to love. I felt it was a big betrayal you chose her over me."

"I didn't choose her, and I'm sorry that you felt that way. I was just trying to help a friend ... and yes, even though she didn't deserve it. But I didn't do it for her. I did it because I don't like to see someone in so much pain. This is who I am," I said. Mable turned, and her eyes met mine. "Why can't you understand you're everything to me?"

She shook her head. "Don't you see? That's not what's keeping us apart. It's our lives that keep putting us on different paths, and a relationship consists of more than just love. Hell, we would have to live in the same country for this relationship to work, or else what's the point?" She eagerly gathered her hair up on top her head. "No one is to blame ... We're just not ready to sacrifice the one thing that takes us apart. I thought we were better off."

"Are you better off? Because I'm not fucking better without you. After you had said you wanted your space, you completely shut me out like I never existed, like I meant nothing."

"That's not true. You mean the world to me," she said, and I stifled a laugh. "I love you, but maybe it's not enough ... that's why I had no choice but to cut ties, because I knew—one look at you and I would be pulled back where we started," Mable said.

"Would it be so bad?"

She revealed the pain on her face. "Let's drop it." When she couldn't find her black elastic, she let her hair fall back on her shoulders in defeat.

"I don't believe you want to be with Julian—not when you still love me." She didn't protest. "Yeah ... you pretend you like it there behind that wall, but I feel a part of you wants me to come and get you. I'm going to try my best. If I can't, then no one else can." With my heart stuck in my throat, I started the ignition and slowly drove the vehicle onto the road.

Two nurses walked by, bringing my attention back. I fed the machine more coins, pressed A3. When the item fell, I reached for it under the lid, placing the chocolate bar in my pocket. My mind went back at that moment in the Jeep. She was leaving, and I was staying. No kiss would have changed the outcome. Here I was, not trying to rewrite the past or invent the future, but I hated when people said that everything happens for a reason. If things are meant to be, then they will surely be …

As faith had it, my home had a new tenant. But he could always be evicted.

Unfinished Business

Mable

When my father dozed off again, I went out into the corridor to stretch my legs. That was when I saw him there—the man who I couldn't get out of my mind, sitting in a seat with his head down. His hair was much longer since I had last seen him. I guess it had been a while.

"Hey, howya holding up?" His blue eyes filled with tenderness.

"As good as I can be, I guess. What are you doing here, Simon?" My eyes slightly turned down in the corners. I couldn't believe he was here.

He stretched himself up as I got closer. "I wanted to make sure you were okay before I left." A weak smile touched his lips.

Left? *Where is he off to now? Again?*

After how we ended things in Rwanda, I shouldn't have been any of his concern, but yet here he was. He knew exactly how to make me fall so hard for him.

"Simon, I—" I took the seat next to him.

"It's all right …" He shook me off. Maybe it was too

painful for him to be near me. I should know. "Did you get any results on your dad?" He changed the direction from where I wanted to take us.

"Not yet." I looked down at my lap where his hand rested on top of mine. "Have you heard the news? My mother is back— what a twist to this messed-up story." I realized that I needed someone to talk to, and Simon was always there to listen.

"Yeah, Gloria filled me in on the details." He permitted himself to brush the hair from my face.

"Can you believe it? It seems unreal … After all this time, 'the most wretched woman'—is my mother? How can I have not known?"

"Those weren't the words I used—were they?" He winced. "Sorry, love I wouldn't have said those things if I knew she was your mother."

"It's all right. I won't hold it against you." I leaned back in the chair. "What?" I said. His eyes were transfixed on my face, the look that could get my heart to pick up the pace. His eyes always had a way of doing that, creating some synergy.

He cleared his throat. "Yeah … now that I look at you, I see the similarity." I didn't believe those were the words he wanted to use. *I know a cover-up when I see one.*

"Oh, shut up," I half-smiled, looking away.

He caught my eyes and continued. "Love, I know this is hard to gather up, but there's a silver lining in this," he said, sounding hopeful.

"Really? Where?"

"Maybe there's a reason this happened. You have a chance to pull your family together. If she wants in, Mable, let her. Everyone makes mistakes, and people do deserve a second shot."

I wondered if there was a double meaning in his words, and to be honest, I wanted there to be one.

"The past is finished; the question is, are you ready to start the future? Who knows, this might work out the second time around." He smiled.

"What if it doesn't?" I murmured.

"Well, that's the chance you have to take."

When I looked at Simon, I thought this should have been easy, but I guessed love demanded to be earned. Only things worth having come with an attachment of struggles and pain. So why couldn't I get myself on track with Simon? Back in Rwanda, I had been so close to giving it another try, if only he had persuaded a little harder—but I didn't want him to think I was the kind of girl who cheated. But then again, I didn't know if I was the kind of girl that needed to settle a score, either. When I broke things off with Simon, I was hurt and confused, and when the opportunity presented itself, I ran into the arms of the first man who wanted me. I knew Simon despised Julian as much as I despised Vanessa. Maybe I had made mistakes, too.

"He's going to be all right."

"How do you know?" I asked.

"Because I have a feeling about these things."

Simon looked me over.

"Oh, before I forget, I have something for you." He reached into his coat pocket and pulled out a chocolate bar.

"There you go again, Simon. Always know how to make me feel better." But this was a bribe; this little treat was to soften the blow. *As much as Simon thinks he knows me, I know him better.* Simon was leaving me again.

I was trying to get over jet lag and hadn't changed my clothing since I left Italy. Which was roughly twenty or twenty-four hours ago. I didn't know anymore. I was so tired I could fall flat on my face at any minute, but luckily I was sitting quietly in the dark next to Simon in his car.

"So are you going to tell me what the problem is?" I said. I knew a silent treatment when I saw one.

"What do you mean?"

"You haven't said two words since we got in the car."

"It's nothing."

"I saw you talking to Gloria before we left. She said something to you?"

"Nah, it's not worth getting into ... just drop it."

"How can it be nothing? Look at the way you're acting."

"You didn't have to take it off on my account, Mable." The tone of his voice had caused me some grief.

"Oh, I see." I followed his gaze down to my hand. There was a white line on my wedding finger. I had taken the ring off after my trip with Julian from Ibiza, a couple of days before my father was hospitalized. I should have clarified things, but he was such a blockhead, and I didn't want to give Simon the satisfaction of telling me he was right.

"Congrats on the upcoming nuptials. When is the big day?" His tone was drier than the Sahara Desert.

"You could try to be happy for me, Simon." I looked out the window. I had forgotten how magical New York was at night, the streets filled with people no matter what the hour. *I miss this city.*

"All right, I could do that—"

When I looked back, he gave me the most bogus smile ever, and it almost had me laughing.

"This is my punishment, right?"

"Punishment?" I asked.

"You knew I despised that sorry arse of a man, and you went right for him." From the tone he used, there was a sense of a long-awaited unfinished business with us.

"I wasn't trying to get you back for anything. I'm not devious like Vanessa." Not intentionally, anyway. "Julian treats me right, if you must know."

"Good on ya ..." Simon nodded. "He treats everyone good until he gets what he wants. Congratulations. It's just a matter of time before he'll drop you like a hotcake."

"Screw you, Simon." I balked. All of a sudden I felt my second wind coming along.

"Well, that's the best thing you've said to me so far," he said, and I shook my head at him. I was in no mood for any of his shenanigans tonight.

"Why isn't Julian here? Hey? Your father's in the hospital, and he's nowhere to be found."

"What did he ever do to you?" I asked. When the expression on his face fell, I knew. I remembered Simon mentioning once that they had gotten into some ruckus because of a friend.

"Ah—Vanessa ... Oh, of course." I wiped my palms on my jeans. Just mentioning her name had me perspiring. "So tell me, how is she involved in this?" I held my lips tight.

He took a long breath before continuing. "Vanessa and Julian had something going on a while back."

"Oh, please ... I don't believe that. Julian never said anything about Vanessa." I gave him a side-glance.

"No surprise there." He snorted.

"Don't be a hypocrite, Simon. Haven't you kept things from me too?"

"Nah, nah, nah—that's not the same."

"Actually for once, you're right. Who Julian dated in the past is his own damn business. You, on the other hand, were keeping things from me while we were together."

"I wasn't keeping it from you. I—"

"Whatever ... It doesn't matter now." I held my hand up. "Okay, so what—they dated."

"That's not the only thing. The relationship ended when Vanessa got pregnant. Julian didn't want to acknowledge that the baby was his. Instead he tried to push her to get an abortion, Mable," Simon said, without missing a beat.

"That's what she told you? Oh, the girl has more stories than Walt Disney." I let out a nervous laugh.

"If she said it, then I have to give her the benefit of the doubt."

"You're a fool, Simon—so you punched him out because you wanted to fight her battles for her?" Simon let out a long breath that only furthered my agitation. "The woman sold you out to a rag magazine after you were trying to help her," I said. "And here's something. She doesn't care about you; she uses you to get herself out of trouble."

"What was I to do? She came to my doorstep crying. So I did the only thing I could … I thought the creep deserved it." He pulled the car to the curb and put it in park.

"Oh, aren't you a valiant knight," I said, opening the passenger door, making my way up the stairs of the apartment I had kept paying rent for all those months. I guessed that, in the back of my mind, I'd known I would be back.

"If you've got something to say to me—then say it. If not, stop acting jealous." He pulled out my duffel bag from the trunk and followed me up.

"Who's jealous?" Obviously, I was envious of whatever hold Vanessa had on him. I should have been over this by now. The hurt. I pushed the front door and it opened to another flight of stairs.

"I understand Julian might have deserved it, but I'm just disappointed that you thought to resort to violence as your best solution."

"Yeah. It might not have been the best option, I agree, but sometimes these things need to be done. It certainly felt great at the time," he said, with contentment in his voice. I paused in my step and looked down at him. I found him grinning. Then I realized why.

"You're such a caveman."

"Because I'm looking at your ass?"

"No, because you're acting like an asshole … I know what you're trying to do," I said, picking my keys up off the step. "This is your last attempt to sway me into believing Julian is a despicable human being, but your sister-in-law is no saint, either."

I knew none of this was making any sense, because the reason for this fight was absurd. I was mad at Simon for being a good friend to a woman I despised and—him? Well, I wasn't too sure why he was upset, but I had a feeling that we probably played for the same team. We were hurting and afraid because what we wanted was not up for grabs, and that just left us desperate for something more.

"You're getting defensive because now you've realized what a prick your fiancée is. And I got news for you. I would do it again." I felt him standing behind me. "If he ever hurts you …"

"He won't do anything, Simon. Stop acting like a possessive ex-boyfriend."

He made a sound, coming from the back of his throat that made me turn around, catching his eyes going soft. "Don't marry him." His eyes were pleading.

"Simon."

"It's a mistake, and you know it. You'll never be happy."

"Did you ever think that maybe I am?" I waved my hand around, my eyes heavily set on his. Of course, I would never be—not with anyone else, because my heart was lost on Simon. I wondered if it would always be like this between us, this dark depth of resentfulness. I couldn't seem to get past it, and he knew it. The truth was never simple, but I realized that I had gone running into Julian's arms because I wanted to throw cold water on it … the possibility of us. Maybe I didn't want to be happy. I was tarnished by the past experience.

He stepped closer and looked at me in a way that made me wish he had enough magic to take us back to where we were—

when things were good. "This thing we have going on here—this cat-and-mouse thing … running around in circles. Maybe it's just a way to distract ourselves from the fact we both know—we are never off the table."

Oh?

When were we ever on the table?

The door from across the hall opened up, and an older woman with a forest-green bathrobe stood there behind us. And even though our clamorous tone was the reason for her dejected look, she'd never liked me since the day I moved in.

"Sorry, Mrs. Tansley, we'll be quieter." And with no change in her expression, she closed the door.

I turned the key and pushed into my apartment. "See, you're always getting me into trouble … you've been nothing but trouble since the day we met." I never intended for it to come out malicious, but my heart had been stalling for time, hoping it would be rescued, and she had become impatient and ferocious. I had walked away from probably the best thing in my life. Maybe I should have told him that, but I was so afraid for history to repeat itself—I feared I would always be stuck in this limbo.

I walked into my living room. When I didn't hear Simon's footsteps behind me, I turned, looking for him, but Simon remained outside in the hallway, looking pensive.

"Aren't you coming in?" I frowned.

"No." He shook his head, and I caught something in his eyes. "I should be going." He placed my bag at the entrance without setting foot in my home.

"Okay." He might as well leave. I had nothing else to tell him, and nothing to give, because he already had it.

"It makes little sense."

"What's that?"

"You were in no rush to get married—yet here you are … And you don't even know him."

"Simon."

"No. No, I get it … It was just something you never wanted with me," he said, hiding his pain behind a half smile. *He couldn't be more wrong.*

"I don't know what it is you want from me."

"I want you to be honest with yourself—because I think you're a liar. You're misleading yourself if you believe it could work out."

I sighed with no motivation to continue. "Can we pretend that none of this matters, because I could use a friend right now?"

"Friend? We could never be friends, Mable. You were like home, and yet we didn't officially live together. I feel like there was so much more left between us that should have happened. I have so much love to spare, you know?"

"Simon."

"I want you to know what I had—with you, it was the best time of my life. You were the most important thing to me, but somehow you lost faith in us, and I can't tell you how gutted I am to know that." He gulped in a long breath, keeping it for a moment before letting it go. "But in no way did I ever see myself as someone who was nothing but trouble for the woman I love. I'm sorry, Mable, if that's all I ever meant. I tried to make you happy—I really did—because all I ever wanted was you."

My heart took a plunge. "Look I didn't mean it like that— Simon." I put my hand on my face in frustration. "I have a lot on my plate right now."

"I realize that." He looked down. "And you don't need any more. That's why I will leave you to get some rest. Get yourself a good night's sleep, love." His eyes washed over me as if he were trying to take a mental photograph, like this was the last time. Why did it feel like the last time?

Then in the next moment, he was gone, leaving me there feeling unresolved.

The Final Departure

My parents were unaware I was watching them through an open door. There my father lay in a hospital bed, and Elaine was sitting on the edge, talking about the past and behaving like nothing had transpired between them. They seemed almost happy. And so I had to question everything I knew about love and forgiveness—could you have one without the other? If my parents had found peace after eighteen years, why couldn't I? After last night, I had wondered where it left me with Simon, especially after how it ended. Somewhere in the back of my mind, I thought I could move on from this, seeing how remorseful Simon was, but I'd allowed my pride to get in the way, and now I'd hurt him.

I heard footsteps coming up from behind me. "Do you see what I'm seeing?" When Gloria came close enough, she handed me a paper cup of coffee. We both watched my mother and father smiling, their hands intertwined like they were a couple of teenagers.

"I guess it could be worse." A faint smile lingered on her lips.

"Yeah, how?"

"They could be killing each other." Leave it to Gloria to reveal the bright side of things.

"You have a point," I said, and we sipped our coffees simultaneously. "I don't know … I just don't get it," I said, without looking at her.

"What is it you don't get?"

"Why love has to be so complicated," I said under my breath.

"Oh, Mable, love is not an easy thing to explain." She shrugged. "We go in blindly, and sometimes we get hurt, we forgive, and we do it all over again, because in love we must be brave. It's the only thing worth fighting for."

I wondered if she was talking about my parents or Simon.

"Look, I owe you an apology," Gloria said after we shared a moment of silence.

"For what?" I asked.

"For not minding my business. I told Simon that you were getting hitched." She gave me an innocent smile. "I know it wasn't my place to tell him."

I knew better; she wasn't remorseful. "It's all right. I'm surprised he didn't know about it sooner," I said, knowing that it would be a matter of time before everyone would see the truth— plastered in every rag magazine even Gloria had no clue about.

"How would he have known?" Her eyebrows scrunched together in the middle. "He's been in India, living in a remote area for the past few months," Gloria said.

At some point, I had stopped asking about Simon's whereabouts. I thought it would be easier not to worry about him if I didn't know where he was.

I turned to look at her. "I wanted to ask you something," I said.

"Okay."

"Did you know Vanessa and Julian had a relationship and that it ended when she got pregnant?"

She hesitated before saying, "I only know about the rumors that were circulating … But you know it happened a while ago."

"Did you know Julian wanted her to get an abortion?"

Gloria slightly shrugged "I wasn't sure if it was true."

"So why didn't you tell me?"

"Because what difference would it make? You always do what you want, and I was afraid that if I tried to discourage you from marrying Julian, it would motivate you even more. I knew it would be a matter a time before you came to your senses."

"What happened to the baby?"

"I was told Vanessa miscarried." Gloria faced me, and I stood there under her watchful eyes. "Why are you asking me this?"

"Something Simon said last night. I'm just curious." I shrugged.

"How did it go with Simon?"

"Not good. I did a great job of pushing him so far away that now I think he might never talk to me again."

"I'm sorry. I feel it's my fault." Her compassionate brown eyes offered no comfort.

"No, it's my fault. I should have been honest with him. Anyways, I'm sure I'll see him around today and I'll try to patch things up."

Her head snapped up, searching my face. "He didn't tell you?" Gloria asked as I felt the heat rise in the back of my neck.

"Tell me what?"

"The man is intolerable. I can't believe he didn't tell you." Gloria took her phone out of her purse. I was not sure what she was looking for.

"What was he supposed to say, Gloria?"

"That he's on an assignment for some European news magazine. This time he's headed somewhere in the Middle East."

"What?" I blinked several times. "When is he leaving?"

"This afternoon."

I looked into Gloria's doleful eyes, and now everything made perfect sense. Gloria had told Simon that I was getting married to provoke something between Simon and me, to stop us from leaving each other. Whatever she had imagined the outcome to be had backfired. An elusive sound of glass shattering was coming from my heart. *If I lose Simon forever, I know there's no coming back from the blow.*

"I wanted to tell you, but then all this stuff happened with your dad. Simon came back two weeks ago looking for you. He had no idea you were living in Italy until I told him. It's clear that with this new lifestyle Simon is leading—the more places he goes, the more chances he will get himself into trouble. I suspect he came back to make his peace and say goodbye … you know … in case."

I couldn't muster a word with a big lump in my throat.

"Why don't we sit down?" Gloria led me toward the empty chairs in the hallway.

"You warned me about Simon," I stated, feeling another emotion creeping in. He was coming, not for me, but to settle some unfinished business. It was to make himself feel better. "I should have never gotten involved with him."

"You don't mean that. I was so wrong to discourage you, and I'm glad you never listen, because think about the good things you would have missed out."

"We were never meant to be."

"Look, Mable, not everyone you love will leave you. I think we miss the point about love, that no human being is bound solely to us. What's important is that they come back."

I sat there focusing on the little hole in the wall across from us. *I love Simon. Shit, it's the ones we love that hurt us the most.*

I wished I loved Nutella more.

"You know, nothing you will say to me is going to make me feel better."

"Oh, the only thing that would do that is seeing Simon before he leaves."

"He doesn't want to see me." I gave her an exasperated look. "It's not like him to leave without saying goodbye."

"Maybe it's too hard for him to walk away from you. Did you ever think of that?" Her eyebrows rose. "You could still catch him at his apartment if you leave now."

"You have a point. I should make things right," I said, slowly getting up from my seat.

"Yes, go!" Gloria said from behind me as I rushed towards the elevators.

I had tripped right into this bitter hole, and now I risked losing the only thing that brought joy to my life. It's hard to swallow when you realize you're the cause of your own demise. And now he was leaving.

Sitting in the back of a cab, all kinds of scenarios played out in my mind, but the one thing I couldn't imagine was my life without Simon. I needed him to be thriving somewhere out there in the world. I didn't think I was a good enough reason to get him to stay after the way I had behaved yesterday. *Am I going to beg him to stick around? Do I even have the right to?*

I looked out the window and caught sight of Simon coming out of his apartment building, making his way to a yellow taxicab at the curb.

"Stop, stop right here," I yelled to the driver. "Keep the change." I scrambled out of the car, and my eyes fell on his.

"Mable, what are you doing here?" His face was clean-shaven, his hair slicked back and damp.

"After everything we've been through, weren't you at least going to say goodbye?" I said, short of breath. "Why didn't you tell me you were leaving?" Again.

"I thought you were mad at me." He shrugged. "And I didn't believe you cared."

"Oh, you're full of shit, Simon Rowe."

"Maybe I am." A slow smile spread across his thin lips. I'd never thought I'd see the day when I would chase after a man, but Simon wasn't just any man—he was mine. A proclamation that was only known to me. *For now.*

"For your information, I wasn't mad at you," I clarified.

"You told me to go to hell." His eyebrows perked up.

"Correction, I said—screw you."

"Oh, right." He smirked.

"Yeah, so ... I say a lot of things. Since when do you take me seriously?"

"Mable, I have to go." His eyes were dispirited, making me think he wished for more time, too.

"I know. I need a minute."

He must have sensed the desperation in my voice, because it was enough for him to walk over to the driver to say something, then make his way back. His duffel bag hung by four fingers behind his back.

"I'm not marrying Julian. We were on a break before I left Italy. So if you want to say I told you so ... go right ahead," I shrugged. "I deserve it."

"No. I'm not going to say anything. None of it matters as long as you're okay. That was the only concern of mine."

"Why are you going?" I said, staring at his face.

"Mable."

"I know I have no right to say this ... to ask you to stay, but I don't want you to go, because I feel like if I do, I'll never see you again." My eyes blurred.

"You think something will happen to me?" His eyes softened.

"I know you're capable of putting yourself in harm's way if

you have a purpose."

Simon was a man in search of truth. I knew that about him. That's what made him good at what he did. His job was to validate reality, and his photographs were a way to document people's lives, getting others to care enough to do something. He was putting faces to statistics. It was only a matter of time before he was ready to do more, even if it meant risking his life, and so I understood why he needed to go out there. This was his calling, but it didn't make it easier for me to accept it. Then I realized I wasn't there to stop him from going, but to let him go.

"Nothing is going to happen to me," he said, calm, with no signs of fear in his eyes.

"How could you say that, knowing there's a chance that something could go wrong?" I said, thinking maybe the art of letting go was more of a process.

"Look, Mable, I know you care about me, but I don't have time to argue." He gave a quiet laugh. "I've got people depending on me. I can't miss my flight."

Care? No, that wasn't the only thing. I was madly in love with him, and there was no more valuable time to tell him than now.

"I wanted you to know you were right about everything. I've been hiding behind excuses because it scared me to be with you, but all this made me realize that I'm even more scared to live without you. What I'm trying to say is I—"

"Just stop." He gave me a weak smile, closing in on the distance between us. "It's okay. You don't have to tell me what I already know."

"But I—"

"Love you." He cut me off and brushed the hair from my face. "I love you. I love you … I will forever love you." He whispered close to my ear. "Just always remember that … I got to go, love." He sighed heavily, then touched his forehead with mine.

"So this is goodbye." I looked down at the concrete sidewalk. If I looked him in the eyes, I would lose it.

"Goodbye? No … It's never goodbye. I could never say those words to you," he stated in a half whisper, making me feel like a puddle of water, my heart in total disarray.

"Don't worry about me, Mable. It will be okay. I'll see you when I get back? Yeah?" His voice was hoarse, kissing my forehead before opening the door to the cab. As I watched him, it felt like the end of the world was near, like the walls were coming down all around us. Nothing mattered, not the things we had fought about, the stupidest things that were keeping us apart. None of it had any meaning at this moment. I had realized it too late.

"Walter," I said.

Simon suddenly stopped midair, and without words, he came right up, pulling me into his arms. He kissed me like it would be the last time. This was the truth—it was home.

"*Shh*—it's going to be all right." He placed his hands in my hair, and everything told me this would be the last time I'd see him. *But my heart whispered,* he'll come back.

"That's an empty promise," I said with teary eyes.

"No, it's not. I need you to know something." He raised my chin up, looked into my eyes. "You're my focal point, Mable. No matter where I go or how far, I will make my way back to you … I always come back to what's mine." He kissed me gently.

I had to trust his words and let him go, because that's what you do when you truly love someone. His eyes dragged over my face just before he slid into the back of the taxi. I stood there, not able to move, following the yellow cab as it drove off, disappearing from my sight, leaving me alone, in full view of anyone who might be watching me.

Epilogue ...
A Few Years Later, or: How It Came to Be

Simon

I often think about life and what it is we are in search of. One way or another, we always seem to want to arrive at something or to someone, but what if we take things for what they are and just relish the present? We might as well. When this moment passes—it will never happen again.

I stood in a white room, watching the people pour in from the streets. The more the room filled up—the more anxious I got. The last time I was this nervous and excited was on my wedding day, but tonight was special, too. It was the opening night for my new exhibition, *The Human Eye*. Everything this project represented was now on the walls: pictures I took from my travels all over the world were now in plain sight. I saw a few familiar faces in the crowd—Gloria, and Tracy, who had been married now for a while, and were processing papers for adoption. Noah, who came to show his support, had brought his boyfriend, Dan. They were introduced by our mutual best friend, Mable. At first, I had told her it would be a bad idea to play the matchmaker, because I had known Noah longer and knew he wouldn't go for something like that. Second, if things went sour, who did she think would be blamed? But her stubbornness persevered like it always does. This time I was glad it did, because Noah seemed happy.

The Harpers were there too, Charlie had made a full recovery and was back together with Elaine, who appeared to be going stronger with time despite the past—they made it work. And Elaine, regardless of what she had missed out on in Mable's childhood, had proven herself to be the mother Mable needed now. The only person I was glad was not there that night was Vanessa. We hadn't spoken to each other since that whole story she'd sold to the rag magazine. All I knew was Vanessa had gotten married to a retired F1 race car driver and was now living somewhere in Switzerland, according to *U* magazine. I wished her well; I did—but she was not for me to worry about, not anymore.

Doesn't everyone deserve a happy ending? Sure—if you're up for the challenge. It takes hard work and choosing the right decisions after making a couple of wrong ones—but you should be able to get there—eventually, according to a very sexy bird. She was the only person I wanted by my side tonight, and she was nowhere to be around. But she was not easy to lose sight of these days. She'd changed in her looks—a little different from the first time I'd seen her, but more beautiful than she'd ever been. I felt a hand on my shoulder. I turned around, and there I met Gloria's smiling face.

"Wow, this is really great, Simon."

"Thank you."

Gloria cast her eyes at me like she was seeing me for the first time. "I don't think I ever saw you this happy."

"I'm in the right place." I felt it. *I'm where I'm supposed to be.*

"You finally have it all, and there's no more deserving guy I know."

"Yeah. Nah … not yet, anyhow."

"What can you possibly be missing?" Her eyebrows gathered up.

"Maybe a daughter?" I said, and Gloria smiled.

"And what does your wife say?"

"She said if I give her another boy, she'll leave me." This made Gloria laugh, patting me on the shoulder.

"Where is your wife, anyway?" Her eyes glanced over the crowd.

"Somewhere around …" My eyes scanned the room with no success in finding her. She'd once told me she was hard to pin down. *Don't I know it.*

"Look what I picked up." Gloria pulled a book out of her green handbag. "And I wanted you to sign it for me." She held up a copy of *Lyrical Lights*, the book I had published a month ago. After I had shown it to Mable, she'd thought I should share it with the world. It was her idea. All the proceeds would go to a charity that Mable had created, World Hearing, a nonprofit charity that supplied hearing aids for developing countries.

"With pleasure," I beamed. "But I don't have a pen." I patted down my navy suit jacket.

"Here you go, Simon." She handed one to me. *Gloria always comes prepared.* That's one thing I liked about her— she'd always had my back.

"To the biggest pain in my ass, and faithful friend. Thank you for keeping this book out of the binner."

She read it back to me, then laughed. "Oh, there's Matthew Norville. Let me go say hi."

"Still keeping up appearances, I see?" I frowned.

"You know a little ass-kissing hurt nobody, right? Anyways, next week Tracy and I have vacation time. It would be nice to get together for dinner with you guys." She pulled me into a kiss goodbye.

"Yeah, let me speak to the missus, but I'm sure it will be

okay."

"All right, we will be in touch," she said.

I watched her go off in the direction of the CEO of Norville magazines. I couldn't blame her. Sometimes you had to play the game to stay in it. I should know. As for me, I had so much to be grateful for. After what I had witnessed, my time traveling to the most censored countries, there were some close calls, but thankfully I had made it back in one piece. I had had to ... I needed to come back to the love of my life.

After going through one refugee camp after another and meeting people who were forced from their homes by war, it wasn't hard to identify my humanity in the misfortune and struggles of others. I couldn't let a moment go by with knowing I was the fortunate one. But it didn't mean I should stop—turn my back on the world. It only motivated me to do more. To make the world better for others ... each life is valuable. Now, becoming a father, my cause only deepened.

I often think back to the day I landed at JFK after being gone for six months, and the last person I had expected to see there, waiting for me, was Mable. I knew I had made a few mistakes in the past, but now I was ready to make the right choices.

"You're quiet," she'd said, in the back of the cab, headed to my apartment, now for good.

"I was thinking," I said to her.

"About what?"

"The Taj Mahal." I stared at Mable like I never had before. Her blond hair was cut at shoulder length, the shortest I'd ever seen.

"What about it?" She smiled with curiosity.

"In fact, I was thinking about Sheh Jahan and the love he had for his wife Mumtaz, that when she died, he built this beautiful monument in her memory."

"Wait, didn't he have seven wives?" She looked puzzled.

"*Right ... and plenty of mistresses, but that's what makes this story so much more unique.*"

"*What are you trying to say, Simon? You want a harem?*" Her brows bunched together.

"*No, no, but I have a point—if you let me finish.*"

"*Okay ... this better be good.*" Mable's eyebrows came together.

"*Sheh Jahan may have had seven wives in his lifetime ... But there's always that one, you know? Everyone gets that one, and for Sheh, Mumtaz had to be his one, or why would he build the Taj Mahal her honor?*"

"*What does this have to do with anything? With us?*"

"*You're my one, Mable ... my Taj Mahal ... and after what I've seen these past couple of months, I don't want to waste any more time being away from you. And if you don't want me, well, I guess I'm prepared to live a lifetime alone. If I can't have you, no one else will do.*" I shrugged.

"*A lifetime is a very long time to be alone.*"

"*Oh, good, you understand my dilemma then ...*"

"*Completely ...*" she said, and I drew her closer.

"*Then marry me?*" I looked at her like she was the only thing that existed. "*I'm crazy about you,*" I said, and she smiled. "*The first time I saw you, I was hooked and in love ... I'm nothing without you. Be my one?*" Her eyes became clear. Now she knew what happened when an unstoppable force meets an immovable object.

I put my glass of champagne down and walked around the room, and that's when I found what I was searching for. My Aphrodite—my wife, standing in front of a mural, a picture I had taken of her in Rwanda with a little girl in her arms.

"This is my favorite picture," Mable said, looking up at me while I stood next to her.

"Mine too," I said, slipping my hand into hers.

"So what's next?" she asked. I loved the softness in her eyes. They had a way of seeing right through me.

"Well, I have something in mind, but first I want to know—are you in?" My eyebrow slightly went up, and she giggled.

"I'm in—with you, all the way," she said, and I pulled her as close as I could.

"You're so beautiful, you know? I'm one lucky man." I searched her face.

"I got pretty lucky, too." We had promised each other we would stop with the rush and concentrate on our growing family. *When I go right, I want her there right beside me, and when Mable goes left, I'll follow—no matter the limit—for her, I will go anywhere.*

"It's so simple, isn't it? You can thrive under the lights as long as you got someone by your side that makes the world feel like your oyster … Only one can do that."

"And now one has become three," she reminded me, putting her hand on her large stomach—my boys, who I'd meet in a month's time.

"And maybe eventually four." I nuzzled her neck.

"Four? Do you think we'll be able to handle more children, Walter?"

"Sure we can. Together there's no limit to what we can do. But keep calling me Walter, and maybe there'll be five."

She laughed, and I kissed her before she could protest.

I guess it comes down to who you become and what you leave behind … But whatever you do, never leave love behind. Never.

The End

Want to read the collection of poems that inspire *Lyrical Lights*?

Subscribe to Maria La Serra's newsletter to receive
a free eBook copy of *Bright Lights*!

Get a copy at:
https://claims.instafreebie.com/free/lJvoswIF

Looking for the next read?

Also by Maria La Serra

The Proverbial Mr. Universe

After finding her fiancé cheating, Olivia Montiano must question what she wants out of life and love. When she finds the mysterious, handwritten letters tucked away in places only meant for her, she begins to see what the Universe has in store for her...

About the Author

Maria La Serra lives in Montreal. Before becoming a writer, she worked as a fashion designer. She will try everything at least once, except for skiing, hiking or camping—okay anything relating to activities done in the great outdoors. When she's not working on her next book, you could find spending time with family. *Lyrical Lights* is her second book.

www.ingramcontent.com/pod-product-compliance
Lightning Source LLC
Chambersburg PA
CBHW020230260626
47156CB00002B/618